BLOOD AND GHOSTS

SHIRA ANTHONY

REAMSPINNER
PRESS

Published by
DREAMSPINNER PRESS

5032 Capital Circle SW, Suite 2, PMB# 279, Tallahassee, FL 32305-7886 USA
http://www.dreamspinnerpress.com/

Blood and Ghosts
© 2015 Shira Anthony.

Cover Art
© 2015 Reese Dante.
http://www.reesedante.com
Cover content is for illustrative purposes only and any person depicted on the cover is a model.

ISBN: 978-1-63476-114-7
Digital ISBN: 978-1-63476-115-4
Library of Congress Control Number: 2015930653
First Edition April 2015

Printed in the United States of America
∞
This paper meets the requirements of
ANSI/NISO Z39.48-1992 (Permanence of Paper).

For Irwin. You will be missed.

Acknowledgments

Special thanks to Helen Pattskyn, Rebecca Cohen, and my amazing editor, Gin.

DRAMATIS PERSONAE

HUNTERS

Adrien Gilbert. An immortal hunter and the youngest son of the fabled Gilbert Clan of vampire hunters, Adrien Gilbert saw his mother murdered by a vampire when he was just a boy. Adrien never wanted to become a hunter and always believed his older brother, François, was the more powerful son. Adrien was given immortality by the ancient vampire Nicolas Lambert. Adrien loves Nicolas.

François Gilbert. Adrien's older brother, François is a hunter who willingly became a vampire after falling in love with the powerful and solitary vampire Charles Duvalier.

Jacques Gilbert. Jacques is the father of Adrien, François, and their sister, Isabelle. Much of Jacques's past is shrouded in mystery. Once a powerful hunter in his own right, Jacques has not been himself since the murder of his wife by a vampire.

Verel Pelletier. An immortal hunter, Verel Pelletier has installed himself as the new regent of the Council of Hunters. He is ruthless and cunning and does not believe in the vampire-hunter treaty that created the Council. Pelletier advocates the use of vampire blood to enhance his followers' powers.

Roland Günter. An immortal hunter and former teacher of Adrien and François Gilbert, Roland has long been a vocal opponent of Verel Pelletier and his cronies. Roland and his longtime companion, Thomas Fournier, keep a low profile, working behind the scenes against Pelletier's forces.

Antonio Giovanetti. A hunter and Verel Pelletier's right-hand man and proxy, Giovanetti is more powerful than most hunters, although he is not an immortal. He serves as acting regent of the Council of Hunters after Pelletier disappears.

Thomas Fournier. Roland Günter's longtime companion, Thomas is a powerful hunter in his own right.

Claus Bremen: A hunter and researcher for Pelletier's faction, Bremen perfected the means to enhance hunters' powers by using vampire blood. Bremen is heartless and cruel and doesn't hesitate to torture for pleasure alone.

Isabelle Gilbert. Adrien and François's little sister, Isa was also trained as a hunter, although she chose to pursue a life with humans.

Victor Sauvage. Another of Roland Günter's students, Victor saves Adrien in a barroom brawl in Paris and becomes one of Adrien's strongest allies.

Robert Aguillon. Former regent of the Council of Hunters, Robert Aguillon was once quite powerful but in recent years has become feeble and struggles to maintain control over the Council.

VAMPIRES

Nicolas Lambert. An ancient vampire (born a vampire, not created from a human), Nicolas is the youngest son of the Lambert Clan. He is several hundred years old but is relatively naïve in the ways of the world since he has been sheltered by his older brother, Jean. Nicolas has offered himself in marriage to Rosina Rousseau to cement a fragile peace between their warring clans. Nicolas loves Adrien Gilbert.

Charles Duvalier. Transformed from human to vampire against his will, Charles is old and very powerful. Charles shuns vampires and hunters alike, and he blames himself for transforming François Gilbert into a vampire. In spite of this, Charles loves François deeply.

Jean Lambert. An ancient vampire, leader of the Lambert Clan, and Nicolas's older brother, Jean Lambert appears cool on the surface, but he genuinely loves Nicolas and wants what is best for him. In spite of his reservations, he permits Nicolas to offer himself in marriage to end the war between the Lambert and Rousseau Clans. Jean and Blaise Rousseau share a history that reignited the war between the clans several hundred years before.

Blaise Rousseau. An ancient vampire and the eldest surviving son of the powerful Rousseau Clan, Blaise hides a painful past and a broken heart.

Rosina Rousseau. Blaise's younger sister, Rosina is a strong-willed ancient vampire who is quick to anger but loyal to a fault. She has begrudgingly agreed to marry Nicolas Lambert to ensure the treaty between their clans.

Caroline Vestry. Charles Duvalier's creation, Caroline would do anything for Charles and would defend him to the death. Caroline also cares deeply for François Gilbert and believes François will make Charles happy.

Rémy Desgrieux. A distant relative of Nicolas and Jean, Rémy is a loyal Lambert Clan member and good friend of Nicolas. Despite their rocky start, Rémy and Adrien Gilbert become close friends.

Reynaud Rousseau. Uncle of Blaise and Rosina, Reynaud became Rousseau Clan Leader after his brother's murder. Reynaud believes in the need to keep his clan strong, even when his choices lead to dire consequences.

CHAPTER ONE:
THE STRANGER

The Present

"ADRIEN."

The voice sounded familiar. Adrien looked around to see who was speaking, but saw no one.

Laughter. Then: *"You won't find me out here."*

Who are you? Adrien hated games. He was too old for them.

"You know who I am, Adrien."

Adrien's head jerked forward as he woke with a start. It took him a moment to remember where he was: Jean Lambert's plane. On their way to the Council meeting in Paris.

Pelletier.

He glanced out the window. A sea of white clouds danced below them, obscuring what he guessed was ocean. His head throbbed. He rubbed the bridge of his nose and pulled his phone from his pocket. "How much longer?" he asked Jean, who sat next to him.

"Less than an hour."

The attendant brought a tray of food and set it on the table between them. Adrien poured himself a small cup of thick black coffee. Maybe the jolt of caffeine would get rid of his headache.

"What do you have in mind?" Adrien asked Jean. Of course it might have been better if they'd discussed plans *before* Jean knocked him out. Then again, Adrien would have refused to come with Jean if given a choice.

"We will attend the meeting."

Adrien nearly spat out a mouthful of coffee. "You're joking. We'll never get near the building, let alone make it inside."

1

"They will permit us entry," Jean replied, nonplussed. "Giovanetti intends to become the next regent if Pelletier doesn't appear. He won't risk alienating Council members sympathetic to the vampires' concerns."

"You really think Pelletier will show?" Adrien swirled his half-finished coffee around. Over the past century, Jean had tried to convince Adrien that Pelletier would appear at other Council meetings. Adrien had flatly refused to attend them, and in the end, Jean had been mistaken. Still, Adrien would humor Jean. He understood that Jean, like him, needed a reason to believe they'd find Nicolas.

"I believe he will. He's always enjoyed putting on a show," Jean replied with obvious disdain. "How much more grandiose an entrance can he make than to reappear after one hundred years? And in the Hall of Hunters, no less?"

"He'll be ready for us."

Jean nodded. "No doubt he has a plan."

Adrien released a long breath. "And we have none."

Jean frowned. "Roland will come."

"That's your plan?" Adrien stood up, careful not to hit his head on the low bulkhead, and ran a hand through his hair. Having his erstwhile teacher at the Council meeting would certainly help should trouble arise, but in the face of so many potential foes, it wouldn't guarantee their safety.

"Unfortunately it's the best I have to offer."

Adrien had nothing better to suggest. After years of searching, he'd almost made his peace with losing Nicolas. Almost. He would have given up looking for him decades before if the niggle at the back of his brain didn't keep reminding him of the hole in his heart.

He looked out the window again as they began to descend. It had been seventy years since he'd visited Paris. He'd continued to perform his duty to the Council in the intervening years, dispatching vampires, but he'd received his orders first as telegraphs and telegrams, then later through texts. Adrien often wondered if the Council required his services only so that Pelletier's cronies might keep tabs on him. Years spent chasing after Pelletier to find Nicolas had yielded nothing but dead ends. A grainy photo he thought might be Nicolas in a newspaper, a glimpse of someone on the street he thought might be Pelletier. Never anything concrete.

Adrien watched as the airplane touched down at the private airport outside Paris. More than ever he was convinced their presence at the Council meeting was a waste of time. Perhaps worse than a waste of time. Dangerous. Still, he'd grown tired of arguing.

A limousine met them at the airport. Adrien paid little attention to where they were going until the buildings and spires of Paris disappeared into the distance and he realized they were traveling away from the center of the city.

"Where to?" he asked.

"Château Rousseau."

Jean wore a grim expression. Years before, Adrien might have taken solace in the fact that Jean, too, had his ghosts. Now he understood all too well the toll ghosts could exact on those they haunted.

Over the years Adrien had managed to piece together some of the bloody history that had rekindled the war between the great vampire clans. He knew Blaise Rousseau and Jean had been lovers. He'd also heard that Jean had murdered Blaise's brother and was responsible for the death of Blaise's parents. Adrien knew few of the actual details, and Jean refused to speak of it. Eventually Adrien had stopped asking.

The limousine pulled up to a large wrought-iron gate, which opened automatically after a few moments, and they started down the long drive to the château.

The peace that had cost both Adrien and Jean so dearly had been a lasting one. Although it had taken time, the Rousseau and Lambert Clans were now allies. Jean's suggestion that they stay here was a testament to this new relationship between the clans, but Adrien guessed Jean was as troubled as he to be back once again.

As they climbed out of the car, Blaise Rousseau stood in the middle of the entryway, green eyes focused and bright. His youthful face had not changed over the years, although his eyes shone with a wisdom born of nearly a century as leader of the Rousseau Clan, a position he had assumed after his uncle, Reynaud Rousseau, left in disgrace.

As always, seeing Blaise caused Adrien's chest to tighten. He saw so much of Nicolas in Blaise's face. Except for their eyes—Nicolas's were brown—they might have passed for twins.

Jean offered Blaise his hand. Though Jean's demeanor remained calm, Adrien saw him clench his jaw. Blaise's smile appeared just as strained, although when he moved to shake Jean's hand, he rested his left hand briefly on Jean's forearm in an unexpected gesture of friendship. He then approached Adrien, but instead of a handshake, he embraced Adrien warmly, as one might embrace a long-lost brother.

"Welcome to my home, gentlemen. It's been a long time." Blaise gestured them into the sitting room while the servants took away what little luggage they had. "I'm sorry my sister isn't here today. She has her own residence in the Sixth Arrondissement." His expression grew wistful. "She joins me at the castle only infrequently." He motioned them to be seated. "Cognac?"

"Thank you." Jean sat so straight in his chair, he reminded Adrien of a statue.

"Yes, please," Adrien added.

Blaise filled two glasses with cognac and offered them to Jean and Adrien. Adrien inhaled the warm scent of the alcohol and nearly sighed into his glass, happy to have something to ease the tension in his body that being back in this place caused. The castle reminded Adrien of Nicolas. He'd spent wonderful days at Nicolas's side here, but it was also where he'd lost Nicolas.

"So," Blaise continued as he sipped his drink, "much as I'm pleased you chose to visit, I realize you're not here to pay a social call."

"We will attend the Council meeting the day after tomorrow," Jean said. "The Council intends to take up the question of who will succeed Pelletier as regent."

Blaise's expression darkened. "Do you think it's wise for you to go?"

"I asked the same question," Adrien said with a chuckle. "But Jean believes Pelletier may appear."

"And if he does?"

"It might give us a clue about where he has Nicolas," Jean explained.

"Jean thinks Pelletier will dangle Nicolas as some sort of bait." Adrien rubbed the back of his neck.

"Bait?" Blaise asked.

"Jean believes all of this is about me." Adrien ran a hand through his hair and this time failed to stifle a yawn.

"We can speak of it later, Adrien," Blaise said with a knowing smile. He stood and put his hand on Adrien's shoulder. "For now, why don't you get some rest? One of the servants will show you to your room."

Adrien had barely slept in weeks, and he couldn't afford to be exhausted in the unlikely event Pelletier did appear at the meeting. He nodded, then said, "Thank you for the hospitality, Blaise. It's good to see you again."

BLAISE TURNED to Jean after Adrien disappeared. "What's this about Pelletier wanting Adrien?"

"Just that. Pelletier might have wanted Nicolas at one time, but now I believe he's set his sights on Adrien." Jean sighed and shook his head. "Adrien's mother was murdered by a vampire when Adrien was a child. She died defending him. I've long suspected that vampire was in Pelletier's employ."

"But it's been more than a hundred years since Pelletier disappeared with Nicolas," Blaise protested. "If he wanted Adrien, why wait so long?"

"A hundred years is nothing for an immortal," Jean answered. "Nothing, and everything, in this case."

"Everything to Adrien."

"Yes. It's quite clever, if you think about it." Jean had thought about this more than he cared to admit. "Pelletier knows that the years will take their toll on Adrien. He's chased Pelletier all over the world since he took Nicolas. Pelletier lets him get close, then vanishes again. And although Adrien's powers may have grown with time…."

Blaise pressed his lips together and frowned. "How is he, really?"

"Adrien?"

Blaise nodded.

"As well as can be expected. He's spent the last century looking for Nicolas. He's discouraged, heartbroken…."

"As are you."

Jean took a long sip of his drink in an effort to mask his emotions. Blaise's presence awakened many of the same feelings in him as the loss of Nicolas. Grief. Heartache. Loneliness. And although Jean's responsibilities as leader of the Lambert Clan meant that he and Blaise were in regular contact, they had only seen each other once since Nicolas's disappearance. The fault was Jean's own. He had failed both Blaise and Nicolas, in the end. Blaise had every right to keep him at arm's length.

"I'm to blame for not protecting Nicolas. I chose this path for him. I should have considered the danger."

"Adrien blames himself as well." Blaise shook his head and let out a long breath. "This self-loathing accomplishes nothing. Nicolas wouldn't have wanted this for either of you."

Blaise was right, of course. It had taken Jean nearly a century to see his folly in letting Blaise go for what it was: penance. But perhaps now enough time had passed that he could say what he should have said back then.

"I too grieve the loss of Nicolas," Blaise said softly.

"I know." Jean finished his cognac and set the glass down on the table between them. For a few moments, Jean hesitated, unsure of how to broach the subject after so long. He knew he must do this. He could not in good conscience chastise Adrien for his self-pity when he was guilty of the same.

"There is something else I wish to discuss," he said at last.

"Of course." Blaise pretended to focus his attention on his drink, but Jean suspected he knew the topic and was steeling himself for what Jean might say.

"It's been more than a hundred years since you learned the truth," Jean began. "I should have spoken to you about it. I have no excuse but that Nicolas's disappearance affected me more than I was willing to admit. But lately I've been thinking about the past. Perhaps far more than I should. I've been thinking about you, and whether we—"

Someone knocked on the sitting room door.

"Excuse me," Blaise said as he went to open the door.

"Blaise, I think—" The man who entered the sitting room stopped when he saw Jean seated there. "I'm so sorry," he added, appearing flustered. "I didn't realize you had company. I can come back later."

"It's all right," Blaise said as he gestured the man inside. "It's my fault for keeping you waiting. I should have told you I'd be delayed."

"Are you sure?" the man asked with a glance in Jean's direction.

"It's quite all right," Jean put in.

Blaise shifted on his feet. He clearly hadn't anticipated Jean and the newcomer would meet. Jean schooled his features. His conversation with Blaise would have to wait. He told himself he hadn't really believed he and Blaise might rectify what had happened years before, but he'd hoped he might use the opportunity to rekindle their friendship.

There's no rush.

"Jean," Blaise said, smiling at the newcomer, "this is Rogier Chastain. Rogier, Jean Lambert."

Jean stood and shook Rogier's hand.

"It's a pleasure to meet you," Rogier said. "I hope I haven't interrupted anything." Handsome and slightly taller than Blaise, Rogier wore jeans with a white button-down shirt and a leather jacket. Dressed for an afternoon outing—one Jean and Adrien had obviously interrupted.

"Not at all," Jean said. "Blaise and I are—" He paused and smiled at Blaise. "—old friends. We'll have plenty of time to catch up later."

"Rogier's in town for the Council meeting," Blaise explained as he took Rogier's hand. No doubt the gesture was meant for both Rogier and Jean. Jean knew Blaise well enough that he'd have understood without it. Blaise had moved on. And why shouldn't he? Jean had done nothing to attempt a reconciliation, even though Blaise knew the truth of his parents' deaths.

"I figured I'd take advantage of Blaise's hospitality." Rogier gazed at Blaise with affection. "With my work, we don't get to spend as much time together as I'd like."

"You're a hunter." He'd stated the obvious, but Jean felt it easier to slip back into comfortable formality than face his own petty jealousy.

Rogier nodded and Jean offered him a pleasant smile. Then he turned to Blaise and added, "I should get some rest. Tomorrow will be a long day. I thank you for your hospitality. It was good meeting you, Rogier."

CHAPTER TWO: DESCENT

RESTLESS, ADRIEN wandered the hallways of the Rousseau castle well after midnight. He felt hunger, but not for food.

What the hell's the matter with me? Since Nicolas had given him immortality more than a century before, there'd been times when he'd craved blood. But each time he'd been able to master the hunger, and it had eventually passed. This time felt different. The bloodlust had come on him suddenly, nearly overwhelming him.

In the hallway he met a servant dusting the statues and paintings that lined the walls. An attractive woman, she looked to be about twenty in human years, but the knowing look she gave him told him she was no child.

"May I help you?" She set down the feather duster and approached him.

Adrien fought the urge to grab her and sink his teeth into her neck. "I… I…," he stammered, furious with himself for his lack of control. He'd fed only days before. Why now?

The servant said nothing but bared her neck to Adrien and smiled. He pulled her roughly toward him, his blunt teeth tearing her tender skin. She moaned with pleasure and his mouth filled with the taste of her until he knew nothing but the sensation of drowning in her blood.

Someone laughed. It took Adrien a moment to realize the laughter was his own.

"You're weak." He recognized the voice—the same voice he'd heard on the airplane hours before. *"You'll suffocate until you learn what it means to be an immortal."*

Who are you?

"You must learn what it means to possess true power."

"Adrien. Adrien!" Jean's voice brought Adrien back to his senses. Adrien was kneeling. The servant had gone limp in his arms.

Jean took the woman from Adrien with surprising ease. He touched her cheek, then frowned at Adrien.

"I…. Is she…?" Adrien's hands shook as horror twisted in his gut at what he had almost done.

"She'll be fine with a rest," Jean said, eyeing him with obvious concern. "Has this happened before?"

"Once," he whispered. "Long ago. I hadn't taken blood in decades…." He didn't add that he'd hoped to die, but he guessed Jean knew this. "But it's been only days since I last fed."

"Wait here." Jean carried the servant into one of the guest bedrooms, leaving Adrien sitting on the floor, staring at the spot where he'd nearly killed her.

When Jean returned, Adrien looked up, still at a loss to explain what had come over him. "I'm sorry. I don't know…. I don't understand…." He'd behaved just like the animals he'd once hunted.

"Let me help you to your room." Jean's expression didn't judge, and for that Adrien was thankful. He already felt like shit about what he'd done.

Adrien tried to speak, but finding nothing to say that might justify his actions, he merely nodded. Jean offered him a hand. Adrien took it, then leaned on Jean for support as he continued to shake.

They reached Adrien's room a few minutes later. "You're troubled," Jean said as he helped Adrien to the bed. "Perhaps it was unwise to force you to come—"

"No. If Pelletier shows, I want to be there. I'm just tired."

"I know little about immortals," Jean said, "but I find it difficult to imagine that such a sudden and overwhelming lust for blood has anything to do with lack of sleep. Perhaps you should speak with Roland."

Adrien furrowed his brow and pressed his lips tightly together. The last person he wanted to speak with was Roland. Still, if it would appease Jean, he'd tolerate another of Roland's lectures.

"All right," he said.

Jean nodded. "You will call me if you should experience the bloodlust again tonight."

"I'll call you."

Jean hesitated a moment, then left the room and closed the door behind him without another word.

Adrien closed his eyes. *You're tired.* The words did nothing to quiet the sensation of unease that had settled in his chest. He breathed in, then out again, tensing, then releasing his muscles as Roland had taught him more than a century before.

He fell asleep to thoughts of blood and the sound of someone chanting a rhyme he'd once heard when he was a boy.

Man of words and not of deeds is like a garden full of weeds… and when your back begins to smart, it's like a penknife in your heart; and when your heart begins to bleed, you're dead, and dead, and dead, indeed.

"NICOLAS!" ADRIEN opened his eyes and shuddered as the first light of morning streamed through the castle window. He'd dreamed of Nicolas, just beyond his reach as always. But this time, when he'd called Nicolas's name, Nicolas had turned around. Adrien had seen his face, not just an amorphous blur of memory. He'd seen kindness and longing in Nicolas's expression. Adrien wiped his eyes and discovered his cheeks were wet with tears.

It was a dream like any other.

"You're weak, Adrien."

Was he going mad, hearing voices? *Who are you?* Adrien laughed at himself that he'd even think to ask the question.

"You already know the answer, Adrien," the voice replied. *"I am you."*

CHAPTER THREE:
WOUNDS TO LICK

Abbeville, France, 1896

PERCHED ON a cliff high above the English Channel, Roland's small house was tiny compared to the Rousseau castle. For Adrien, however, it was a welcome relief from the trappings of nobility. He felt far more comfortable here, with no servants hovering, eager to attend to his every need. The house reminded him of his family's home in Saint-Gervais: cozy and warm. The meals Thomas, Roland's constant companion, provided for them reminded him of his sister's cooking. The beds they slept in were small but comfortable. The location was idyllic, but Adrien had barely noticed.

Six days since the ill-fated engagement celebration. Six days that had healed Adrien's body but had done nothing to quiet his feeling of dread. He'd asked after Nicolas every day, hoping for news and yet fearful that he might learn something had happened to him.

"Jean is with him and Rosina," Roland had reassured him. "He will keep them both safe."

Since regaining consciousness three days before, Adrien had done nothing but train with Roland and Charles, with only short breaks for eating and sleeping. The nearly constant training kept him from brooding over the loss of his sword, although he thought of it much of the time he sparred. Today's training had been particularly taxing, and now, seated on the roof of Roland's house with the salty breeze on his face, Adrien remembered with frustration how he'd once again been outmatched by Charles.

"May I join you?" François asked.

"Please." Adrien motioned for François to sit beside him.

"I've barely seen you the past three days," he said. "How is your training progressing?"

"It's not," grumbled Adrien, his frustration getting the best of him. "I can't fight either of them without my sword."

"But I've seen you attack without your sword."

"My power is too weak all on its own. The sword magnifies it," Adrien explained. François already knew this, but for Adrien, speaking the words felt like well-deserved penance for his failure.

"Why don't you try attacking me?" François asked as he stood up.

"You?"

"And why not?" François glared at him. "Or have you finally realized you're stronger than I am?"

"I couldn't," Adrien snapped.

François laughed. "Are you afraid to fight me, then?"

"No, but—"

"Then what? Are you worried you might hurt me?" François raised his hand and summoned his sword, then met Adrien's gaze in challenge.

"No." He truly had no good reason for turning François down if he wasn't afraid of hurting him. *Except that you're afraid to lose to him.* Adrien *was* weak. A hunter without his soul's weapon was no more than a magician performing paltry tricks for entertainment.

"Well?" François's expression told Adrien his brother understood his fear, even if he refused to acknowledge it was justified.

"All right."

"Let's go, then." François grinned.

"Now?"

"Are you too tired?"

Adrien's body ached and his stiff muscles protested as he got to his feet. "No." He could do this.

Ten minutes later, they faced each other inside the enormous cave Roland used for training. Cut out of the hard rock of the cliff overlooking the ocean, it was unlikely to collapse even after repeated vampire and hunter attacks. The light inside was dim, the few torches inadequate to illuminate the enormous space. In spite of this, Adrien had little difficulty seeing François. His vision now matched that of the vampires, thanks to Nicolas's blood. He saw the reddish glow of François's eyes as François raised his sword. Adrien stood ready to defend against his attack, resolved not to obsess over his lack of a weapon.

François whipped his sword backward and forward, launching an arc of fire toward Adrien. Adrien raised his palms and deflected the energy upward. Bits of rock and dust fell from the roof of the cave, forcing him to move to avoid being hit.

"I've been watching you train," François admitted. "I guessed having an audience would make you uncomfortable."

Adrien frowned in surprise—he'd seen François at the house, but he hadn't realized he'd been in the cave. François was right; it did make him uncomfortable.

"Vampires are skilled at hiding their presence," François continued with a look of sympathy. "It's a skill immortals also possess, I'm told."

"How do you know about immortals?" Adrien asked with genuine interest.

"I'm curious, and Roland likes to talk." François's soft chuckle reminded Adrien of how much he'd missed his brother. "Do you want to know what else I've learned?"

"Of course." Adrien hadn't considered asking Roland about immortals' power because he'd been too busy trying to avoid the feelings training with Roland recalled in him.

"Immortals possess powers similar to both vampires and hunters. I suppose that makes sense, since we all share the same blood. There is one key difference, though."

"What is that?" Adrien asked.

"Vampires' powers are more offensive in nature, whereas hunters' are primarily defensive."

It made sense. Hunters were supposed to protect humanity from the unchecked power of the vampires, whereas for millennia, vampires had been primarily predators.

"What did Roland say about immortals' defensive abilities?"

"He wasn't very specific," François said as he leaned against the cave wall and folded his long arms over his chest. "You know him." Adrien chuckled and shook his head. "But he implied that immortals were able to combine the strength of the vampires' offensive techniques with those of the hunters to create a stronger defense. I suppose the same might be true of offensive attacks."

Adrien looked down at his hands. He'd been using them strictly as offensive tools. He thought about the techniques he had learned as a child, of using his sword to absorb the energy of a vampire attack.

"Try attacking me again," he told François.

"All right." François moved to the center of the chamber, raised his weapon, and swung it down in an arc. This time he showered Adrien with bursts of ice that swirled about the room like a hurricane. Adrien raised his hands as he'd done before, but this time he focused specifically on the energy of his attack. His palms warmed and he imagined absorbing the energy as he'd done with his sword.

A hum filled the room, and Adrien instinctively turned his hands toward François. He felt François's power gather in his hands, then move to his arms and chest. He breathed in deeply, allowing the strength to build within him, focusing on the feel of it. Then, when the intensity peaked, he aimed his hands toward one of the large rock formations at the edge of the cave.

Streaks of black and gold flew from his fingertips, and the pitch of the hum rose as the power discharged. The light hit the rocks with a resounding explosion, shaking the floor of the cave and sending fragments of rock flying like projectiles.

"Not bad," François said as the dust cleared.

"Thanks for the suggestion." Adrien smiled for the first time since the fight with Pelletier at the castle.

"So how about some dinner?" François asked. "You haven't eaten anything since breakfast and it's nearly midnight."

"I'll stay." Learning to use his newfound abilities was more important than food.

François frowned and his sword vanished. "You're more stubborn than I remember, little brother."

Adrien laughed. It felt strangely good to laugh. The last time he'd laughed, he'd been with Nicolas….

"You love him, don't you?" Adrien saw no judgment in François's face.

"If you'd told me a year ago that I'd care about a vampire…." He sat on one of the rocks and rubbed his eyes. "But what I feel doesn't matter. He'll marry Rosina and—"

"He loves you too."

"François," Adrien warned.

François smiled. "Dinner?"

"If I agree, will you drop the subject of Nicolas?" Adrien didn't have the energy to argue. His body ached even though the cuts and bruises from training had healed.

14

"All right." François put his arm around Adrien's shoulders. "For now, at least."

"I missed this," Adrien admitted. "Sparring with you."

"This was nothing. Tomorrow, when you're rested, we'll spar for more than a few minutes." He smiled, then added, "You've gotten stronger. Even if you don't realize it yourself. And it's not just the blood."

For once Adrien didn't argue. An hour later, he lay in bed, exhausted but satisfied. It was a start.

CHAPTER FOUR:
RELEASE

ADRIEN AND François began their practice early in the morning. Charles arrived a few hours later and took François's place.

"François told me about last night," Charles said as he readied himself with his sword. "Shall we see what you've discovered?"

Adrien nodded, then waited for Charles to launch his attack. Adrien raised his hands as he'd done with François and felt the warmth of the energy run up his arms and through his body. During his session with François that morning, Adrien had gotten quite good at directing the stream of energy back at his opponent. He did as he'd done before, allowing the energy to build inside his body, then focusing it back from where it had come.

This time, however, instead of the narrow beam of energy he'd managed to direct with François, when he aimed for Charles, the energy did not release. His hands burned as though they were on fire, and he shouted as he tried to let go of the building energy.

He glanced at his hands as the red flames grew brighter, flickering at the edges with tinges of white. This felt different than with François. And in spite of the pain, his skin appeared unmarred beneath the bursts of energy.

His attack was more powerful. Different somehow.

Adrien struggled to control the flames. It felt as though time had slowed and he was watching this unfold at his own pace.

The attack isn't burning me. He needed the reminder as pain seared through his fingers and made its slow trek up his body. The flames poured from his arms and shoulders now, as if his hands were too weak to contain them. This thought led to another: why not use his entire body to reflect the energy the way he'd used his hands before?

He breathed in and allowed the power of the attack to permeate his skin, allowed it to heat his muscles, then warm his blood. He struggled to focus on Charles, who seemed frozen in place, his sword still where he'd raised it before he'd unleashed his weapon. When Adrien felt the heat in every pore of his body, he imagined it flying toward Charles. A high-pitched shriek like the sound of a bird of prey diving from high above echoed throughout the cavern.

A ball of blue fire shot from Adrien's chest, spinning and undulating as it flew toward Charles. Adrien watched Charles react, turning his sword sideways and lifting it to meet the attack. Adrien relaxed, trying not to shout in excitement at this new development. But at the same moment, the fiery orb exploded short of its target, sending out sparks of light that disappeared as they met the solid walls and ceiling of the cave.

"What?" Adrien took a step backward and stared in disbelief. Nothing was left of the volley. No marks from the impact were visible on the rocks. "It did nothing?"

Charles eyed Adrien with a mixture of surprise and amusement. "You shouldn't be surprised."

"I…. Why? It should have knocked you off your feet at the very least."

"You thought it would hit me," Charles replied. "But you lost your focus."

Damn. Adrien had done exactly that. He'd thought the attack would meet its mark. He'd thought once he'd launched it that it would behave as any normal attack would. *But it's not the same.*

"You've seen this attack before?" he asked Charles.

Charles nodded. "It's similar to one the ancients use." He laughed, then added, "Some call our kind parasitic. Perhaps it's true for reasons other than our need for blood."

"I see it differently. If someone attacks me, why shouldn't I use their power against them?"

The corners of Charles's mouth edged upward in a knowing smile. "There's a reason few humans know of our existence," he said. "Power like that doesn't endear us to them any more than our bloodlust."

Adrien wouldn't argue. Even as a hunter, he'd sensed that humans tolerated him, at best. Hunters were necessary evils, like the rat catchers who got paid by the carcass. He shrugged off the thought.

"Attack me again."

This time Charles smiled outright.

ADRIEN AND Charles sparred on and off until nightfall, joined at last by Roland. They would have kept sparring, but Thomas came to the cave to let them know that dinner was ready. After some prodding, Adrien followed Charles and Roland back to the house.

"Where is François?" Charles asked as he swirled his glass of wine around but barely drank from it.

"He went for a walk on the beach a few hours ago. He said he'd be back for dinner." Thomas set a large terrine on the table, then brought several baguettes, which he placed in the center. The heavenly scent of duck and spices filled the room.

Adrien was so hungry by this point that he had little interest in anything but ladling out the food onto his plate. "Wasn't he in his room?"

"No." Charles stood abruptly.

"Something wrong, Charles?" Roland broke a piece of the bread off with his hands, then handed the baguette to Adrien.

"Nothing, I'm sure," Charles answered. "I'll be back shortly. Please don't wait for me."

Roland raised an eyebrow, then began to slice the terrine. Adrien watched Charles leave as he absentmindedly chewed on his piece of bread.

"He's worried," Adrien said as he helped himself to some of the terrine. The scent of spices and meat made his mouth water.

Roland nodded but said nothing more.

"Should he be worried?" Adrien pressed.

"What do you think?"

Too tired to protest, Adrien just sighed in response.

THE SMELL of burned wood wafted on the night breeze. François smelled it, even from where he sat at the top of the cliff. The night before, he and Charles had sat beneath those trees. Tonight, he'd pointed his sword at the trees, he'd used his hunter power, and he'd watched them burn.

The waves below crashed against the rocks. He felt like the water, tossed around by forces beyond his control. He imagined the rocks being pummeled by the water. How long, he wondered, did it take to turn boulders into sand?

He stood and walked along the edge of the cliff. In the distance, the moon rose over the water, casting shadows.

Vampire whore. You like it, don't you?

He tried to ignore the echo of the past and focus on the sound of the surf. He began to run. The breeze felt good against his cheeks. The stars over the water flickered.

Pretty beast.

He ran faster now, trying to leave the whispers of memory behind him. He pushed away the recollection of the rough touch, the pain of the violation, the sense of powerlessness. He'd wanted to die.

He tripped and fell headlong into the grass, and he lay there, tears burning the corners of his eyes until he stopped fighting and just let them fall. Tears for his lost self, the strong and independent self who'd loved life more than anything. The man he had once been.

An hour later he wiped his wet face on his shirt and stood. He watched the waves crest and crash upon the sand. After jumping off the cliff and landing softly on the beach, François undressed and walked naked into the surf.

He waded out until the water covered him completely, then forced the last bit of air out of his lungs and sank to the bottom. Darkness swallowed him as he closed his eyes.

A COLD fear gripped Charles as he walked along the sandy beach. He'd been to the cave and he'd walked the fields in the hopes of finding François.

"Come to me, Charles." François's voice resonated in the recesses of Charles's mind.

Charles saw something floating in the surf. Clothing.

Where are you?

"Not far."

Charles walked into the water, not caring that he was still fully clothed. *I was worried.*

"I'm waiting for you."

The water reached his shoulders, but still Charles saw only the shimmer of moonlight on the surface. A wave broke, nearly causing him to lose his balance. Two strong arms encircled his waist, steadying him.

Cool lips pressed against his neck, and the sharp edge of teeth barely broke the skin.

"François." Charles turned to see François, naked, his hair wet. Smiling.

François leaned in and claimed Charles's lips without parting them. Water rose and foamed, swirling around them, sending drops skyward, painting their bodies.

"You needn't worry," François said as he released Charles's mouth. "I really will be fine."

Charles sighed, unconvinced.

François clearly sensed this, because he pulled back his wet hair to expose his neck and said, "I won't hide from you again. My soul is yours."

Charles licked a line over François's skin until he felt his pulse. He inhaled the scent of the salt water and of François's blood, then bared his teeth and slowly sank into the soft, cool flesh. François's moan mingled with the sound of swells breaking on the sand as Charles lost himself in the blood.

The world outside faded, replaced by the steady beat of François's heart and the wave of emotions that accompanied the memories Charles tasted. But for the first time since they'd brought François back from the hunter prison, those memories were not dark. Instead, Charles felt François's love not only for him, but for Adrien, Nicolas, and the others. François's bleak recollection of the prison cell became power Charles hadn't sensed before. He saw François drink Roland's blood and felt François call upon the power of the immortals. He understood now that François had survived only because of that blood. He silently thanked Roland for that gift.

Charles's thoughts wandered as he relived François's time spent at his side. He saw himself as François saw him, and although he still felt unworthy of François's love, he would never doubt it again. These thoughts mingled with François's physical desire for him. As Charles drank, he felt François respond to the bloodlust, and his more primal instincts directed him outward, beyond François's soul. He released François's neck and came back to himself as François kissed him once more.

Charles shivered as the wind raked the waterlogged fabric of his clothing.

"Let me help you out of those," François said with a chuckle as he opened the buttons of Charles's shirt, then worked his way downward until Charles was as naked as he. In spite of the cool water, Charles's skin warmed as his body adjusted to compensate.

Centuries before, Charles had learned that his body would adapt to extreme temperature. Even fire could not kill a vampire. He'd never thought this ability interesting in the least. Not until he'd understood the freedom François discovered in his own body. He'd chosen not to see the beauty in his vampire existence, but François, even fledgling that he was, understood that beauty.

You've taught me so much.

LATER, THEY lay sated on the grass, legs entangled. François looked up at Charles, his expression serene. How had Charles not seen it before, the love François felt for him? *Easy to miss when you don't believe you deserve it.*

François kissed the base of his neck, then laid his head against his chest, just over his heart.

"François," Charles whispered, "welcome home."

CHAPTER FIVE:
RESTLESS HEARTS

Paris, France

BLAISE AWOKE to bright sunshine streaming in his bedroom window. He hadn't slept well since the confrontation with Pelletier, and the guards his uncle had posted around the castle did little to ease his sense of foreboding. Knowing that Jean Lambert slept several rooms away from his hadn't helped, either. If it hadn't been for his and Rosina's insistence that Jean remain to ensure Nicolas's safety, Blaise guessed Reynaud would have been more than happy to see Jean go. But Reynaud was a pragmatist who understood the benefits of an alliance between the clans. Whatever his connection to Pelletier and the hunters, he would not risk Nicolas or Jean withdrawing from their bargain if he could prevent it.

Blaise dressed in riding clothes and took the servants' stairway in an effort to avoid his uncle, who preferred to take his breakfast early. "Unless you intend to challenge me for the leadership of our clan," Reynaud had told Blaise the third time he'd attempted to speak to his uncle about Pelletier and the clan's continued contact with him, "you'd be far better served carrying out your duties than concerning yourself with mine."

As the eldest son of the former clan leader, Blaise could challenge Reynaud. But a vicious fight to the death would do nothing to improve the lives of his clanspeople, and he did not aspire to power. There might come a time when he'd be forced to take Reynaud's place, but for now he would defer to his uncle. It was with these dark thoughts that he saddled his horse and rode for the forest and the rolling hills beyond.

He became aware of Jean's presence as he reached the farthest corner of his family's land. He didn't need to hear Jean to know he was there—even without having shared their blood, they had been too close to ever completely extinguish the bond between them.

Blaise rode harder. *Let him follow.* He'd given Jean too many chances to explain the past. Too many times Blaise had struggled to retain the pieces of his heart Jean hadn't stolen. He wouldn't let him have what was left of it.

Time passed. Blaise nearly managed to forget Jean as the wind brushed his cheeks and wove its fingers through his hair. The sun rose and warmed the late spring morning, but sheltered by the trees, the air in the forest still felt cool against his skin. He had nearly reached the small lake near town when, with the skill of an accomplished horseman, Jean overtook Blaise's horse, cornering him so quickly that neither Blaise nor his horse had time to react.

Blaise glared at Jean. "Your horsemanship has improved over the centuries, but your manners have not."

"My apologies." Jean's cool expression belied the intensity Blaise saw in his eyes—eyes that appeared to see right through him.

Blaise dismounted and walked past Jean toward the water. Jean followed, jumping from his horse and landing so close that Blaise felt the brush of his jacket against his shoulder. "You're not sorry." He took a breath to calm his racing heart, then added, "I'm neither blind nor stupid. You enjoy taunting me."

Jean's smile took Blaise by surprise. "I could never fool you, Blaise." Jean spoke his name like a caress.

Blaise drew a long breath and schooled his expression. "What do you want?"

"I wish to make amends."

"How self-serving of you." Blaise didn't care that he sounded bitter.

"You still care for me, don't you?" Jean's dark eyes glittered momentarily with pain.

"Does that please you? Does it make you happy to know how even now, you have the ability to wound me?"

Damn him to hell. Blaise turned and walked to the water's edge, where he stood, back to Jean, gazing out over the sunlit surface. How many hours had they spent here? How many times had they made love on the shore?

"It matters a great deal to me," Jean said.

Jean stood so close that Blaise felt his breath on his neck. He shivered in spite of himself. There was nowhere to retreat to this time. No party to occupy him. He stood his ground but did not turn around.

"*You* were the one who left on the day we were to be handfasted. You were the one...." Blaise couldn't speak the words. He clenched his jaw and willed the pain back to the place where he could master it. He'd gotten quite good at it over time.

"Blaise." Jean's voice reminded Blaise of the wind as it blew through the wheat of the farmers' fields. Soft. Resonant. Deep.

Blaise was unprepared for Jean's hand on his shoulder, turning him so that he couldn't avoid meeting Jean's gaze. He was even more unprepared for the way his body betrayed him as he leaned into Jean's touch. For a moment they remained that way, their lips a hairsbreadth apart. And yet neither of them closed the distance to claim the kiss. "Please. Leave," Blaise said as he came back to himself and pulled abruptly away.

"I truly am sorry," Jean said. "Please forgive me."

Jean mounted his horse and galloped away, leaving only dust from the trail in his wake.

Blaise closed his eyes. This many years later, there were no tears, only the deep pain of emptiness that tore at his heart, reopening the wounds of the past.

CHAPTER SIX:
ECHOES OF THE HEART

BLAISE RETURNED his horse to the stables, thankful he didn't run into Jean once again. As he often did when he needed to think, he retrieved his sketchpad from his room, sat under his favorite tree, and allowed his pen to guide his thoughts.

As often happened when he drew, time passed quickly and he lost himself in his work. It wasn't until he heard the sound of hoofbeats on the gravel that he realized he'd completely lost track of time.

"You've been sitting there for hours, Blaise," Rosina said, peering down at him from the gray mare she was riding. "Something's troubling you."

He looked up from his sketchbook and smiled at her. "You worry too much about me."

"I only have one brother," she replied with a glint of mischief in her eyes.

"And I have a firebrand of a sister," he laughed. "Perhaps you will find happiness in your marriage, Rosina."

Her smile became a frown.

"You still oppose this marriage?" Blaise asked, knowing he should have kept his opinions to himself.

"I'll do what is asked of me," she said, lifting her chin as she often did when she disagreed with their uncle.

"Uncle wishes only what is best for you."

"*Lord* Rousseau," she said, stressing the honorific, "wants only what is best for the *clan*."

"Is that so wrong?"

"I am tired of mourning those I love," she said, the bitterness in her voice obvious.

Blaise sighed. "Mother and Father were hardly pawns in this struggle. They fought for what they believed was right."

SHIRA ANTHONY

"No," said Rosina. "Perhaps not."

"Nor was Paul."

"He didn't deserve to die so young," she retorted. Anger and pain flashed through her deep green eyes.

"No. Of course not." He walked over to her horse and gently stroked its head. "I miss him too," he said softly.

"I know." She gathered the reins and turned to leave.

"Where is Uncle?" he asked.

"Inside. Meeting with the hunter again."

"You don't trust Lord Pelletier, do you?"

"No," Rosina replied. "They're all the same, hunters. They want power, and they'll use our clan to attain it. They can't be trusted."

"Have you spoken to Uncle about your concerns?"

"He's too blind to see," she replied angrily. "The prospect of victory over the Lamberts is an obsession with him. He chooses to look the other way." She smoothed a strand of hair that had escaped the ribbon that bound it back. "I will tolerate his poor choices for now. But if there should come a time when those choices threaten those I love, I won't hesitate to use my blade in battle."

Blaise sighed. "Rosina Rousseau," he said, "you're a woman of honor. Still, I hope your fears are never realized. I should hate to see you in harm's way."

"And what of you, Blaise?" she asked. "Will you look the other way as well?"

"I...." He hesitated. He had done his best to leave the past alone, even if he would never forget it. "I've been taught well. I do not interfere in the affairs of the clan. When it's time for me to take Uncle's place, I will do my best."

She pressed her lips together and shook her head. "Sweet Blaise," she said. "Your poet's heart is not meant for war, in spite of your resolve. Yet you fight what your heart leads you to do."

"And what might that be?" he asked, knowing full well what she would say.

"It's time you ask Jean for his blood, that you may know the truth." She narrowed her eyes and added, "At least you will know whether to kill him—"

"Or love him?" Blaise finished.

She nodded. "But that's the crux of your hesitation, isn't it? To kill him would destroy you."

26

Blaise clenched his jaw. What could he say? She spoke the truth.

"You deserve some happiness," she said as she began to ride away. "At least as much as I."

He watched her disappear over the next ridge and once again took his seat under the tree. *Happiness.* He laughed. *Not in this world.*

Blaise closed his eyes and recalled a time when he was younger, before the deaths of his beloved older brother and his parents—before the horrors of war had stolen the joy from his life.

He'd first met Jean in winter, after his parents had finally consented to let him attend a party at the château of a noble family. He had been to Paris many times before, but he'd never seen Paris quite like this. Beautiful women with porcelain skin floated gracefully across the marble floors, laughing, fluttering their fans, smiling at the men who stood talking at the edge of the room. Sumptuous food filled tables adorned with fresh flowers from southern climes where the sun still shone warm.

Men conversed in undertones while they drank thick ruby wines that made Blaise's nostrils tickle and his head spin. Some of the men danced with the women, others with men. Still others withdrew to private rooms where they shared their blood and more. Blaise wondered what delights he might find in those rooms, although they frightened as much as called to him.

He had just come of age—a boy in a man's body, unsure around both sexes but intensely curious. He knew little of how to dress. His older brother had told the tailor to make him a suit of the finest silk velvet in deep green, to match his eyes and emphasize his dark hair. Far more comfortable in the riding clothes he preferred, he'd felt strange and awkward. Out of his element.

He'd learned to dance, a skill expected of a young man of his status, the second heir to the Rousseau dynasty. That skill served him well that night, as countless men and women sought to partner him in the latest *contradanses*. They danced in a group to the carefully prescribed steps, smiling at each other and flirting.

Tired after dancing for hours without rest, he had shed his uncomfortable shoes and escaped the warm ballroom into the cold winter air. There he stood, watching his breath rise as the snow caused his bare feet to tingle.

Someone grabbed him from behind and spun him around—one of the men he'd seen when he'd danced and who had, on several occasions, tried to entice him to join him for a drink in one of the adjoining rooms.

His brother had warned him to be careful of such men, who preyed on those too inexperienced to know better. He'd refused, but the man had been persistent. Now the man pulled Blaise against him and, in spite of Blaise's protests—or perhaps because of them—stole a kiss. The man's breath reeked of hard spirits, and his beard burned Blaise's lips.

Blaise fought the man with all his strength, which was considerable for a young man his size. But Blaise was far smaller than his amorous suitor. The man put his hand to the ribbon that held Blaise's hair at his nape and untied it. Blaise's hair fell over his shoulders in a tousle of black.

"Stop!" Blaise yelled as the man pushed Blaise's hair from his neck, then bared his teeth, panting in anticipation. They struggled, but Blaise could not free himself from the man's grasp.

"Leave him be." The warm baritone resonated against the windows that led back to the ballroom.

"A beautiful boy is meant to be savored," Blaise's suitor laughed.

"Release him," the newcomer said. He was handsome—tall, pale-skinned, with dark blue eyes and hair the color of night. The contempt in his chiseled face was plain. "Clearly he does not wish your attentions."

The older man pushed Blaise away and materialized his sword. Blaise tumbled headlong into the snow, twisting his ankle as he fell.

"Who are you to tell your elders what a boy wants?" Blaise's tormenter growled.

"A man who values honor," the stranger replied. He didn't call his sword but continued to glare at Blaise's attacker. "That is all you need to know."

Blaise's would-be suitor swung his sword, firing a blast of blue toward the newcomer and laughing unabashedly as he did so. The stranger remained still, raising only the palm of his hand to the attack and reflecting it back whence it had come. "Leave, or I'll be forced to injure you," the stranger said in a calm, controlled voice.

Blaise's attacker aimed his weapon at his challenger's chest.

A powerful wind blew from his rescuer's fingers into the attacker's face. Blaise's attacker began to laugh but then stopped abruptly as the stranger flicked his wrist. His attacker flew into the air and landed with a thud yards away. He groaned weakly, then lay still.

Blaise struggled to his feet. A strong arm encircled his shoulders, helping him.

"You're injured." The stranger's deep voice sent shivers up Blaise's spine.

"My ankle," Blaise said as the man lifted him into his arms. Blaise blushed with embarrassment. His body would heal by morning, even if his fragile ego might not.

The man carried Blaise into a small sitting room and laid him on a settee, accidentally brushing Blaise's face with his hands. The touch was electrifying, and for a moment Blaise forgot how to breathe.

"Thank you." Blaise thought he saw a flash of crimson in those dark blue eyes, but then he blinked and it vanished.

"May I call someone to assist you?" the man asked, his beautiful face inscrutable. "Is there someone here with you?"

"My… my mother," he stammered as his heart pounded so loudly he was convinced the man could hear it. "Lady Rousseau."

The man said nothing but bowed deeply and turned to leave the room.

"Please," Blaise said, knowing he sounded like the child he was. "I would like to know the name of my rescuer."

The man paused as if considering whether to answer. Then the edges of his mouth turned upward in the makings of a smile. "Jean," the man said. "Jean Lambert."

BLAISE GAZED down at the sketchpad as he came back to himself and the sound of the leaves as they crackled on the nearly bare trees. When Rosina had stopped to speak to him, he'd been drawing the garden with its dying roses and mounds of straw meant to shelter the tender plants in the coming winter. In the middle of the sketch he'd drawn a man, his dark hair and proud bearing instantly recognizable.

Jean, how long will you run from me?

CHAPTER SEVEN:
NO SMALL PRICE

JEAN'S HORSE galloped across the field and jumped the low fence separating it from the wild hills and copses beyond. A skilled horseman, Jean had managed to lose the Rousseau guards Reynaud had posted to him after a few minutes. He rode until his mount was too tired to continue, then led the horse to a small stream and sat down on the soft moss, his back pressed against a gnarled tree.

Here, where no one could see, he allowed himself the luxury of dropping his practiced façade. He picked up a smooth rock and held it in his palm, rolling it around distractedly.

You had no right to taunt him. Blaise. Beautiful, loving Blaise. Jean had tried to forget Blaise. He thought he'd become inured to the pain of loss, but here, faced with Blaise again, he'd been unable to restrain himself.

You've accomplished too much to risk it on your own foolish heart.

He imagined Blaise's older brother, Paul. Even now, he half imagined Paul would join him here. How many times had they laughed as they'd raced their horses over these hills? At times Jean missed Paul's friendship nearly as much as Blaise's affections.

"You worry far too much," Paul had told him a few days before he and Blaise were to be pledged to each other. *"You'll be happy. You are meant to be together."*

He'd laughed and called Paul a romantic fool. But Jean's heart had been full to know that not only would he and Blaise be joined for eternity, he would truly be able to call Paul "brother."

"Paul," Jean said as he watched the water hurry over the stones, "can you ever forgive me for what I've done to him?" The rushing of the stream was his only response.

He sighed and glanced at his hand. Nothing was left of the stone but a handful of dust.

Darkness had fallen over the castle when Jean finally led his horse back to the stables. He dismissed the stable hands and tended to the horse himself, removing the saddle, brushing the horse's coat, feeding and watering it. He had no desire to rush back to the castle.

"Did you enjoy your ride, Lord Lambert?" said a voice from the door to the stall.

Jean turned to face Rosina. "It was… enlightening."

"Why do you insist on torturing him?" She glared at him. "Isn't it enough that you came here in the first place? After what they say you did, I should run you through."

"I'll leave once it's safe for Nicolas." He deserved her anger, so he'd bear it.

"Blaise and I can protect him without your help." Her eyes flashed in open challenge. He didn't doubt she would make a powerful foe.

"You underestimate Pelletier."

"And *you*, monsieur, underestimate *me*." Her expression darkened. "I was only a child when they told me you'd slaughtered my parents and my brother," she continued. "They said you did it for my brother's blood, that you stole every drop in his body. They say you and your men killed my parents because they stood against you."

"What would you have me say, Rosina?" Jean asked.

"I would like the truth," she replied, her gaze fixed on his.

"What has been done cannot be undone with my words."

"I don't believe you killed my parents or Paul. Blaise doesn't believe it either." She spoke these words in obvious challenge.

Jean stared at her. He knew Blaise didn't believe it, but Rosina too?

"This surprises you, doesn't it?"

"Yes," he answered truthfully.

"Until a week ago, I believed what I'd been told. But after what Pelletier did…."

There were few times in his life that Jean had hesitated to respond, but now he struggled to find the words. Why, after all that had happened, did both Rosina and Blaise believe in his innocence? In the end, he said only, "The truth has been spoken. There is nothing more to say."

"I *will* know the truth, Lord Lambert," Rosina said as Jean turned and walked out of the stables. "For my brother's sake, as well as my clan's."

NICOLAS WATCHED the stars from the balcony outside the dining room. Jean still had not returned to their rooms, although one of the servants had told Nicolas he'd seen Jean around the stables that afternoon. Nicolas knew it was childish to worry about his brother—Jean was one of the most powerful vampires alive, and the connection between them was strong enough that he could sense Jean's presence even now.

He'd grown up hearing the accusations that Jean had murdered Paul Rousseau and his parents. He'd not dared to ask more about it. Whatever Jean had done, he'd had his reasons. Nicolas and Jean had lost their own parents in the fight between the clans. Still, knowing that Jean was here, in the midst of their enemies, worried him. Jean might be strong, but what they'd witnessed with Pelletier and his men....

The door behind him opened. He smiled to feel Jean's reassuring presence, then turned to face him. "I was worried about you."

"I'm sorry to have returned so late."

"You look tired," Nicolas pressed a hand to Jean's cheek.

"You worry too much, Nicolas," Jean replied, taking his hand and squeezing it gently. "But I'm grateful that you care."

How could he not? Jean was more like a father to him than a brother. Jean had protected him, taught him everything he knew. "Cook saved you some dinner. I'll ask him to warm it."

"Thank you."

Nicolas followed Jean inside and settled into one of the chairs by the fireplace.

Jean poured himself a glass of wine, sipped it, then gazed into the flames. He took a deep breath and seemed to steady himself, as if trying to shed the weight of an ancient burden. For the first time Nicolas could remember, Jean appeared vulnerable.

"What do you fear?" The question was impertinent, but Jean would forgive him.

Jean appeared to consider the question, then said with a melancholy smile, "Despite what you believe, I fear many things. But most of all, I fear I will hurt you."

"Hurt me?" Nicolas shook his head. "You've given me so much. How could you hurt me?"

"Perhaps I should have resisted when you suggested this marriage. Perhaps I should—"

"This isn't like you," Nicolas said.

"It isn't like me to doubt my choices?" Jean sighed audibly, then took another sip of his wine. "Perhaps not. But I hope when all is said and done, you'll forgive me for them."

"You needn't worry. There is nothing you can say or do that will change how proud I am to call you brother. The choices I've made are mine and mine alone." Nicolas got to his feet and gently touched Jean's forearm, hoping to reassure him.

"You're still young, Nicolas."

"I'm old enough to die fighting should this war continue. I'm more than old enough to be married. And although I know you've seen far more than I, I am old enough to understand the consequences of my actions." He met Jean's gaze and added, "If my choice to marry Rosina prevents more death, I will have no regrets."

"I, also, am proud to call you my brother," Jean said as he embraced Nicolas.

CHAPTER EIGHT:
CROSSROADS

"FASTER, ADRIEN!" Roland shouted as Charles and Adrien flew around the cave.

A flash of light and a shower of ice burst from the place where their attacks met in midair. Adrien dodged artfully, then, using his newfound strength, somersaulted over Charles. He stretched his hands out as he soared, sending twin beams of black-and-gold-tinged energy that barely missed Charles. As he landed on the floor of the cave, Adrien saw François seated high on an outcropping near the ceiling. François smiled and nodded his approval.

This time Charles swung his sword wide, creating a wall of ice that blocked Adrien's path. Adrien leaped over the ice and landed only a few yards away from Charles. Before Charles could raise his sword to attack again, Adrien moved directly in front of him and grabbed Charles's blade with his bare hand to hold it in check.

Adrien ignored the bite of the blade. The wound there would heal. Charles's ego, on the other hand, might take a bit longer, judging by his dour expression.

"Nicely done, Adrien," Roland said as he stood and walked over to them. Charles's sword vanished and he walked away without comment. Adrien followed on his heels, ignoring Roland's rambling discourse on the use of angles to determine the trajectory of attacks.

"Come to rub it in?" Charles asked with a scowl.

"I came to thank you," Adrien said as he repressed a grin, "for letting me win."

Charles stared at Adrien in obvious surprise.

"You didn't think I knew, did you? But I've seen you fight Pelletier. I know what you're capable of." When Charles said nothing, Adrien continued, "I can't best you without my sword. But I *will* best you, eventually."

"Impudent brat." The hint of a smile on Charles's lips belied his words.

"Thank you." Adrien bowed theatrically, then headed over to the waiting Roland, who sat cross-legged on the dirt floor, drinking from a silver flask.

"Nicely done," Roland repeated as he offered the flask to Adrien. "Either of you care to join me in a celebratory drink?"

"Later, perhaps," Charles said.

Adrien waved the flask away. "Not particularly."

Roland shrugged and took another sip of what Adrien guessed was homemade spirits. "So," Roland said with obvious relish, "you've mastered the use of your hands as a weapon. Perhaps now you're ready to do the same with a sword."

"If I could call my sword, I wouldn't have spent the last four days training with my bare hands."

"An interesting point." Roland grinned and leaned back against the cave wall. "Then perhaps it's fortunate that you have no sword."

Adrien shot Roland a withering look.

"Thomas brought a sword for you to train with." Roland gestured to a bundle that lay a few feet away, propped up against the rocks. "It will have to do for now."

Adrien reached over and opened the wrappings. He inhaled slowly, hoping his expression wouldn't betray his surprise.

"You remember it, then?" asked Roland with a sly grin. "Is it acceptable to you?"

"I-It...," Adrien stammered, at a loss for words. "It's far more than just acceptable, Roland."

He knew the sword only too well. He'd found it when he was a child, tucked away in a steamer trunk in the attic of his family's home. His mother's sword.

"She was a hunter?" he'd asked his father after he'd explained who the sword had belonged to.

"Yes," his father told him with a sad smile. "When your brother was born, she chose to relinquish her hunter powers. She wanted to be a mother to you and your siblings. She chose to live her life as a human."

Adrien knew that unless a hunter chose to give up his or her powers and become fully human, the Council's commission was for life. Still, he had never considered what that choice might mean. The realization of what his mother had sacrificed for them made his gut clench.

"Charlotte was a powerful hunter," Roland said, bringing Adrien back to himself. "I see much of her in you, Adrien."

Adrien stood abruptly and walked to the cave entrance. François, who had been seated nearby and had no doubt overheard the conversation, followed.

"Are you all right?" François asked as Adrien watched the waves crash against the rocks below.

"Sometimes I forget she was a hunter too," he said.

"You were a child," François said as he clasped Adrien's shoulder. "You killed the vampire who murdered her."

"The vampire wanted *me*."

"You? But how do you—"

"He said he wanted me. But I knew it even before he said it. He came for *me*, François." He'd never told François this. He wondered now why he'd withheld the information. Maybe he hadn't wanted François to know. Maybe he'd once thought he needed to bear the guilt over her death alone. It didn't really matter now. Maybe it had never mattered.

François seemed to understand because his words didn't judge. "She wouldn't blame you. She wanted you to live, to become strong. She'd be proud of you."

Adrien swallowed hard and met François's gaze. "Thanks."

François smiled and nodded.

"Charles," Adrien said as he walked back into the cave, "I'm ready."

Roland stood and walked to the center of the cave. "Charles will not be your opponent this time," he said with a coy smile. "*I* will be."

Adrien met Roland's gaze, smiled, and shook his head. "No doubt you think I'll be easier to trounce after you've set all the others on me."

Roland returned the smile, then turned his palms upward. Adrien had always thought Roland's weapon a beautiful one. Jeweled, as were all hunters' swords, but with an etched design on the flat side of the blade. Unlike the more typical scrollwork Adrien had seen on some weapons, Roland's featured a more primitive design. Angular, with areas of dark and light, it reminded Adrien of some of the tribal patterns he'd seen in the history books he'd loved to read as a child.

Adrien drew his mother's sword, and it warmed to his touch. But when he reached out with his soul, he found nothing there but cold metal.

He forced back the ache of regret for the loss of his beloved Ianus. Regret would do him little good if he was to protect Nicolas.

Roland nodded, as if he'd understood the uneasy peace Adrien had made with the sword. "Of course it's not Ianus," he said. "But it is powerful. You must connect with the source of its power or it's as worthless to you as if a human bladesmith had cast it out of steel."

Leave it to Roland to state the obvious.

Adrien had no time for small talk. He pointed his weapon at Roland, then charged him without delay. The blades scraped, the metal singing throughout the cave as the swords vibrated against each other.

"Do you know what makes a hunter's weapon different from that steel blade?" Roland asked as they pressed their wrists against each other.

Adrien sighed, then pushed back to dislodge himself. He stepped backward and held his weapon pointed at the ceiling, then got down on one knee. "There drew he forth the brand Excalibur," he recited in English, "and o'er him, drawing it, the winter moon, brightening the skirts of a long cloud, ran forth and sparkled keen with frost against the hilt: for all the haft twinkled with diamond sparks, myriads of topaz-lights, and jacinth-work of subtlest jewellery."

"And I thought only your brother recited Tennyson," Roland said with a chuckle. He swung his sword and sent a blaze of fire and ice toward Adrien, an easy volley to dodge. Adrien jumped and rolled, then got quickly to his feet.

"I used to imagine Ianus *was* Excalibur." Adrien smiled as he recalled how, as children, he and François would pretend they were Knights of the Round Table as they practiced their swordsmanship.

Adrien didn't wait for Roland's response but gripped his weapon with both hands and focused his power within his body and outward through the blade. Roland used his weapon to deflect the black-tinged flames toward Adrien, but this time Adrien didn't dodge. He held up his left hand and imagined taking the power back into himself. He breathed through the rush of energy and the pain of the heat, then shivered with pleasure as his body warmed in response to the power.

"This isn't so different," Roland said with an appreciative smirk. "You, like the mythic Arthur, must be worthy of the blade."

"Arthur was born to it," Adrien pointed out. He set himself for another volley, then watched as his power soared high and descended on the spot where Roland stood.

"As were you to Ianus," Roland said. He vanished, then reappeared several feet away.

"How did you do that?" Adrien demanded.

"Do what?"

Adrien scowled and used both his hand and his sword to answer Roland's question with a blinding flash of fire that scorched the rocks behind Roland. Roland, however, vanished again, then reappeared behind Adrien and put his blade to Adrien's neck. Five minutes into their match and Adrien had already lost.

"Do that," Adrien hissed between clenched teeth.

Roland released Adrien, who sheathed his mother's sword. "You'll be able to do the same," Roland finally answered, his eyes twinkling with mischief. "In time."

"I don't have any time," Adrien snapped. "And without Ianus...."

Roland rested his left hand on Adrien's shoulder. "Have you considered that your own lack of faith in yourself and your mother's weapon may be the reason for your frustration?"

"I can't feel the sword," Adrien said. He looked at his hands, turning them over and back again. "I'm stronger than before, but it won't be enough to defeat Pelletier. I don't understand what I can do to become stronger."

Roland released Adrien's shoulder and raised his own sword. For a moment Adrien thought he saw the markings on the blade move. The metal seemed to stretch and thin.

Adrien stared at Roland. "What was that?"

"An immortal's blade is not like a hunter's," Roland said. He inhaled audibly, and the metal began to glow red, as if it were being forged.

Adrien reached out to touch Roland's sword but stopped several inches short as he realized the blade *had*, in fact, become molten metal. Just as quickly, the blade shimmered with blue light and ice crystals formed on its surface.

"An immortal's blade," Roland continued with his usual coy smile, "is far more malleable than even a vampire's. It is our connection to our swords that gives them substance, not the other way around. The Ianus you wielded is no more. You cannot recall it. Someday you may become strong enough to forge a new weapon with your immortal power, but until then, you must learn to make the most of the weapon you have.

"With your soul's weapon, you had no need to establish a bond. No need to prove yourself worthy. But with your mother's weapon"—Roland glanced to the sword at Adrien's waist, then met Adrien's gaze once again—"you must work harder. Learn its secrets."

"How?"

Roland's expression grew somber. "Accept that Ianus is gone."

CHAPTER NINE:
TRUTH IN THE DARK

ADRIEN DANGLED his feet in the river and hummed as he watched the clouds sail overhead. One of the clouds sprouted wings, and he laughed and raised his hand, jabbing as if it held a sword.

"Dragons?" his mother said as she gazed down at him.

He grinned up at her.

"Do you talk to them?" she asked.

"Talk? Why would I talk to them?"

"Maybe the dragon isn't a bad one." She smiled as he sat up and considered this.

"What if they don't speak French? How can I talk to it?" he said with a frown. Dragons didn't understand words. Dragons were evil. Why else would the knights of his imagination kill them?

She pressed her lips together and the corners of her mouth edged upward in an understanding smile. "Not everyone speaks French, Adrien. Sometimes you must learn a new language to make a friend."

He looked up again. The dragon was now a bird with a long beak and downy feathers. Another cloud pressed in on the bird, devouring it like a fox did its prey.

"The more things change," Roland had told him at his last lesson, "the more they stay the same."

The scene changed. Still the river, but this time he stood over his mother's dead body. Nearby, the vampire who had killed her lay headless, unmoving.

Tears streamed over Adrien's cheeks, mingling with the raindrops. His hands trembled violently, causing him to drop his sword into the mud. The loss of contact with the blade brought him back to his senses. He stooped to retrieve his weapon, and as he stood, he sensed a presence nearby. He turned to see a figure standing at the water's edge. A man, cloaked, his eyes obscured by a pair of spectacles.

The man smiled at Adrien, but Adrien felt nothing warm in the gesture. The man had come to see him. To watch.

"I'll wait, Adrien," he heard the man say, although his lips didn't move. "I'll wait until you grow strong."

ADRIEN AWOKE to the sound of the surf against the rocks. He hadn't meant to fall asleep—he'd just needed to rest a bit after the last round with Roland. He took a deep breath and pulled himself to his feet. Every muscle in his body screamed in protest.

"Adrien." Charles leaned against a nearby tree.

"Watching me sleep?" Adrien asked with a chuckle.

"I take no great pleasure in it," Charles said, deadpan. "You snore quite loudly, in fact."

Adrien lifted his hands over his head, then moved from side to side to stretch his stiff shoulders. "What can I do for you, Charles?" he asked.

"I need to say something," Charles replied somberly. "Something I should have said before." He shook his head and added, "It seems I frequently fail to speak my mind in a timely fashion. More often than not, others suffer for my silence."

Adrien raised his eyebrows but said nothing.

"I nearly lost the one truly good thing in my life," Charles continued after a pause. "The one thing that makes my life worth living. For centuries, I wandered like Ulysses"—he smiled wistfully—"seeking, but never finding the thing I craved above all else.

"And then your brother found me. Adrift with no land to set my sights upon. With nothing but my guilt and sorrow. Pitiful. He wouldn't let me be, even though I tried to push him away. And now...." Charles looked out over the dark ocean as if seeing something there Adrien could not.

"Why are you telling me this?" Adrien asked as the silence stretched.

"My motivation is purely selfish," Charles said, his blue eyes now lit from within. "I haven't always done the honorable thing. I didn't choose to become what I am, but I've made an uneasy peace with my existence. What I've learned about life, I've learned only relatively recently, and I credit your brother with that knowledge." Charles sighed, clearly uncomfortable with sharing such a heartfelt revelation.

"Immortality is worthless if you spend your life in isolation. I cannot change *what* I am, but I am willing to change *who* I am. I don't wish to live my life without your brother. Do you want to live without Nicolas?" he said. "Whether fifty years or a thousand and fifty, loneliness makes for a miserable existence.

"Once a vampire marries," Charles continued when Adrien did not speak, "there's no going back. A vampire mates for life; the price of infidelity is death. Our bodies know this, and they offer us no second chances. Choose your future carefully."

Adrien had no words to answer with, no learned argument with which to counter the truth of Charles's words. Instead, he nodded to Charles, then watched him leave.

Honor and duty leave no room for love.

"I WANT the truth," Adrien said as he stood in the doorway of the small sitting room at the back of the house. He'd let Roland string him along. He hadn't been ready to hear the truth, even if he'd told himself otherwise. Now he'd demand it. He smiled in the knowledge that Roland had no doubt understood this as well.

Roland sat cross-legged on a well-worn chair by the fireplace, reading a book. He looked up, smiled broadly, and motioned to the other chair. "Please join me."

Adrien hesitated. He was more inclined to pace than sit after his conversation with Charles, but his sore muscles protested and he thought better of it.

"Chocolate?" Roland asked, handing Adrien a bowl filled with brightly wrapped confections. Too tired to argue, Adrien took the bowl, unwrapped one, and popped it into his mouth.

"Thomas made them. He wraps them too." Roland chuckled. "He quite enjoys it. Sometimes I wonder whether he'd have done better taking over his parents' patisserie than traipsing about with me." A flicker of sadness shone in Roland's eyes, but it vanished a moment later. "Quite good, aren't they?"

Adrien nodded, his mouth full of a second chocolate. He hadn't really considered that Thomas had a past apart from Roland. He also hadn't realized how hungry he was, having left the baguette and cheese nearly untouched.

"Your appetites are more demanding now that you're no longer human," Roland said.

"I need to speak with you." Adrien knew he was referring to more than just his need for food, although he'd hardly give Roland the satisfaction of knowing how many nights he'd awoken craving Nicolas's body and his blood.

"So I guessed." Roland set the book down on the small table between them. "There is something you wish to know, then?"

"Yes," Adrien said as he set the bowl next to Roland's book. As he did so, Adrien noticed the book's title, *Idylls of the King*. He smiled in spite of himself and looked up at Roland, who pressed his lips together as the wrinkles at the corners of his eyes deepened.

"I always did love Tennyson."

Adrien inhaled, then exhaled slowly. *No more distractions.* He would do what he'd come to do, and he wouldn't leave until Roland told him the truth. "The night my mother died," he began after a minute, "her murderer said he wanted *me*. He said my mother was... expendable."

Roland raised an eyebrow.

"I need to know why he chose me, Roland. I think you know."

Roland reached for the bowl of confections, ran a single finger through the pieces, then finally chose one wrapped in bright green paper. "I can guess," he said as he slowly unwrapped the chocolate and lifted it to his lips.

"Explain."

Roland took a bite and licked his lips, as if he enjoyed making Adrien wait. Adrien gritted his teeth, and just when he thought his temper would get the best of him, Roland spoke.

"You're a particularly intriguing specimen, Adrien."

"Specimen? I don't understand."

"You understand the value of the ancients' blood, of course," Roland answered. Adrien nodded. "But some blood is even more precious."

"I understand why it might be precious *now*, but when I was a child...?"

"What do you know of your family?"

Adrien shrugged. "The Gilberts have been hunters for centuries. Our bloodline is powerful."

"Yes," Roland agreed. "That's true. Although there are other hunter clans at least as ancient as the Gilberts, and just as powerful."

Adrien rubbed the bridge of his nose, where a headache threatened. "Tell me, then. What don't I know about my family?"

"What do you know of your *mother's* family?"

"My mother? Nothing much. She was from the Bardon Clan," Adrien said. "I'm told they were a small clan, but powerful as well."

"All that is true." Roland tilted his head to one side and asked, "But did you know that her father was a vampire?"

"What?" Adrien frowned and ran a hand through his hair. "No," he said. "I had no idea. But if what I've learned about hunters is true, there must be other hunter children born of vampires."

"None born of an ancient vampire."

"An ancient? But he died before I was born. I thought—"

"Even the ancients can die. Surely you know this." Roland appeared to study Adrien's reaction.

"Yes, of course."

"Claude took his own life," Roland said, his expression somber for once. "His wife, your grandmother, did not desire immortality. When she died, Claude couldn't bear to be without her."

A few months ago, Adrien might have had difficulty understanding. But now…. "Surely there are others with blood purer than mine. There must be something else you haven't told me."

Roland nodded. "Half a millennium ago, a hunter saved the life of a small vampire child—an ancient," he said as he plucked another chocolate from the bowl. "That child's name was Jean Lambert."

"Jean? Someone from the Gilbert Clan saved Jean's life?"

"Yes." Roland unwrapped the candy and lifted it to his lips.

"I still don't understand," Adrien blurted, at the end of his patience. He stood up and stalked over to the window. "What difference does it make to me that a distant relative—one who lived a thousand years ago—saved Jean's life when he was a child?"

"Because, Adrien," Roland answered, no doubt drawing out his response for dramatic effect, "that relative was your father, Jacques."

"My *father?*" Adrien turned and stared at Roland. Had Roland finally lost his mind? "But my father is—"

"An immortal. Like you, Adrien."

CHAPTER TEN: OUT OF TIME

ADRIEN AWOKE with a start with Nicolas's name on his lips. Nearly three months had passed since he'd left Nicolas in Paris, and the wedding would be held in less than a week. Three months he'd spent away from Nicolas. Two months he'd spent training. And for what? True, he'd grown stronger with Roland's help. But he'd still failed to master his mother's sword, and none of Roland's reassurances convinced Adrien he was strong *enough*. He'd not forgotten Pelletier's immense power, and although Roland had managed to pry him from Pelletier's death grip, Pelletier would not be as easily deterred the next time they met. Pelletier knew to expect them at the wedding, as they knew to expect Pelletier.

"I still don't understand why the vampires wanted me," Adrien told Roland after he'd learned the truth about his bloodline. "Why not François?"

"It could just as easily have been François. Had you both been with her that day, they might have tried to take him as well."

"And my mother…. Even without her sword, shouldn't she have been able to defend herself?" Adrien pushed away the memory of the vampire tossing his mother's body onto the muddy ground like a rag doll.

Roland sighed and shook his head. "To do what she did—to relinquish her powers—she had to sever her soul from her sword. She became entirely human."

"My father allowed it?" Since he'd learned the truth about his parents, not a day went by when he didn't wonder why his father had told him so little. The little voice at the back of his mind told Adrien he'd simply *chosen* not to see the truth.

Roland laughed. "Your mother was a strong woman, in spite of what you might think. You remind me a great deal of her. Intelligent. Hard-headed. Determined to protect those she loves at all costs…. Your father objected, of course, but he couldn't stop her. After her death, your father enlisted help to keep you children safe."

"Help?"

"Hunters. Friends he trusted," Roland explained. "Do you remember Madame LeFavre?"

"The housekeeper?" Of course Adrien remembered the tiny, wrinkle-faced woman who'd helped care for them after their mother's death. Until he'd left home, he still visited her from time to time. "She was a hunter?"

"She was, years before." Roland rubbed his jaw and smiled. "When your father and I couldn't watch you, Isa, and François, *she* did."

Would his father have told him this if he'd asked? Adrien remembered many times his father had opened the door to just such a conversation, but Adrien had promptly shut it. He'd been afraid of the truth, and he hadn't wanted to revisit that horrible night. The dreams were bad enough.

Even now, Roland's revelations left Adrien feeling uneasy, as if the foundation on which he'd built his life had inexorably shifted, causing him to rethink many other things he'd taken for granted. He thought of Nicolas and of Charles's admonition about choosing his future wisely. He thought of his grandfather, who'd ended his life because he hadn't wanted to live without the woman he loved. He thought of his father, who'd survived his mother's death but had never been the same.

And then there was the shadowy man in his dreams. He no longer knew if the vague presence he recalled from the day his mother was murdered was born of his imagination. Sometimes he believed that man to be Pelletier. Had Pelletier sought him out back then? None of this changed the fact that Adrien had resolved to kill Pelletier if given the chance.

Adrien made his way downstairs around noon. He walked onto the terrace carrying a cup of coffee, eager to feel the midday sun on his face. The weeks spent in the relative darkness of the cave had left him feeling both disoriented and hungry for the light and warmth.

Today, Sunday, Roland had given them all a day of rest from the unrelenting training routine. Adrien had been training with Roland from dawn until well after dusk, while François and Charles sparred in an adjoining cave. They were unquestionably not on the list of official guests at Nicolas and Rosina's wedding, but they had every intention of attending the festivities. Adrien knew he needed to make a choice: fight for Nicolas, or allow him to marry Rosina and accept that he and Nicolas would never be together.

He set his cup down on the rickety wooden table on the back patio, then leaned back in his chair and closed his eyes. At first he'd protested the time off from practicing, but now that he had a moment to rest, he realized how tired he felt. The exhaustion wasn't physical. His body healed quickly. But his mind and his heart—

"You're lazy, monsieur."

Adrien stood and spun around. "Rémy!" He extended his hand and Rémy shook it hard, clasping his forearm with his free hand. "What are you doing here?"

"Thought you might like some company at the wedding." Rémy grinned. "I have no intention of missing all the fun this time."

"You didn't miss much."

"Because you lost?" Rémy laughed and shook his head. "You weren't the only one who lost that day. I heard Charles chased a few of Pelletier's dogs away, but he didn't kill them, did he?"

Adrien pressed his lips together. Knowing they'd all been outmatched didn't make him feel any less impotent.

Rémy nodded. "I'm sorry I wasn't there to help."

"I'm glad you'll be with us the next time." And he was, too.

"So," Rémy continued, clearly undaunted by Adrien's somber mood, "I was hoping you might show me a few of your new tricks."

"Tricks? Without my sword, they aren't all that interesting."

"That's not what I heard. Charles was impressed."

"Could have fooled me," Adrien replied. "Then again, he's not exactly the easiest person to read."

"New sword?" Rémy gestured to Charlotte's blade, which hung from Adrien's waist.

"A very old one. My mother's." Adrien touched the hilt. "It doesn't like me much."

"Roland told me. Sometimes it just takes a little time." Rémy offered him a reassuring smile.

"Time isn't something we have a lot of," Adrien said. "What have you heard from Nicolas?" He knew his concern was obvious, but he was long past pretense. Rémy knew how he felt about Nicolas.

"Only that he and Jean are making preparations for the wedding and that Reynaud and his men have given them no trouble."

Adrien hated himself for feeling disappointed at this news. *What did you expect? That he'd be pining away for you?* Nicolas had been honest and never anything but resolute in seeing this marriage through.

"You're far too transparent." Rémy jumped onto the wall next to Adrien and gazed down at him with a self-satisfied grin.

"And you're far too interested in the affairs of others," Adrien snapped.

"Why are you going back to the castle if you don't intend to stop the wedding?" Rémy asked with eyes full of mischief.

"I swore to protect Nicolas. What better reason do I need?"

"Fine." Rémy shrugged. "I won't discuss it again."

"Good." Adrien turned back to his coffee.

"Still obsessed with the Lambert princeling?" a voice behind Adrien said.

Adrien felt a strong hand on his shoulder and turned around.

"Victor, Caroline." Seeing them buoyed Adrien's spirits. Caroline, a powerful vampire and Charles's creation, would be a welcome asset should Pelletier attempt to interfere in the upcoming wedding. Victor, another of Roland's former students, was a strong and experienced hunter. From what Roland had told Adrien, Victor had been organizing opposition against Pelletier in the Council.

"You look better than you did when we saved your skin in Paris," Victor said.

"And Roland looks very much alive," Caroline added, the edges of her mouth quirking upward.

"I'm happy to be proven wrong about that," Adrien admitted. "Victor Sauvage, this is Rémy Desgrieux."

Rémy offered Victor his hand as he glanced at Caroline. She frowned back at him, but Adrien saw the glint of amusement in her eyes.

"Roland told us you might need some help." Victor's canny grin vanished as he tensed his jaw.

"Happy to have it," Adrien said. They could use all the help they could get, if the last skirmish at the castle was any measure.

"There's talk in the Council that Pelletier is planning to make his move soon," Caroline said with a scowl. "As if the bastard hasn't done enough harm."

"I've heard rumors that Bremen has perfected the means to strengthen hunters using vampire blood," Victor added. "Several more vampires have gone missing in Europe and Asia. Word has it Bremen's trying to capture an ancient. What better place to try than at the wedding, where there'll be dozens of them in one place?"

"Pelletier wants Nicolas," Adrien said with a glance in Rémy's direction. "That's the reason he's allowed the wedding to go forward. He won't touch the Rousseaus for fear of damaging the alliance, but he cares nothing for the Lamberts or any of the others."

"That's why we're here." Victor winked at Caroline.

"Coffee?" Rémy said. "Then a bit of swordplay?"

THE SUN had nearly risen by the time Adrien slept. He had sparred with Rémy, Victor, and Caroline until Thomas interrupted them with a tray of food and an admonition. "Roland wants you rested," he said when they tried to argue.

That night, as he often did, Adrien dreamed of Nicolas. Nicolas wrapped his arms around him, pressed his head against Adrien's back. He dreamed of Nicolas's blood and of the sound of Nicolas's voice in his ear when he awoke. Dreams would have to be enough.

CHAPTER ELEVEN:
BLOOD AND GHOSTS

AVOIDING THE stone bench and choosing the soft grass instead, Blaise sat in the shade of an ancient oak tree, then attempted to read a book. The afternoon went by slowly, like so many others since Jean Lambert had reappeared in his life. It had been almost a week since the near kiss, and true to his word, Jean had scarcely crossed paths with Blaise except when Jean accompanied Nicolas to meals in the main dining room.

However, while Nicolas served as a welcome buffer between Blaise and Jean, his stalwart presence did nothing to calm Rosina. She remained irritable, moody, and had taken to riding for hours on end in an apparent attempt to avoid contact with the other inhabitants of the castle. This had been particularly troublesome for Nicolas, who had on several occasions approached Blaise to inquire after Rosina.

"I know she's unhappy to be marrying me," Nicolas told Blaise, "but I thought we'd grown to be friends. Now I'm not sure. I rarely even see her."

Blaise had tried to reassure Nicolas that Rosina was neither disappointed in Nicolas nor did she have second thoughts about the upcoming wedding. He wasn't sure he'd done a particularly good job of it, but he guessed Nicolas understood her misgivings about Jean.

What are you hiding, Jean? What secret do you keep at the cost of your heart?

Blaise sighed, then went back to reading his book. But the words seemed to dance in the sunlight, and once again Blaise had to force his focus back to the page. Time passed, but he made no progress. Finally, having read the same paragraph for the fifth time, he closed the book in frustration and gazed back at the castle.

"You might get further reading your book if you opened it."

"Rosina." Blaise glanced up to see his sister dismount from her horse.

"I suppose I am a bit preoccupied," Blaise admitted.

"Just a bit?" she asked with a sympathetic smile.

"Am I that obvious?"

"You're thinking about him again," she said as she sat down beside him.

Blaise frowned.

"Why don't you ask him for the truth?"

"Why do you believe he'd share it with me?" he asked, knowing he sounded defensive.

"He loves you."

"He loved me once." Blaise set the book down on the grass and rubbed his face.

"He still loves you. You love him too. The two of you only fool yourselves."

"Coming from someone who wanted to see Jean dead, this conversation seems a bit disingenuous. Are you telling me you no longer believe that he killed Paul and our parents?"

"You don't believe he did, either," she retorted. "Maybe if he were to tell us the truth—"

"And what then?" Blaise laughed bitterly and retrieved his book. "If you find out he really did kill them, will you kill your husband's brother? What good can possibly come of the truth?"

Rosina ignored the question. "You must ask him, Blaise. For both our sakes." Without waiting for his reply, she rose and mounted her horse and rode away.

BLAISE RETURNED to the castle long after dark. He'd chosen to walk the grounds rather than risk meeting Jean in the stables. The gnawing hunger in his belly was nothing compared to the discord in his soul, but the simple need to eat kept his mind sharply focused.

Rosina was right. For nearly two hundred years, he'd gone about his life with the memory of Jean banished deep within his heart. But no longer. By design, or perhaps inadvertently, Jean had awakened the sleeping prisoner of memory when he'd returned to the castle. Blaise must learn the truth, and he knew of only one path to Jean's soul. With each day that passed, the anger and pain grew. He would learn the truth one way or another, even if he had to take it from Jean by force.

Your blood cannot avoid my questions.

Jean and Nicolas's rooms were located in one of the newer additions to the castle, far from the Rousseau family's quarters. Reynaud had insisted on stationing guards at the entryway, although Blaise didn't think they were there for Jean and Nicolas's protection.

One of the guards startled and stared at Blaise in obvious surprise. "My lord. I don't think your uncle—"

"Stand aside, Guy," Blaise snapped.

The guard yielded, allowing him to pass. "Of course, my lord," Guy said, cheeks pinking, no doubt realizing he had no authority to prevent the clan's heir apparent from visiting.

A moment later Blaise stood at the door to the sitting room, which opened as he knocked. Hardly a surprise—they'd been too close, he and Jean. They'd shared too much blood. Jean had surely felt his presence long before he'd come near the room.

"Blaise."

Jean wore a silk robe tied loosely at his waist, his pale skin visible in the gaslight. Blaise hoped the breath that caught in his throat wasn't entirely obvious. He waited for Jean to invite him in. Jean owed him that.

"Please come in." Jean gestured him inside, his expression inscrutable as ever.

Blaise knew these rooms well, the furnishings having changed little since Jean had lived here in the time leading up to what should have been their handfasting. Back then he'd spent nearly every night in Jean's arms and nearly every day at Jean's side as they explored the surrounding countryside on horseback.

"I sense this is not a social call."

"I've come for answers." Blaise met Jean's gaze with determination. "I will have them, whether you wish to cooperate or not."

"Answers," Jean repeated. "Yes, I expected you'd come eventually. Still, I'd hoped you might have come for… different reasons."

"I'm tired of these games." Blaise stood so close to Jean he could hear his slow, steady breaths.

"This is hardly a game. The stakes are far too high."

"I must know your heart," Blaise said. "I claim your blood. The right is mine, as Rosina's brother." Jean probably knew he would not truly force his hand, but he'd reached the end of his patience and he was tired of feeling powerless.

Blaise thought he saw something like amusement flash through Jean's eyes, but it vanished an instant later. "A barbaric custom," Jean said in an even voice. "But it is your right as her brother to question our clan's motives. Still, the truth is not always liberating. I do not wish to cause you more heartache than I've already done."

"You're as stubborn as ever, and I'm far stronger than you realize."

Jean's self-control appeared to falter. His eyes widened almost imperceptibly and he pressed his lips together as he reached out to touch Blaise's cheek. Blaise grabbed Jean's wrist but did not push him away. Instead, he leaned in and grasped the back of Jean's neck, claiming his lips with a hunger that took him aback. Jean's mouth softened to admit Blaise's tongue.

Jean moaned and Blaise's body responded to the siren call, his cock hardening, pressing against Jean's thigh. Blaise tasted Jean's desire and felt the bloodlust rise. It overwhelmed him. He wanted Jean. Wanted his body, his blood, his soul. He would take them all if he needed to, but he would have them.

Their lips parted. Jean, too, seemed shaken by the contact. But instead of fighting, as Blaise expected him to, he closed his eyes and offered the delicate skin beneath his ear in submission.

Blaise growled and bared his teeth. There was nothing controlled about the way he tore Jean's skin and found the pulsing artery beneath. The sweetness of Jean's blood rushed past his lips, and Blaise was transported to a place of memories and emotions: Jean's soul, laid bare for him to see.

He saw himself through Jean's eyes as he sketched the Cathédrale Notre Dame de Paris, not long after the ill-fated dance when Jean had come to his aid.

"I often come here to think," Jean said.

Jean's control faltered. Blaise hadn't sensed Jean's bloodlust, hadn't understood that Jean had been watching him since he'd arrived at the castle. Few vampires could hide their hunger so completely.

"My lord."

"I almost didn't recognize you in your riding clothes," Jean said. "For a moment, I thought you a street rat."

Jean had been nervous? Blaise had been too nervous himself to see Jean's outward calm as a façade.

"I'm no rat." Blaise crossed his arms over his chest. How painfully young he'd been then! The papers of his portfolio scattered in the wind, and he chased after them as his cheeks pinked in embarrassment.

"Indeed you're not." Jean picked up several of the pages and gathered them, studied one of the drawings, then realized he was the subject. Blaise had been too mortified to realize that Jean had been more than simply amused—he'd been both pleased and flattered.

Blaise retrieved the papers from Jean. Their fingers brushed, and through Jean's blood, Blaise heard Jean's long-ago thought—*Charming young man*—for the first time, as he snatched away his drawing of Jean as he'd been when they first met: dressed in his red velvet suit, his long hair secured with a ribbon at his nape.

"So you draw more than just cathedrals." Jean's chuckle covered his discomfort.

"I… no… it's not what you—"

"It's quite a fair likeness," Jean said. "Although perhaps I look a bit broader in the shoulders in your imagination."

Their hands brushed again. "I… I'm not interested in taking a lover." Had he really said that? He'd been afraid of his own intense bloodlust and afraid he would displease Jean. He'd wanted Jean, but he'd wanted more than a simple dalliance. And why would the Lambert Prince want more than that from someone as inexperienced as he?

Jean leaned in and claimed Blaise's lips. Again, Blaise felt Jean's intense hunger for him and for his blood. Jean's body responded as he struggled to reclaim his self-control.

"I hope someday to change your mind, Blaise Rousseau," Jean said, his deep voice resonating like the plucked string of a mandolin. "But until then, the memory of your lips will warm my nights."

The scene faded, the stone plaza now replaced by the castle's grand entryway, where Jean waited at the foot of the long staircase.

"Blaise," Paul said, "I'd like you to meet my friend Jean Lambert. Jean, this is my brother, Blaise."

"Pleased to meet you," Jean repressed a smile as he offered a very surprised Blaise his hand.

"And I you." He blushed to the roots of his hair, and yet Jean found his schoolboy's response endearing. Still, Jean didn't see him as a boy. Where Blaise thought himself awkward and inexperienced, Jean saw him as charming and full of youthful excitement. The very things Jean found irresistible in him were the things that embarrassed Blaise.

The realization that Jean had loved him even then struck Blaise with particular force. His heart ached for them both. For what might have been.

The scene changed once again. Blaise's father stood in the garden, having just given his blessing for their handfasting. Pleasure danced on his father's handsome face, his deep green eyes lit with pride. Blaise sensed Jean's warmth and genuine respect for his father.

"Immortality is worth little if not spent in the company of those we love." Blaise's father, Stéphane, smiled at Jean. "You are fortunate to have earned the love of a good man."

"Thank you, my lord," Jean said.

Stéphane walked to the edge of a small pond set in the center of the gardens. "Blaise will be a strong leader for our clan. And perhaps together you will find a way to unite our clans for good."

"I am fortunate to be blessed with four children," Stéphane continued, turning back to Jean.

"Four?" Jean knew of only three children: Blaise, Paul, and Rosina.

"Yes," Stéphane replied. "Anaïs and I are expecting our fourth child soon. Another son, she tells me. She has felt the child's soul. We will call him Nicolas."

"A lovely name," Jean said.

"Only Paul knows of this," Stéphane explained. "And although I know I have no right to ask, I wish you to keep this a secret until tomorrow. I would like to share our good news with our guests at the wedding banquet. I humbly ask your permission to toast our good fortune."

"I'm honored that you would choose to share this news at our handfasting."

Jean had never wished for anything before. He had always been a practical man. But now, as the sun began to set, he closed his eyes and wished that this new child would know peace.

The memory changed once more. Jean stood on the balcony, gazing out over the fields below. For nearly an hour, he breathed in the crisp spring air as he watched the sun rise over the hills. It was the day of their pledge, at last.

Blaise, Jean thought, *I truly am fortunate to have found you.*

As he made his way inside to dress, Jean heard a muffled cry. He ran back outside, then jumped and landed several stories below, following the sound.

Jean felt the presence of guests arriving for the ceremony. Nearer still were two familiar souls, Blaise's parents. But Jean also sensed another soul. Evil and cold, with a singular purpose and intensity that even at this distance Jean could taste. A hunter's blood and yet something more. Not vampire either. Powerful. A frightening presence.

He rounded the corner onto the small courtyard behind the servants' quarters. Blaise's mother, Anaïs, lay on the ground, unmoving, the folds of her full skirt splayed about her like the colorful wings of a butterfly. Stéphane shielded her body from attackers, who crouched behind bales of hay to avoid Stéphane's powerful attacks.

As Jean ran to assist, Stéphane shouted, "Watch out!"

A blast of red fire soared through the courtyard, passing close enough to Jean that he felt the heat of the attack on his cheek. A moment later the fire joined with a stream of ice.

Hunters fighting with vampires?

"What's happening?" Jean shouted over yet another attack.

"Anaïs was attacked…. They took her here. I felt her and followed," Stéphane gasped, still leaning over his wife's body. Stéphane bled profusely from a wound to the neck. The wound smoked, growing larger instead of healing as Jean might expect it to. "I… I chased them away… went to her… but she…." Stéphane's voice broke.

Arcs of fire and ice roared toward them, illuminating the courtyard like a brilliant sun. Jean called his sword and deflected the attacks toward where they had come from. The reflected power hit one of the stone walls and sent bits of rock and mortar showering onto their attackers.

"I must get you out of here." Jean tried to pull Stéphane away from Anaïs's body, but Stéphane resisted.

"No! I won't leave without her."

"We can bring Anaïs with us," Jean told him. "Perhaps she can still be saved."

"I tried to revive her." Stéphane grimaced in pain. "Their weapons are like none I have ever seen before. Our wounds won't heal…. Anaïs… is gone…."

Jean raised his sword and shot a burst of silver in the direction of their attackers. Smoke rose as the bales of hay and several of the thatched buildings nearby erupted in flames with another of the fire attacks. Several figures ran through the smoke and into the gardens. "I must get you out of here. Please, you're injured."

"No!" Stéphane shouted. "You must save the child." He grabbed Jean's arm. "The attack caused…. I could save the child, but not…. They would want him…. They'd want his blood. I was able to chase them away without them noticing him."

"The child? Which child?"

"Our son." Stéphane pulled Jean by his shirt so that their faces were inches apart. He gasped, his voice barely a whisper now. "You must save him. Hide him. Don't let them have him. Keep him safe. Please. You must promise me this. Swear it. Please, I beg you!"

Jean had thought Stéphane had doubled over to protect his wife's body, but when Stéphane straightened, a tiny hand reached out from the folds of what remained of Stéphane's coat. "There was nothing else to wrap him in…. He's so small… so fragile."

Stéphane had used himself as a shield for his child. A child so tiny that Jean marveled he could survive outside of his mother's body. *A child whose will to live is strong.*

"Paul must know of this treachery. You must find him." Stéphane handed Jean the baby, still wrapped in the velvet cloth. "Leave. Make sure they cannot follow you. Please, I beg you…."

"I'll find him. Then I'll come back for you."

Stéphane smiled at Jean, but Jean saw death in his dimming eyes. Stéphane got to his knees, then lay next to his wife's still body and pulled her tightly to him. "Please go now, before it is too late," he whispered. He shuddered, then became still.

Who would do such a thing? Jean had no time to ponder the question because in the distance he heard more shouts and explosions. He would protect the child. Blaise's brother.

Blaise! He must find Blaise. Make sure he was safe. From his chambers on the other side of the castle, Blaise probably hadn't heard the fight. If Blaise should come upon the attackers….

No. First Jean would entrust the child to Paul. He couldn't risk the child Stéphane had died to protect. He'd have to wait to make sure Blaise was safe. Clasping the baby to his chest, Jean ran through the gardens to the front lawn. He slipped into the castle through the servants' entrance, hoping to avoid the guests who had begun to gather in anticipation of the ceremony. He took the steps four at a time and kicked open the door to Paul's chambers.

The heavy drapes were drawn, and the sitting room was cloaked in shadow. The smell of blood and death hung heavy here. Jean sensed Paul's presence, heard moans from the bedroom.

"Paul!" Jean opened the door and found Paul on the bed, pale and still.

"Paul!" Jean set the baby next to Paul's head and put his hands on Paul's cold face, which was covered in blood. "Paul!" Jean shook him by the shoulders.

Paul's eyes fluttered open, then closed and opened once again. "Jean," he gasped. "He has taken the gift. He's no longer human."

"Who has taken the gift?"

Paul's eyes darted to the window. Jean stepped back and called his sword.

"Pelletier," Jean said as he moved to confront Pelletier. He'd protect both Paul and the baby if it cost him his life. "You've taken his blood without permission, and you've not returned it to him?" To claim the gift without asking was incomprehensible—to steal it and leave the donor to die was an abomination.

"Immortality can be taken as well as given," Pelletier replied. He pointed his sword at the bed.

"Even an immortal can be killed with the proper blade," Jean hissed.

"Then your friend and the child will die as well. Your friend is in need of blood. Not that it will do much good. You cannot protect them and defeat me. You have a choice, Lord Lambert—save them or kill me. What will you choose?"

Nicolas stretched his arms and cooed. Jean held his sword pointed at Pelletier but glanced quickly at the bed. Pelletier was right—in such close quarters, he could not protect Paul or Nicolas from Pelletier's attacks. The risk was too great, the cost incalculable.

"No," Paul whispered. "You must save Nicolas. If you give me your blood...." Paul coughed and gasped. Jean felt his soul fading. Paul was right. Even if he gave Paul his blood, Jean doubted it would do much good. The gift was a bargain. A life for a life. His own blood might buy Paul some time, but only Pelletier could save Paul now.

"Give him your blood," Jean demanded.

"I will do nothing of the sort." No doubt Pelletier believed himself stronger for having taken Paul's life. Perhaps he was.

"Everyone will know what you've done." Jean considered his devil's choice. If he attempted to force Pelletier to return Paul's blood, he would risk Nicolas's life. If he took Nicolas to safety, Paul would surely die.

"If you speak of this, I will kill the child. I will hunt him down and I won't stop until I destroy him. You cannot watch him all the time," Pelletier said with obvious relish. "I will kill him, if not today, then tomorrow, or a hundred years from now. He will die."

"Jean," Paul whispered. "Let him go. The child must live. Nicolas is the only thing that matters. Please."

Jean glanced back at Pelletier, but he had disappeared through the window. Paul grabbed Jean's wrist and pulled him closer. "Raise him as your own brother. Protect him from that bastard. Someday you can tell him how much he was loved. How much I loved him."

Jean's eyes burned, his self-control weakening in the face of his overwhelming grief. "I will keep him safe. I swear it on my life."

Jean squeezed Paul's hand and gathered up the bundle that lay by his head, hiding Nicolas beneath his jacket. "Farewell, my friend," he said. He knew Paul was already gone.

The door flung open to reveal Reynaud and several of his guards. One of the guards charged Jean, but Jean ran at the nearest window, shattering the panes and shielding the child in his arms from the razor-sharp glass. He landed silently on the grass below, then ran, dodging icy bursts of power from the guards' swords.

Forgive me, Blaise.

SHIRA ANTHONY

CHAPTER TWELVE:
THE WAITING GAME

BLAISE RELEASED Jean and gasped for air, staggering backward. He leaned on the back of a chair to steady his shaking legs. He met Jean's gaze, numb. He tried to banish the image of his mother and father from his mind. He could still smell their blood.

"Why? Why would Pelletier…?" he asked as he regained some semblance of control over his fragile emotions.

"I believe Pelletier and Bremen hoped to use Rousseau blood to give other hunters power. And when they realized your mother was carrying a child…. You know how few children are born of the ancients. You know of the myths told of their power."

Of course Blaise had heard the stories of the power of an ancient infant's blood. No vampires healed faster. That power had most likely helped Nicolas survive although he'd been born far too soon. The thought that Pelletier sought to steal Nicolas to gain the power of the ancients made him physically ill.

"Where did you go after you left the castle?" he asked.

"I took Nicolas and hid for nearly fifty years, until he was no longer a child. During that time, I learned my parents had died in the fighting. When I emerged, I told everyone Nicolas was their child and that he'd been hidden to protect him. Nobody ever doubted me, although I believe your uncle always suspected Nicolas was Stéphane's child. More so now that he's seen Nicolas—he looks so much like you."

"You kept him away from other vampires because you feared someone might notice how much we look alike."

Jean nodded.

Blaise clenched his jaw. "You never came to me for help," he said. Jean's eyes shimmered with regret. "You said you loved me."

Jean nodded. "You saw my soul. You know—"

60

"*What* do I know?" Blaise demanded as the dam holding back his anger crumbled. "What I saw in your blood?"

Blaise grabbed Jean by the collar and pushed him hard against the wall. Jean didn't fight him. "Did you believe I was too young? That I would doubt you?" He shook his head in frustration. "For two hundred years, I grieved you. And you—" Blaise released a long breath. "—you could have trusted me. Told me the truth. I could have helped you protect Nicolas."

"I am sorry." Jean spoke the words with obvious regret. But of what use were words after so much pain?

Blaise tightened his grip on Jean's neck. "For two hundred years, you've hidden something precious to me," he hissed. "My brother. *Rosina's* brother." Blaise held Jean's gaze unflinchingly. "You didn't object when Nicolas suggested he marry Rosina. He was a card to be played to your advantage."

"I regret my actions," Jean said. "I believed the danger to Nicolas was too great. I feared if I let him from my sight, he might be killed, if not by Pelletier then by his own clan."

"Did you think me so weak that I couldn't help protect him?" Blaise snapped. He knew this wasn't true. He'd seen himself in Jean's blood, but his anger burned in spite of his reason.

"No."

Blaise frowned and released Jean. This wasn't about strength or weakness. "No," he repeated. "This is about something more than just your fear that Nicolas might be killed."

For the first time that night, Jean flinched in response to Blaise's words.

"This is about something far deeper, isn't it?" Blaise asked, his anger abating somewhat with the realization.

A muscle in Jean's cheek twitched, but he remained silent.

"You love him like your own brother," Blaise said. "It was there, in your blood. But you hoped I wouldn't see it, didn't you? Because if I saw how much you loved him, I'd realize you kept his birthright a secret in part because you were selfish. You didn't want to lose him. You didn't want to give him up." He paused to catch his breath as anger once again burned his heart. "You've gotten quite adept at hiding the truth. How else could you share your blood with Nicolas and not have him know who he really was?"

"I don't deserve your forgiveness," Jean said. "Nor will I ask for it. I only ask that you help me keep Nicolas safe. I intend to speak the truth. I will no longer perpetuate this sham. He deserves to know his birthright."

"Why now?" Blaise demanded.

"Our clans need to unite," Jean explained, his expression softening with what Blaise recognized as concern. "The Council of Hunters is in turmoil, just as Verel Pelletier meant it to be. Without the truce between our races, we are all at risk. When Nicolas approached me about a marriage...." Jean frowned and rubbed his forehead. "I knew there could be no better time for the clans to put aside their differences.

"Pelletier cannot touch Nicolas once he's been publicly accepted as a Rousseau, and your uncle won't dare oppose a truce if he risks being implicated in Pelletier's scheme. And how better to ensure Nicolas's birthright is acknowledged than to have the most powerful ancients in attendance?"

Blaise's head felt as though it might explode with all the implications. "And what of my uncle? If he knew...."

"Reynaud must know Pelletier killed Paul to obtain immortality, since Pelletier hasn't aged since that day," Jean said. "But Reynaud is weak. Pelletier knows your uncle fears what will happen if war breaks out between our clans again. He needs Pelletier's protection.

"I *will* stop the marriage," Jean continued, "although I don't understand why your uncle wishes the wedding to go forward."

"I can't believe he'd permit them to marry." Was Reynaud so desperate that he'd risk the entire clan by allying with Pelletier? The thought horrified Blaise.

"Millennia ago, the ancients didn't consider marriage between kin an abomination. There were too few of us, and marriages to commoners or humans were not permitted. Reynaud would likely justify their marriage in such a way. Besides, once bound, there would be no going back. It would make little difference what anyone believed."

Blaise remembered his father's words, spoken centuries ago. *Do you love him, Blaise? You will be forever bound to him by blood. Nothing but death can release our kind from such a vow.*

"We must stop this," Blaise said. He might not be able to forgive Jean for keeping his secret for centuries, but he'd not let Nicolas suffer.

He'd seen how Nicolas looked at Adrien. Once, he'd understood Nicolas's willingness to sacrifice himself. But now—

Jean nodded, clearly sensing his thoughts. "I know about the hunter," he said. "And I know of Nicolas's feelings for him."

Blaise's anger warred with the realization that once again he'd underestimated Jean. How easy it was to forget the loving heart beneath the cool exterior. Easier than acknowledging he still loved Jean.

"I also know Adrien Gilbert is an immortal, and that Nicolas gave him the gift," Jean added. "Adrien has demonstrated himself to be a man of honor worthy of Nicolas's affections. But it is no longer my blessing to give should Nicolas seek to pledge himself."

For just a moment, Blaise felt the weight of Jean's guilt. "I would hardly deny him happiness," he said, knowing full well Jean understood both his anger and pain.

Jean did not shrink from his gaze. Instead, he inhaled and said in a voice surprisingly filled with emotion, "I hope someday you and Nicolas will forgive me. I realize I don't deserve forgiveness. But know that I will gladly die for him, should it come to that." He paused for just a moment, then added in an undertone, "I would die for you as well."

Blaise nodded. He had no answer to give. No words of forgiveness he could find in his heart to speak. Instead, he steeled himself and said only, "We will find a way to end this. Pelletier will pay for his crimes. There must be peace. We have all lost far too much to settle for less."

Chapter Thirteen: Confluence

The castle shimmered with blue and silver, the colors of the Rousseau crest. Large panels of midnight blue fabric covered the cold stone walls, and deep blue candles replaced the white ones that usually lit the many chandeliers and sconces. Tiny silver balls hung from every fixture, creating an illusion of a starry sky indoors despite the drab weather.

The wedding, which was to have been held outside, had been moved to the castle's large conservatory on account of days of rain. Droplets fell steadily on the glass ceiling and walls. Outside, the garden teemed with brightly colored flowers in contrast to the otherwise gloomy countryside.

Nicolas had slept fitfully the past several days, his mood echoing the gray sky in spite of his resolve. He often dreamed of Adrien, dreams punctuated by a longing that had only deepened since Adrien left. Now, as he dressed in his wedding suit, he studied himself in the mirror. His skin appeared nearly translucent in the dim light of his room. Dark circles underscored his eyes, and his normally brown irises shone with a distinctly reddish cast.

He knew this for what it was: bloodlust. He had come to crave Adrien's blood in the short time they'd spent together. And although myths of the sweetness of hunter blood abounded in vampire lore, Nicolas knew only Adrien's blood could ever affect him so. Tradition proscribed the taking of blood the week before a marriage or handfasting, or Nicolas might have hunted to quell the bloodlust. The ceremony where vampires pledged their lives to each other ended with the ritual sharing of blood—the blood that bonded them for eternity and ensured that unfaithful spouses would meet a painful death. Nicolas would wait and hope that Rosina's blood satisfied him.

"My lord?" The servant tending to Nicolas held up the dark blue jacket embroidered with silver thread and tailored from the finest silk. It did nothing to improve Nicolas's spirits.

"Thank you." Nicolas smiled at the servant, whose expression brightened. He slipped on the jacket and allowed the man to fasten the buttons.

This was not the time to be looking back. He would look only to the future. He cared for Rosina, and she cared for him. *She is a good woman,* he told himself as he looked in the mirror and ran his fingers over the silver thread of his lapel. *She will be a good wife to you.*

These words had become something of a mantra to Nicolas. The reality of his future dawned as gray as the sky outside. In spite of the words, he knew he would never truly be free of his love for Adrien but that with time, the pain of separation from the man with whom he had shared his soul would begin to dim.

After the wedding, my heart will have no choice but to obey.

ADRIEN, FRANÇOIS, Charles, Rémy, Victor, and Caroline arrived at the Rousseau castle not long before the wedding was to begin. Roland stayed behind, feigning exhaustion from the long hours spent training with Adrien in the cave. Adrien guessed Roland's true reason for remaining behind was that he hoped to empower Adrien by having him lead the group of vampires and hunters to Paris.

Their plan was simple: protect Nicolas and Rosina and ensure that neither Pelletier nor anyone else who might have reason to wish them ill interrupted their wedding. None of them wanted all-out war. The most unpredictable part of the plan, of course, was Pelletier himself. Roland believed Pelletier would do anything to rekindle the war between the clans and exploit it for his own purposes. He believed, as did Adrien, that Nicolas was the key. If Pelletier were to kill Nicolas and blame his death on the Rousseaus, Jean would have no choice but to answer.

There was only one way to protect Nicolas: Adrien must kill Pelletier. The wedding would go forward and the clans would solidify the fragile peace between them. Adrien would be satisfied with nothing less. And when all was said and done, Adrien would return to his family and the vineyard. He would resign his commission, give up his hunter powers, and do his best to forget Nicolas.

Given their last visit to the castle, Adrien and the others assumed Reynaud would not grant them access to the building. They were, however, surprised to find that although Reynaud's guards appeared to recognize them, they did not prevent their entry.

"Nothing has changed," Charles said in response to Adrien's questioning look. "It's simply one less fight to be won."

As agreed, they broke into smaller groups and mingled with the large crowd of invited guests: Charles and François, Rémy and Adrien, Caroline and Victor. Although none of them believed a discussion with Reynaud would accomplish much, they had hoped to find him and at least attempt to reason with him about allowing the marriage to proceed. Reynaud, however, was nowhere to be found.

Adrien and Rémy reached the conservatory and made their way to the simple platform where Nicolas and Rosina would exchange their vows. Some of the guests murmured in surprise, but no one moved to stop them. A brass quintet played Mozart as people milled about, most holding a glass of wine or champagne. Adrien glanced around the room and spotted the other members of his group, all in their designated locations. Outside, rain fell steadily, running over the windows and into the gardens. From time to time, Adrien heard the rumble of distant thunder.

Adrien saw no sign of Pelletier, his men, or Reynaud, but he felt Nicolas's presence. He did not reach out to Nicolas to reassure him, knowing this would only cause Nicolas more grief. Nicolas knew he was there. That was all that mattered.

As night fell, the pale gray of the sky turned darker. Servants lit the remaining candles so that glimmers of flame danced over the glass walls and ceiling.

Perhaps noticing Adrien's curious gaze, Rémy leaned in and said, "Vampire weddings are quite simple. Both bride and groom enter the place of marriage hand in hand. The clan leader officiates and the couple exchange short vows. The marriage is consummated by the sharing of blood before witnesses. Far more time is spent celebrating afterwards than at the ceremony itself."

Adrien was about to thank Rémy when Jean entered the room, followed a minute later by Blaise. As always, Jean wore an expression like stone. Blaise looked far more like the future clan leader, greeting guests and making small talk as he made his way across the room.

Adrien caught Jean's eye and inclined his head, gripping the hilt of his sword in a silent acknowledgment of why he had come. In the months leading up to the wedding, he'd naïvely hoped for a different outcome.

Adrien hated himself for wishing Nicolas would change his mind. But he'd known Nicolas would not. He loved Nicolas as much for his kind heart as for his strength of conviction, and true to that strength, Nicolas would do this for the good of his people.

The delicate music that had nearly been drowned out in the guests' chatter now rose. The horns cut through the din, their bright melody heralding Nicolas and Rosina's arrival and causing the guests to grow silent. Moments later the sea of guests parted as Nicolas and Rosina entered hand in hand and made their way to the platform. Wearing a blue silk dress with silver embroidery at the hem and sleeves, Rosina looked beautiful with her dark hair swept off her neck. Diamonds dripped from her ears and wrists, but her throat was bare.

Rosina's beauty was remarkable, but it was Nicolas who held Adrien's attention. Dressed in a perfectly fitted suit, his hair secured with a silver clasp to reveal the smooth skin of his nape, Nicolas strode with purpose, his head held high, his eyes focused. The bloodlust rose unbidden in Adrien, who inhaled slowly in an effort to maintain his self-control.

Nicolas turned and met Adrien's gaze, perhaps sensing Adrien's physical response. Nicolas smiled at him, but the shadows of longing and sadness in his eyes nearly broke Adrien's heart.

As Rosina reached the first step of the platform, she picked up her train and smiled at Nicolas as one might a beloved brother. He returned her smile, and they climbed the platform before turning to face the guests.

Reynaud Rousseau entered next, flanked by several guards. Pelletier, Giovanetti, and Bremen followed close behind. There was no mistaking the message Reynaud was sending to those in attendance: Pelletier and his men were honored guests.

More hunters swept into the room, some gathering in groups near Adrien's comrades, others disappearing into the crowd. Pelletier had clearly expected them and had planned for their arrival. Adrien gripped the hilt of his sword tighter and tried to slow his galloping heartbeat. The thunder roared, closer still, a flash of lightning briefly illuminating the sky.

Reynaud climbed the first step and stopped in front of Nicolas and Rosina. He bowed to them, then turned to face the room. The crowd assembled bowed and curtsied, some shouting, "Lord Rousseau!"

Reynaud nodded solemnly, then turned back to Nicolas and Rosina. "Nicolas Lambert," Reynaud said loudly enough for all to hear, "I wish you a long life."

Nicolas inclined his head.

"Rosina Rousseau," Reynaud continued, "I wish you a long life."

Rosina nodded.

"Today we celebrate not only the union of Lady Rousseau and Lord Lambert," Reynaud said, "we also unite two clans who have been at war for centuries. With this marriage, there will be peace between our clans."

Next Reynaud turned to acknowledge Jean. "Jean Lambert, I ask your permission that these two be married."

Jean stepped forward so he stood only a few feet away from Reynaud. Reynaud blinked and paled beneath Jean's intense gaze.

"Monsieur," Jean said, his deep voice resonating throughout the room, "as we stand here before our kin in peace and reconciliation, I ask that you do now what you have failed to do for more than two centuries."

From the guests' surprised looks and loud murmurs, they had not expected Jean's response. Reynaud glanced quickly toward Pelletier, who ignored him completely, his expression unchanged.

"I don't understand, my lord," Reynaud said as if testing the waters. "We are here to unite our clans and bring lasting peace to our people."

"It is not that particular wrong I seek to right," Jean replied serenely. Blaise, who had been standing on the other side of the podium, now crossed in front of the guests and stood at Jean's side.

Nicolas and Rosina exchanged quick glances. When Adrien shot Charles a look of concern, Charles just shook his head. Adrien glanced at Rémy, who appeared just as surprised as the others.

Reynaud shifted on his feet and frowned. "This is the time to put aside the past and move toward the fut—"

"There will be no marriage," Jean said as he walked over to Nicolas and Rosina, Blaise at his side. The crowd's chatter grew louder. Adrien schooled his expression, knowing Pelletier and the others watched him. Dare he believe there might be another outcome—the possibility that there might be more for him and Nicolas?

"Jean," Nicolas said, "have I done something to displease you?"

Jean shook his head. "You have done all I have asked of you and more. I could not be more proud, Nicolas."

"Lord Lambert, you have pledged your brother's hand in marriage." Reynaud's voice shook, and beads of sweat glistened on his forehead. "Is your promise so easily broken?"

"I have allowed this farce to continue," Jean said evenly. "It's time to exorcise the ghosts of our pasts. It's time to heal a festering wound inflicted centuries ago."

Pelletier, who had been standing off to the side watching the proceedings with interest, now walked over to Reynaud and Jean. "Every action has its consequences," Adrien overheard him tell Jean.

Jean nodded. "Indeed. I have withheld the truth for far too long. But you will not harm him." Jean glanced at Adrien and nodded. In a heartbeat, Adrien stood at Jean's side, sword drawn.

What the hell is going on? Adrien glanced at Charles again, then Rémy. They appeared as confused as he. He tightened his grip on his sword and scanned the room, ready to move to intervene should someone threaten Nicolas.

"Tell him your *precious* truth, then," Pelletier said. "It matters little now."

Reynaud blanched.

"Truth? What truth?" Nicolas's Adam's apple bobbed as he swallowed.

"The truth of what happened to your parents two hundred years ago."

"My parents? They died in battle when I was very young," Nicolas said. "But why—"

"*Your* parents were killed by Verel Pelletier," Jean explained. "He killed your brother as well."

The whispered murmurs from the guests rose to a din as Reynaud again shifted uncomfortably on his feet.

"My brother?" Nicolas asked. "But *you* are my only brother."

"In my heart, Nicolas, you will always be my brother." Jean lowered his voice so that only those nearby could hear. "I couldn't have loved you more." Then, turning so that he would be heard by all present, he continued, "But the truth is that you are a Rousseau, and brother to Blaise and Rosina."

The room erupted in loud chatter. Adrien positioned himself between Pelletier and Nicolas, happy to have something to do rather than stare at Jean in shock. Caroline, François, Rémy, and Victor had drawn their weapons and taken up positions between Pelletier's men and the platform.

Nicolas, a Rousseau? Of course there would be no marriage.

Nicolas appeared even paler than before. For a moment Adrien feared he might collapse under the weight of Jean's revelation. But before

Adrien could do anything to assist, Nicolas straightened visibly and drew a long breath, regaining his poise. "I'm a… Rousseau?"

"Lord Lambert," said Reynaud pleadingly, "I beg of you…."

"You didn't kill Stéphane or Anaïs, nor did you assist in Paul's death," Jean acknowledged. "Still, you must live with the consequences of permitting this lie to be perpetuated. As must I. You knew the truth centuries ago, Reynaud, yet you chose to do nothing."

Reynaud remained silent, but he looked to Pelletier.

"Jean," Nicolas asked, "how is this possible?"

"Pelletier," Jean replied, glaring at the hunter, the accusation plain in his eyes, "stole the gift of immortality from your older brother and left him to die."

"Stole…?" Nicolas gasped and shook his head.

By now the guests crowded around so that they might better hear. François and Charles moved closer to Pelletier's men. Adrien's heart beat wildly in his chest. A single movement of those men might spur a battle.

A flash of lightning preceded a sharp crack of thunder that struck nearby.

Jean nodded. "Pelletier's men killed your father as he shielded you with his body."

Blaise still stood by Jean's side. From his expression, Adrien guessed he already knew the truth.

"For two centuries now," Jean continued, his face ever impassive, "I have kept this a secret. I told myself I did so to protect you, Nicolas. But I've come to realize that although I genuinely feared for your safety, I also feared I might lose you should the truth come to light. I should have revealed the truth of your birthright long ago. I beg your forgiveness."

The room became suddenly silent. Adrien watched in stunned shock as Jean fell to his knees before Nicolas, his head bowed low.

"No," Nicolas whispered, his dark eyes now filled with tears. "Please don't." He stepped from the dais and laid a gentle hand on Jean's shoulder. "You owe me nothing, especially not an apology. That I am not your brother by blood, and that I am brother to Rosina and Blaise… I don't deny this is quite a shock."

Jean remained on his knees in supplication.

"But I understand one thing above all others," Nicolas said as he put his hand to Jean's chin and gently raised his head until their eyes met. "You will always be my brother. You have loved me as your own, and you have protected me with your life. There is nothing to forgive." He helped Jean to his feet, then embraced him warmly.

Throughout all of this, Pelletier watched patiently. Had he known this would happen? He made no move to deny Jean's accusations, nor did he seem to care that all those present might know such a terrible truth.

He wants this. Adrien knew as surely as he knew Pelletier would die in this fight. Pelletier had expected this. He'd *welcomed* it. Adrien grew cold with the realization that he had no idea what Pelletier expected to achieve in allowing Jean to speak the truth.

"You bastard!" Rosina charged down from the platform toward Pelletier. Her sword materialized in her hand and her eyes flashed black with hatred.

Pelletier held his ground.

"Rosina, no!" Reynaud shouted.

Before Nicolas or Adrien could stop her, she aimed her sword at Pelletier, who appeared mildly amused but entirely unconcerned. "Draw your weapon," she snarled.

"No." Pelletier waved his hand like someone batting away a fly. The flash of power that flew from his fingers sent Rosina flying against the wall some ten yards away. She landed with a hard thud and lay still.

"Rosina!" Nicolas ran over to her and put his hand on her chest. He breathed deeply as he met Adrien's gaze. "She's alive." Nicolas gathered her into his lap and glared at Pelletier.

At the same time Nicolas went to Rosina's aid, Jean and Blaise closed ranks to protect him. Seeing this, Adrien placed himself between Pelletier and those gathered around Rosina. Several people screamed as a burst of energy from the back of the room hit the glass ceiling and sent shards of glass flying in all directions. Out of the corner of his eye, Adrien saw Charles respond with his own attack as François met another hunter's sword. The wedding guests scattered, most running from the room. The few who remained stood near the doors, too curious to leave but clearly unsure if it was wise to remain.

Reynaud walked quickly toward where Rosina lay, still cradled in Nicolas's lap. Adrien watched in stunned horror as Pelletier shook his head and sent a bolt of black fire at Reynaud's back. Reynaud fell forward onto the tiled floor and lay still.

Adrien met Jean's gaze for just an instant. As Jean moved toward Reynaud, Adrien aimed a burst of blue-and-red fire at Pelletier to cover him. Jean moved so fast, Adrien could barely follow him as he retrieved Reynaud's limp body from the center of the room and set him down near the wall. Pelletier neatly deflected Adrien's attack with his bare hand, but not before Blaise crossed behind him and stood guard over Jean and Reynaud. Jean ran his hands over the wound on Reynaud's back, his fingers glowing white as he worked to heal him.

CHARLES GRITTED his teeth as Giovanetti and Bremen moved to engage him, Rémy, and François. Rémy sent several chairs flying into the air, and Charles maneuvered into position to fight Giovanetti. Out of the corner of his eye, he saw that some of Pelletier's men now battled Caroline and Victor in a far corner of the room. More glass shattered, and some of the blue-and-silver wall hangings blew against the candles and ignited. Charles sprayed the fire with ice from his sword, dousing the flames to keep them from spreading.

Nearby, François shouted as he charged Bremen, who had moved away from Giovanetti. Charles's blood ran cold. He prayed François was ready to fight again, prayed he was strong enough.

"Time to die, bastard," François hissed, his face contorted with rage. François struck Bremen's sword and a loud clang rang through the room as the two men struggled for position. After a minute François disengaged and pushed Bremen backward. He aimed his sword at Bremen and shot a stream of blue fire. Bremen deflected the attack and the fire hit the windows behind him, which melted from the heat.

François jumped into the air, never taking his eyes off Bremen. He spun around and, as he began to fall, aimed another broad swath of fire in Bremen's direction. Bremen shot a burst of black energy toward François as he landed lightly on the floor.

"François!" Charles shouted, panic zinging through his body as François dodged another attack.

"This is my fight, Charles!" François yelled from inside a cloud of dust and debris. "I'm stronger than you give me credit for."

Charles gritted his teeth. There were too many of Pelletier's men and too few of their own to allow himself to be distracted. His skills would be better served fighting than worrying about François. François would be all right—Charles wouldn't allow himself to accept any other outcome.

Charles dodged an attack from a hunter standing behind Giovanetti—the man Rémy had been fighting.

As the dust cleared, a cloud of brilliant blue-and-white energy swirled around François. Bremen lunged, aiming for François's chest, but when his weapon met the surface of the energy, he was thrown backward and nearly lost his balance.

"What is this?" Bremen's eyes widened. "A new technique?"

"You won't touch another soul," François said as the barrier faded. He pointed his sword at Bremen with a look of utter determination. Charles smiled as he headed off another powerful shot from Giovanetti. He'd never seen François fight, and he'd never seen François as focused or determined. Bremen would die here.

"Soul?" Bremen appeared to contemplate the word. "Do you even have a soul, I wonder?"

François answered by lunging at Bremen, catching the edge of his sleeve with his blade, and cutting through the fabric with ease. Blood blossomed where François made contact. Bremen hissed, but did not back down, instead moving with incredible speed, turning and thrusting his sword at François's chest. François, however, moved even faster.

"You thought the blood of innocent vampires would make you stronger," François said as they faced each other, circling, their weapons only a few feet apart.

"But I *am* stronger," Bremen replied.

"Not as strong as I," he said with a glance in Adrien's direction. "I am the blood of a hunter, the blood of a vampire, and the blood of an immortal." François touched the edge of his weapon to his left palm. He raised his hunter's sword and swung the blade. With a movement both grotesque and strangely graceful, François severed Bremen's head from his shoulders.

CHAPTER FOURTEEN:
THE SPACE BETWEEN HEARTBEATS

THE LOOK of satisfaction on François's face and the expression of surprise on Pelletier's buoyed Adrien's spirits. With renewed determination, he pointed his sword at Pelletier, who had yet to draw his weapon. A loud hum filled the room as Adrien's mother's sword glowed and sent waves of light soaring. The resulting vibrations shook loose some of the broken glass overhead and knocked over the marble statues that still stood amidst the chaos. Gripping his weapon with both hands and channeling his strength through the tip, Adrien focused his thoughts on the blade. Waves of gold and blue spiraled around the weapon in tight circles, growing in size until Adrien drew the weapon back, then brought it down so that the rings flew toward Pelletier.

Pelletier moved quickly out of the line of fire. The rings of gold and blue soared unimpeded toward the windows, obliterating what was left of them with such power that nothing, not even the metal, remained. The entire side of the conservatory was now open to the elements, and droplets of rain blew into the room. The iron supports that had held the glass ceiling in place began to collapse. Both Adrien and Pelletier jumped backward to avoid a web of twisted metal as it fell with a resounding crash onto the marble floor.

"Interesting." Pelletier appeared far more amused than concerned by Adrien's display of power. And Pelletier had yet to draw his weapon.

With a quick flick of his wrist, Adrien ran the blade across his left forearm, cutting deeply into the skin. The cut burned like fire, but Adrien did not flinch. Blood ran down his arm toward his palm and began to pool. Adrien gathered the blood in his hand and then ran the blade across his palm, coating it in the viscous red liquid.

Adrien's fingertips began to tingle with the mixture of heat and power from his mother's sword. He breathed in deeply, imagining combining the sword's power with his own immortal strength. He reached out to the sword and felt it respond much as Ianus had in the past. He opened his soul to the blade, as if the metal had cut open his heart and poured its power into him. The power of his ancestors, vampire and hunter alike.

He recalled the moment when he had heard Nicolas's voice in his mind after they had first sparred. *"You must grow stronger, Adrien. For both of us."*

For you, Nicolas. I am strong.

Pelletier did not move.

"Die, you bastard," Adrien said, his voice calm in spite of his fury.

An arc of blue-and-gold fire flew toward Pelletier, growing wider as it left the blade, obscuring the place where Pelletier stood. Vampires and hunters alike stopped fighting and covered their ears, so painful was the high-pitched hum that accompanied the flames. Adrien hadn't expected the lightning to combine with his power, but he opened himself to the flashes of silver from the storm and drew power from them.

Flames swirled around Pelletier, forming a sphere of gold and blue that completely engulfed him and grew so dense it appeared nearly solid. Adrien felt Pelletier within the sphere, fighting to maintain the integrity of his body, which threatened to dissolve under the weight of the circular mass.

I have him. I just need to keep it up long enough for him to weaken.

Maintaining the attack took every bit of strength Adrien could summon. The room around him vanished as he focused solely on the sphere while Pelletier attempted to break free. Adrien felt fingers of weakness claw toward him. At first he thought this was the result of the incredible amount of power he was channeling through his weapon, but then he sensed something more familiar. Something terrifying and sinister—Pelletier reaching out to him as he'd done the last time they'd fought.

Adrien's arms grew hot as energy flowed back into his body, snaking its way into his muscles and through his shoulders into his chest. Bands of energy like invisible ropes tightened around his chest, making it difficult for him to breathe. His heart struggled against Pelletier's power, slowing down, hesitating, skipping beats.

No! I won't let him do this to me again.

He gasped for breath against the pull of Pelletier's counterattack. His heart slowed. He only had seconds before he would lose consciousness. He had to maintain the integrity of his attack.

His heart skipped a beat. The pain in his chest exploded. He tried to take a deep breath, but his body was frozen. Pelletier controlled him.

Two beats... then another. Agony, like a knife stabbing him through the heart. Another beat, out of time, erratic.

Just a little longer....

A single beat now, then a long pause, then another, feeble beat, and the pain began to fade.

No!

Adrien's heart stopped. He struggled to stay on his feet.

Beat, dammit, beat!

No pain, but a feeling of floating. Peacefulness. Release.

I... won't... die!

It would be so easy. If he just let go.... He imagined he saw himself standing in the middle of the room, hands grasping his mother's sword. The sword exploded in a flash of red light, the bits of metal cutting into his hands and chest like knives. His mother's sword. Gone. Like Ianus.

Beat, heart, beat! You must live. For him. For all of them!

One beat, weak, barely enough to feel. Then another, slightly stronger. Three beats, four, five.... The pain returned. He saw through his own eyes, grounded once more in his own body.

If I can feel pain, I'm not dead.

His heartbeat steadied. He gasped, then inhaled deeply, filling his lungs until they hurt. Flashes of silver light filled his vision. His head spun, but he didn't care. He was alive, and that was all that mattered.

"You may actually be stronger than I," Pelletier said as if he had heard Adrien's thoughts. "But you still have much to learn."

A sword materialized in Pelletier's right hand, the blade of the weapon twisting and swirling like molten metal on the jeweled hilt. Pelletier swung his blade in a circular motion from just a few feet away. The air grew thick and hot.

Knowing he had not recovered enough to face another of Pelletier's attacks, Adrien moved quickly out of the line of fire. The blade barely missed its mark.

Pelletier again swung his sword at Adrien.

"Adrien!" Nicolas screamed.

Molten black metal flew at Adrien's chest, hardening into glittering steel like the razor-sharp teeth of a snake seeking its prey. Adrien raised his hands, hoping to slow the blade.

"No!" Nicolas shouted again, closer than before.

Time slowed. Pelletier's blade pierced the soft white skin of Nicolas's neck. Nicolas spun with the blow, falling soundlessly in a blur of silver and blue.

"Nicolas!" Jean's voice this time, rough with fear. A moment later Jean cradled Nicolas in his arms.

No, Nicolas! Pelletier's sword had nearly killed Adrien, a hunter. What might it do to a vampire?

François, his blade still wet with Bremen's blood, now stood between Adrien and Pelletier, keeping Pelletier at bay. "Don't move!" François shouted at Pelletier as Charles appeared instantly by his side. Pelletier, however, did not appear concerned, instead fending off their attacks with lazy movements of his sword. He seemed to be enjoying the results of his handiwork and waiting to see how Adrien would react.

Adrien ran to Nicolas. "How is he?" he asked as he kneeled next to Jean, whose hands glowed white on Nicolas's chest.

"I can't stop it," Jean said. He shook his head. "The wound... it's nothing I've seen before. It's like fire... it's consuming his flesh."

No. Nicolas would be all right. The only way to kill an ancient was to injure him and cut off his head. Roland had taught him that. *But you've seen Pelletier's attacks firsthand, haven't you?* And he hadn't been cut by Pelletier's blade. This wound appeared far worse, growing larger and consuming Nicolas's flesh.

"Nicolas," Adrien said on a voiced sigh.

Nicolas smiled weakly, his eyes fluttering open.

"You were supposed to let *me* rescue *you*," Adrien whispered as he stroked Nicolas's cheek.

Nicolas's laugh came out as a strangled cough.

Adrien glanced at Jean, who nodded in assent. Adrien reached out and gently gathered Nicolas in his arms. He sensed Pelletier waiting. *Waiting for me.*

"You've... grown... stronger." Nicolas coughed again.

Adrien put his hand over the wound on Nicolas's neck and ignored the pain of the heat in his palm. "Let me give you my blood. Your blood saved my life. I can save yours."

"Your blood won't save me." The sounds of the battle faded as Nicolas spoke in Adrien's mind. *"You can feel it too. The only reason you*

survived at the prison is that you aren't one of us. His hunter's blade was meant to destroy me."

We have eternity. You gave that to me. Please. You must survive, you must—

"You must kill him, Adrien. You must protect those who love you and protect those whom I love."

No. My blood might—

"Please, Adrien. Promise me this."

A moment's hesitation, and then: *For you... I promise.*

Nicolas smiled and sighed.

Nicolas. Beloved Nicolas.

"Nicolas," Adrien moaned as his eyes burned with tears. *Nicolas!*

There was no reply.

CHAPTER FIFTEEN:
THE SUMMONING

ADRIEN CRADLED Nicolas's body, losing his battle with his tears as the pain overwhelmed him. The room fell silent but for Rosina's crying and the sound of the storm. Some of the guests had returned as both hunters and vampires momentarily ceased their fighting, curious to see what had happened.

The battle began anew. The guests shouted and ran as several explosions shook what remained of the conservatory. In spite of the chaos, Adrien remained at Nicolas's side. Tears and raindrops mingled on Adrien's face as he gently laid Nicolas's body on the ground, then brushed the smooth skin of Nicolas's cheek one last time, memorizing his beautiful face. He kissed Nicolas, willing himself to remember his taste. That memory would have to last an eternity.

Blaise and Jean fought nearby, back to back, keeping Pelletier's comrades from advancing toward Adrien and the fallen Nicolas. And throughout it all, Pelletier calmly deflected swordfire. He was watching. Waiting for Nicolas to die. Pelletier knew what Nicolas meant to Adrien. Adrien was sure of it. He enjoyed it!

Through the throbbing pain of heartbreak, rage took hold of Adrien. "Damn you to hell!" Adrien shouted as he launched himself at Pelletier. He reached for Pelletier's neck, but Pelletier touched his palm to Adrien's chest and Adrien flew backward and hit the stone wall. Bits of rock and plaster tumbled onto him, cutting his face and shoulders.

Adrien got to his feet and ran at Pelletier again, this time aiming an arc of black fire as he moved. Pelletier deflected the attack with the edge of his sword, then used both his sword and his hand to respond. Again, the attack sent Adrien into the air until he crashed into the wall. A trickle of blood ran down his cheek.

"Addie! No!" François shouted. He and Charles had reengaged Giovanetti and another of Pelletier's men and were circling them like a twisted dance. The rain had begun to abate, but all of the combatants were drenched. With each step, water splashed from the marble floor, sending droplets flying about alongside powerful attacks.

Adrien stood and dusted himself off once more. His shoulder ached where it had hit the wall. The pain in his chest—broken ribs, he guessed—flared, then subsided to a dull throb as his bones knitted and began to heal. Pain was good. Pain would help him focus on something other than the loss of Nicolas.

Again and again, Adrien attacked Pelletier with everything he could muster. Each time, Pelletier repelled him with ease.

Let him kill me. If he couldn't defeat the bastard, he'd die here. Better that than to live without Nicolas. Better than to live with the shame of knowing he was too weak to defeat Pelletier.

Adrien walked with purpose toward Pelletier, hands at his sides.

"Adrien, no!" Jean stepped between them, sword aimed at Pelletier. Nearby, Blaise watched, his sword also aimed at Pelletier. His face was pale with grief and fear.

Pelletier brushed his hand over his sword, which glowed and lengthened as Adrien watched. From where he stood, Adrien could not see Jean's expression, but the sudden tension in his body told Adrien that Jean hadn't expected this. Adrien felt the thrum of power build—it vibrated through his body, causing his bones to ache. Not pain precisely, but discomfort. The room seemed suddenly quiet, as though he'd dipped his head under water and his mind was drowning.

"You're weak, that you let him win so easily."

Adrien looked around to see whose thought he'd heard, then dismissed it as his own. Who was he to deny the truth? He *was* weak. He feared a life without Nicolas, without the possibility that one day, he and Nicolas might find a measure of happiness. A dream, perhaps, but to sacrifice himself was to admit weakness. There was more at stake here than any one of them. The future his great-great-grandfather had handed him, the lives of his father and sister, the Council of Hunters that had survived for so long and that Roland believed was vital to the future of vampires, hunters, and the humans Adrien had sworn to protect.

"No." Adrien moved to Jean's side, ignoring the pleasure in Pelletier's face. To hell with him. Let him take joy in the fight, because he would die here. He *had* to die here. Adrien wouldn't let Pelletier kill Jean as well. He'd promised Nicolas. He'd given Nicolas his word.

Adrien slid his palm over the edge of Jean's readied sword. Blood hissed on the metal, imbuing it with a reddish cast, as though it had been dipped in the smithy's fire. Adrien rubbed his palms together, then aimed his power at Pelletier just as Jean did the same. The ribbons of blue and red from each attack swirled about in an eerie braid of light, then combined as they flew toward their target.

Pelletier's gaze darkened, but Adrien thought he saw excitement where before his bespectacled eyes had only held calm detachment. Was Pelletier enjoying this new challenge? Adrien's thought fled with the onslaught of Pelletier's counterattack, black wisps that reminded Adrien of hawks, their sharp beaks aimed at unsuspecting prey.

Adrien pushed Jean out of the way, the urge too strong to resist. He *knew* the attack must not touch Jean, that this attack was different from those of the other hunters. Pelletier's power grazed Adrien's arm, slicing through the skin like a knife. Pain blossomed red-hot as the wound smoked and hissed.

Not this time. Adrien breathed deeply and imagined the damaged skin healing. The pain subsided as Pelletier watched Adrien. The last thing Adrien expected was Jean charging Pelletier, his sword drawn, taking advantage of the lull in the fight.

"Jean, no!" Adrien shouted, too late. Pelletier moved faster than Jean, the blade of his sword glancing off Jean's shoulder. Barely a flesh wound, but Jean staggered backward and dropped his weapon. It vanished a moment later as Jean fell to his knees.

"Jean!" Blaise sent a shower of ice flying toward the hunter who blocked his way to Jean. "Jean!"

Pelletier looked directly into Adrien's eyes, then moved toward Jean with his sword parallel to the floor. A hunter's move, practiced and deadly. Sever the head with a hunter's blade, and even the most powerful ancient would fall. Pelletier had no need to use his immortal power—his blade would end Jean's life.

"No!" Adrien stepped in front of Pelletier and raised his arm. The blade bit into his still-recovering flesh, bone deep. Blood ran down his arm, warm and welcoming. He would endure the pain. It would pass. Out of the corner of his eye, he saw Blaise strike the hunter through the heart. He moved to Jean's side before the man collapsed onto the muddy tiles.

"Jean." Blaise gently carried Jean out of the line of fire, then bared his arm and offered it. Adrien prayed Blaise's blood would be enough to heal Jean.

"No more," Adrien gasped. He alone was to blame for Jean's injury. He alone was the reason Nicolas was dead. *No one else will die on my behalf.*

The memory of his mother's death resurfaced, called by the loss of Nicolas, which burned a hole in his soul as surely as Pelletier's blade. He remembered how he'd summoned Ianus through his pain and fear, how he'd killed the vampire who'd taken his mother's life. How the sword had heeded its master's call even though he didn't even know he'd ordered it to appear.

This is no different. Even the rain is the same as that day.

He thought of Nicolas, and this time he didn't fight the tears. This pain would not pass. This pain would stay with him for eternity.

Nicolas. His mother. Gone forever. His sword, Ianus, gone as well.

Adrien's soul cried out for his blade as it had years before. *Come to me!*

What had Roland told him? That he must accept that his sword was gone forever? *No. I refuse to believe it.* If a hunter's sword was a reflection of its wielder's soul, if a vampire's sword was as much a part of the vampire as it was a solid, material thing, then how could an immortal's weapon die if an immortal lived forever?

Ianus! Return to me!

Rosina's sobbing, the sound of the rain on the tile floor, the sigh of the wind through the trees—all of these sounds faded. Adrien heard only the cry of his soul.

Come to me, Ianus!

No more was Adrien the student calling his master. Now he was the master calling his servant. Adrien knew the sword would heed his order. He had grieved its loss, but he'd forgotten that he had never been beholden to it. The sword was his to command. His soul's sword.

He felt the weapon take shape in his right hand, warm and solid. It vibrated with his pain. Pain like power. Pelletier still studied him with keen interest. Pelletier, who could have killed him long before. Why had he waited?

He wants an opponent he cannot easily defeat.

Adrien moved the sword about, feeling its weight, testing its balance. Ianus had changed, just as he had changed. The blade was longer than before, thinner, too. But there was no mistaking the *feel* of it in his palm. This was his sword, transformed, just as he had been transformed through Nicolas's blood.

We will kill him together. Adrien felt a nearly imperceptible vibration from the hilt of the weapon in silent response.

Pelletier stood with his sword at the ready. He did not appear to be afraid, but he no longer seemed amused. He aimed his sword at Adrien's chest, and the invisible strings with which Adrien had become quite familiar began to wrap around his body, snaking their way up his arms toward his fast-beating heart.

My heart belongs only to him. You cannot touch it.

Pelletier laughed, no doubt having guessed or even heard Adrien's thoughts. "You're a fool and a dreamer," he said.

Around them, the battle continued. Adrien allowed Pelletier's attack to permeate his body, winding its way through his muscles, his skin, and his veins. The invisible ribbons of energy squeezed around his chest as Adrien knew they would.

It's time, Adrien told Ianus as he tightened his grip on the sword.

Ianus's blade glowed. Adrien imagined Nicolas's blood running through his veins as he drew on both his own power and Nicolas's. This new power was more subtle than his own—it glowed brightly but was cool like newly fallen snow. Nicolas always reminded him of the snow. The memory made him smile.

Adrien cut into the skin of his wrist and watched the blood flow freely onto the blade before dripping onto the floor like thick raindrops. He coated both sides of the blade and ran the bloody blade over his lips, licking the traces of blood left there. Where before he'd experienced only anger and rage, now he felt power grow within him. A new power. The power he'd not acknowledged before. The power he'd feared. Nicolas's power, running through his body, alive in his blood.

Pelletier appeared surprised that his attack had not achieved its intended effect. He narrowed his eyes, his brow creased in concentration, and the bonds grew tighter around Adrien's chest. Still, Adrien's heart continued to beat.

Adrien raised Ianus. *This is for you, Nicolas.*

Bands of silver and dark blue shot from all over Ianus's surface. The temperature in the room dropped and snowflakes of the purest white fell from where the ceiling had once been. Silver and blue twisted and turned through the air toward where Pelletier stood unmoving, either believing that Adrien's attack would not harm him or that he would succeed in breaking Adrien's concentration. Neither assumption proved correct.

The floor shook under their feet like an earthquake as a hum grew louder and louder. The other fighters struggled to remain standing as the floor buckled. Only Adrien and Pelletier were unaffected.

Adrien's attack began to attach itself to Pelletier's body. Once again Pelletier fought back. Adrien's heart skipped a beat, then resumed its steady pace. Perhaps realizing Adrien would not succumb as before, Pelletier attempted to withdraw. Adrien latched on to Pelletier's connection and drew on the power there to increase the strength of his own attack. Adrien bound Pelletier to him, refusing to let him go.

Now, Ianus!

The humming sound increased in volume and the room shook again. The silver-and-blue ribbons from Adrien's sword now completely bound Pelletier's body like ropes. The shimmering strands undulated over his skin, expanding to cover even Pelletier's face. The attack enveloped Pelletier. Adrien breathed in deeply, then exhaled, imagining his power expanding. The resulting explosion sent a shockwave of such intensity that all the other occupants of the room covered their faces to avoid the impact.

Nothing remained of Pelletier's body. His bladeless weapon clattered to the floor. Pelletier was dead.

CHAPTER SIXTEEN:
TWISTED TIME

ADRIEN'S SWORD vanished. No one spoke. Pelletier's fighters fled along with Giovanetti.

Adrien walked slowly to where Nicolas lay and gathered him once again into his arms. He cared nothing for the shouts of appreciation from his comrades, who were now chasing the retreating hunters. Nothing mattered. This was the one outcome he had never planned for—he had never considered that he could lose Nicolas forever.

No. I won't accept it.

Adrien felt Jean's hand on his shoulder. He glanced up and met Jean's steely gaze. He sensed Jean's grief, sensed his practiced control begin to slip. At Jean's side, Blaise stood with eyes red from tears, his face deathly pale.

We were supposed to have all the time in the world.

He held Nicolas tighter, shutting out the world around him. Let them tell him to let Nicolas go—he wouldn't listen to the platitudes. The only thing he heard was a voice inside his mind. A familiar voice, urging him on.

"My power is yours, Adrien," the voice said. *"But only a little taste this time. The best is yet to come...."*

Adrien suddenly floated in whiteness, as if his soul had been freed from his body. He imagined anticipating Pelletier's attack. Someone laughed—a voice inside of his mind. The same voice that had spoken to him before. He opened his eyes to see who spoke and the room blurred around the edges as though his eyes were momentarily out of focus, and everything took on a bluish cast. His head spun and he fought the urge to vomit. Then, just as quickly, the nausea and dizziness passed.

"Just this once, Adrien," the voice whispered. *"The next time will be of my own choosing."*

The room dissolved into a blur of color. Adrien came back to himself and realized he no longer held Nicolas but was standing facing Pelletier once again—Pelletier, unarmed and implacable.

Adrien watched in shock as Bremen's head flew into the air.

Nicolas! He felt Nicolas nearby. Alive. Whole. *What on earth...?*

"You may actually be stronger than I. But you still have much to learn." Pelletier spoke the same words he had moments before Nicolas had been injured.

Had time *reversed*? Had he done that? Adrien would contemplate this strange turn of events later. He called his sword, but Pelletier did not draw his weapon as he had done before. Instead his eyes grew wide.

He knows what I've done.

"But that's not poss...." Pelletier's frown faded and his lips parted in surprise. "Apparently I've underestimated you. Or perhaps I've underestimated the strength of his blood." Pelletier glanced toward Nicolas and smiled.

Nicolas was alone. Unprotected.

He wants Nicolas's blood.

"No!" Adrien shouted as time began to gallop forward. Adrien pointed his weapon at Pelletier, every muscle in his body, every fiber of his being focused on killing him. Pelletier vanished and reappeared at Nicolas's side.

"Nicolas!" Adrien yelled as Pelletier pressed the blade of his weapon against Nicolas's throat.

"You've lost this fight." Pelletier clamped a hand over Nicolas's mouth. Drops of blood were visible where his blade met the pale skin of Nicolas's neck. Nicolas struggled, but Pelletier held him fast.

"Let him go," Adrien said. "He's nothing to you."

"You're wrong," Pelletier said with a barely repressed smile. "Your little demonstration has proven he's quite valuable to me."

"Regardless of what you try," Jean said as he struggled to his feet, "the Rousseaus and the Lamberts will know lasting peace. If you harm him—"

"As long as I control the Council," Pelletier answered, "your peace will be of little consequence. And if either of you openly oppose me, I *will* kill your little prince."

Adrien's chest tightened at the impact of those words. "There's nowhere you can go where we won't find you," he said as he waited for the opportunity to retrieve Nicolas from Pelletier's grasp.

"Perhaps." Pelletier's smile faded, replaced by a look of determination that made Adrien's blood run cold.

"*Adrien*!" Nicolas kicked Pelletier in the shin and struggled to free himself from Pelletier's grasp. Pelletier's hold on his sword slipped, cutting deeper into Nicolas's skin.

Adrien and Jean both lunged for Pelletier, but neither moved fast enough. Pelletier regained his grip on Nicolas, smiled in triumph, then vanished into thin air.

"Nicolas! No!" Adrien's voice echoed through the room. He stared at the place where Pelletier and Nicolas had disappeared. *Do it again*, he implored the voice he'd heard. *Take me back!*

He closed his eyes and waited for the strange sensations to occur, for the room to dissolve, for something—*anything*—to change.

Nothing happened.

CHAPTER SEVENTEEN:
NO WAY FORWARD

ADRIEN TRIED to recreate the moment he'd traveled back in time once more. He closed his eyes, he called out to the voice he'd heard, and he waited for the sensation of floating outside of his body. And again, nothing happened.

"Adrien."

Roland's voice brought Adrien back to himself. When the hell had Roland arrived?

"I arrived just after Pelletier disappeared," Roland said.

Had Roland heard his thoughts? Adrien tried to focus, but he felt disoriented, disconnected somehow from his body. But how had Roland known to come? The cottage near Abbeville was days away at best. Adrien pushed aside these thoughts and tried to concentrate.

"You won't accomplish anything like this," Roland said. "You're exhausted. You need to rest."

"Not now. I have to—"

"You've been at this for hours." Roland offered him a sympathetic smile.

Hours? But just a moment ago, Nicolas had been standing there. "I can do this," he insisted. He struggled to clear his fuzzy thoughts. If he could *think*, he'd know what he should do.

Roland put his hand over Adrien's, forcing him to lower his sword.

For the first time, Adrien realized the conservatory was completely empty but for the two of them. Where had everyone gone?

"Jean and the others are tending to the wounded," Roland said.

Stop reading my thoughts.

Roland chuckled.

"How do I go back again?" Adrien demanded.

Roland frowned. "Back?"

"Back in time."

"Time?" Roland stared at him. Adrien couldn't recall Roland ever appearing surprised before.

"Yes. Something happened. Nicolas was...." Adrien couldn't speak the word. "I killed Pelletier. I couldn't lose Nicolas. And then...." *Nicolas!* God, he'd lost Nicolas when they finally had a chance together.

"You turned back time?" Roland's frown deepened.

"And I'll do it again." Adrien wouldn't leave until he'd brought Nicolas back. "I'll just go back further in time and stop him from taking Nicolas."

"You'll get nowhere in your present state," Roland said as Adrien began to shake uncontrollably. "You need blood and you need to rest."

Adrien moaned and rubbed the bridge of his nose. "Head hurts," he mumbled.

"Let me help you?"

Adrien nodded, allowing his shoulders to slump in defeat. He'd lost. Yes, he'd saved Nicolas's life, but he'd lost the battle. Worst of all, he'd lost Nicolas.

Roland put his hand to Adrien's forehead and whispered, "Rest now."

ROLAND HAD done something to make him sleep. Probably a good thing, since Adrien guessed he wouldn't have slept at all without Roland's help. When he awoke, he found Roland waiting in the sitting room.

"Tell me everything you know about this power—about what I did to turn back time," he said after dutifully eating the breakfast Roland provided and agreeing that he would find someone willing to give him blood. The thought of taking anyone but Nicolas's blood disturbed him, but if satisfying his bloodlust would make him strong enough to travel into the past again, he'd willingly do it.

"Unfortunately I know very little about what you did," Roland told him as he tore off a piece of bread and buttered it. "Can you tell me about it?"

Adrien told Roland what he could. The entire fight seemed to blur in his memory. He thought he remembered someone speaking to him, but he couldn't recall a face. "I don't remember much of anything," he finally admitted.

Roland appeared to study him for a moment, then said, "I know of no immortal who can turn back time."

"What?" He hadn't even considered the ability was unusual.

"There are stories of ancient vampires who could manipulate time. Myths. At least I thought they were myths," Roland confirmed. "It's possible the Rousseau Clan—"

"But Pelletier *knew*. He knew something had changed." This thought frightened Adrien.

"I'm at a loss to explain that," Roland said with a shake of his head. "Just as I'm at a loss to explain what you must do to recreate what you did to bring Nicolas back. Perhaps the ancient powers are not as dead as I thought."

"What if Pelletier also…?" If Adrien possessed the ability because of Nicolas's blood, Pelletier could have gained a similar power when he stole Paul Rousseau's life blood. *And with Nicolas a prisoner, he might well reinforce that power by stealing Nicolas's blood.*

No. He wouldn't think about that. He *couldn't*.

Then, Adrien had been too tired to think much more about it. Now, as he sat on the roof of the castle, gazing out over the grounds as the sun dipped below the horizon, Adrien knew he'd been naïve to believe that repeating what he'd done would be simple. He had nothing to show for another day spent attempting it but another headache.

He was a failure. He'd failed to protect Nicolas. He deserved the pain that wracked his body and tore at his heart.

"You saved his life," Jean said as he sat beside him on the roof.

"And still I lost him." Adrien drew a long breath and rubbed the bridge of his nose.

"He's alive," Jean said. "We will find him."

"There's so much I don't understand about the gift he gave me. So much I need to learn."

"And therein lies our hope."

CHAPTER EIGHTEEN: FLEETING TIME

THAT NIGHT Adrien dreamed he walked in the shadow of enormous towers of glass. Taller even than the Eiffel Tower or the cathedrals he had seen in Paris, the buildings soared to the heavens, shining like the blade of his sword. In the distance he heard unfamiliar sounds, a low rumble like hundreds of horses on cobblestones, the droning roar of something overhead. A carriage screeched by, but there were no horses pulling it, no steam rising up from its belly. He looked up and saw a metal bird overhead, its wings unmoving. And yet it did not fall.

Ahead, a man walked quickly toward one of the buildings. He wore no coat or vest but was dressed in strange clothing. The wind lifted the ends of his ebony hair.

"Nicolas!" Adrien shouted.

Nicolas turned to look at him. Adrien saw no recognition in his brown eyes. He turned and began to walk faster.

"Nicolas, wait!"

No matter how fast Adrien ran, Nicolas moved faster.

ADRIEN STRUGGLED to catch his breath. A dream and yet somehow more. *An omen, or perhaps a premonition?*

He got to his feet and walked into the sitting room. The glass doors were open to let in the cool evening air. Outside, the stars flickered and the wind rustled the leaves of the nearby trees.

Adrien pushed open the door to the adjoining room. Just the night before, Nicolas had slept here. The bed had been made, but Nicolas's scent lingered on the furniture and in the clothing that hung in the armoire. Adrien picked up the book that lay on the nightstand next to a sheath of writing paper. *Poetry* by Alfred Lord Tennyson.

He leafed through the pages and read:

91

What is that which I should turn to, lighting upon days like these?
Every door is barr'd with gold, and opens but to golden keys.

Every gate is throng'd with suitors, all the markets overflow.
I have but an angry fancy; what is that which I should do?

I had been content to perish, falling on the foeman's ground,
When the ranks are roll'd in vapour, and the winds are laid with sound.

He closed his eyes against his tears. Tears were weakness and a fool's refuge. Tears would do nothing to bring Nicolas back.

"Pathetic," a voice said.

Adrien looked around the room but saw no one.

"Ever the romantic fool."

"What…. Who are you?" Adrien asked.

"Do you need a reason to go on living?" Laughter echoed throughout the room. *"So be it."*

Adrien shook his head. He needed more sleep if he was hearing things. He set the book back on the table, and as he did so, something metal beneath the papers caught the light. He pushed the papers aside and picked up the familiar gold pocket watch. Nicolas's watch. He clicked open the face and a piece of yellowing paper fell onto the floor. He leaned down and retrieved it.

He gasped as he realized his name was written above the fold. With shaking hands, he opened the paper. At the top, a date: *March 3, 1894,* written in Nicolas's beautiful script.

Beneath the date were three words: *I remember you.*

CHAPTER NINETEEN: THE COUNCIL

The Present

ADRIEN WATCHED the sun rise from the roof of the Rousseau castle. The cool air hinted at impending autumn. He thought of his father's vineyard and the coming harvest. By now the grapes would be ripening. He wondered if his father still helped with the vines. He hadn't visited his family home in more than fifty years, but he often imagined himself returning there with Nicolas. Over the decades the dream had faded, even if it refused to die.

More than a hundred years spent traveling the world, chasing after Pelletier with nothing but heartache to show for it. Each time Adrien thought he'd located Pelletier and Nicolas, they vanished. Cat and mouse. A twisted game Pelletier clearly relished. The years of travel had given birth to Adrien's shipping empire but hadn't given him the one thing—the one *person*—he cared about.

Now, back in Paris after so long, Adrien wondered if he'd done enough. If he'd worked hard enough to change time again. He'd become stronger, but that strength had brought him no closer to bringing Nicolas back. Adrien had not been able to recreate the power that had saved Nicolas's life.

Faced with the prospect of yet another disappointment, Adrien felt hollow. Why had he lost control of the bloodlust?

"Because you've given up," the ever-present voice in his mind replied. *"Because you're weak."*

ADRIEN, JEAN, Blaise, and Rogier left the castle for Paris just after midday. They'd been prepared to be turned away at the Council Chamber, but they encountered no resistance when they met the guards stationed outside. Instead, the guards escorted them to seats in the gallery on the bottom level of the chamber. Several other people were already seated there, none of whom Adrien recognized. This didn't surprise Adrien. The only hunters he knew were now Council elders who would sit in the balconies above them.

Shaped like an oval and carved into the bedrock underneath Paris, the Council Chamber rose seven stories high. At each level jutted balconies hewn from stone and edged with wooden railings. Hunters from all over the world filled the balconies. Centuries ago, the Council was comprised only of hunters from Europe. But the number of hunters and vampires had dwindled over the past century, and similar councils located in Asia and Africa had joined the European Council.

Adrien thought he saw Roland peer down from one of the lower balconies, where the Council elders were seated. "Call me," Roland had said in the message he'd left on Adrien's cell phone the night before. Adrien hadn't returned the call. He had no wish to revisit the past—it only reminded him of his own powerlessness.

A balcony, slightly larger than the others, faced the main entrance. Carved with the Council's seal and covered in gold leaf, this was the place of honor assigned to the regent of the Council. For more than a hundred years, it had sat empty, as Giovanetti had chosen to lead the Council as acting regent from the box he held as a Council elder. When Adrien was a child, his father had told him stories of the Council and of the former regent, Robert Aguillon.

Fairy tales. Hollywood and knights in shining armor. Reality was far less appealing. Over the past hundred years, Adrien had heard darker stories of treachery and murder. Even in his absence, Pelletier still managed to manipulate the membership. With Giovanetti as his surrogate, many of the men and women Adrien had known had left or simply disappeared.

In the dim light of the hall, Adrien could not see how many Council members were present, although nearly every chair appeared taken. The dim lighting was by design, since most Council members preferred anonymity. The Internet presented a challenge for most of his brethren, not to mention the vampires who lived thousands of years. Centuries before, hunters and vampires might move from one city to another to avoid detection. Now, many were forced to hide for decades before emerging to live a public life. Humanity, most hunters believed, had not sufficiently evolved to accept their kind, let alone the vampires they hunted.

A very old hunter Adrien recognized as Tyrol Vassilskya called the meeting to order. The room grew quiet as he spoke. "Welcome, brothers, sisters, and honored guests, to this meeting of the Council of Hunters. This meeting has been called to elect a new regent, a position left vacant by the disappearance of Lord Verel Pelletier more than a century ago.

"By law, the Council is charged with electing a new regent when the current regent is no longer able to serve, has become incapable of serving, or has died. Several weeks ago the Council Elders officially certified the death of Lord Pelletier. You will be asked to vote upon his successor in a few minutes. Before then, however, the Council must open the floor to anyone wishing to express an opinion as to the worthiness of the candidates. There are three: Sir Ralph Watson, Lady Valeria Estanza, and Lord Antonio Giovanetti."

Vassilskya motioned to one of the guards posted by the gallery, who escorted a participant seated there to a small dais in the center of the main floor. One by one, the speakers addressed the Council, advocating for particular candidates. Adrien caught himself yawning several times as the speakers droned on about the virtues of their candidate and the dangers of another. Not a single person mentioned Pelletier's name.

"This is a waste of time," Adrien whispered to Jean after nearly two hours of speeches. Blaise, sitting on Adrien's other side, frowned as he looked around the room.

"They will call us soon," Jean said.

"Even if they don't care to listen," Adrien added with a frown. Jean's only plan had been to wait and see what happened and hope Pelletier would appear. No plan at all. Not that Adrien had any better ideas. If Pelletier did show, Adrien might engage him and learn where he'd hidden Nicolas.

"The Council will hear next from Lord Reynaud Rousseau," Vassilskya said after the last speaker had finished.

Blaise's expression darkened. Reynaud was nowhere to be seen.

"Reynaud?" Adrien said under his breath. "What could the bastard possibly have to say to the Council?"

Clearly those present shared Adrien's sentiments. Vampires were permitted in the Council Chamber, but allowing them to speak on matters pertaining to the affairs of hunters was unheard of.

Reynaud entered through the large doorway near where they sat and made his way onto the dais. His hair was nearly white, his face gaunt.

"How dare he show his face!"

Adrien ignored the voice.

"Members of the Council, honored guests," Reynaud began, his deep voice resonating throughout the Chamber, "I thank you for allowing me to speak on behalf of Lord Giovanetti."

"Will you sit and listen to his lies, Adrien?"

Adrien took a deep breath and rubbed his eyes. Jean glanced at him with obvious concern. Adrien ignored this and focused once more on Reynaud, who droned on about the rift between hunters and vampires and about the war between vampires, which had resulted in a lasting peace. Through all of it, Adrien sat and schooled his expression so as not to show his impatience.

"I've had enough of his ceaseless prattle," the voice in Adrien's mind said. *"Suppose we take a little trip, you and I?"* The voice paused for a moment, then continued, *"But perhaps first I should show you how much more interesting your future could be...."*

A sudden wave of dizziness accompanied a low hum that grew so loud, Adrien could barely hear Reynaud's voice. Adrien looked around, but no one else in the room appeared to hear it. He grabbed hold of his chair as the room spun and he fought not to vomit. The dimly lit chamber began to glow with familiar blue light and Adrien's vision blurred.

"...this is why I ceded my position to my nephew, Blaise Rousseau.... Lord Pelletier sacrificed himself to protect him.... The Council should support Lord Giovanetti."

Adrien tugged at his tie, then loosened it and unbuttoned the top of his shirt. He took a deep breath, then another.

Reynaud finished speaking and bowed to the Council members.

"Sacrificed himself? Pelletier? Now that's an interesting twist."

Laughter echoed like a buzz saw in Adrien's mind. Adrien was just about to tell Jean he needed to leave—he wouldn't tell Jean he was hearing voices—when the room seemed to shift. Adrien felt a presence he hadn't felt in more than a century.

"Nicolas." Adrien's heart galloped as he sat upright, fingers tingling. His sword awaited his call. He tried to slow his breathing. He wouldn't overreact and give Pelletier the upper hand.

Reynaud stepped off the podium and headed back toward the heavy oak doors. A man stood there in the shadows, dressed in a modern suit, dark hair gathered at the nape of his neck. He began to walk toward Reynaud. Pelletier was nowhere to be seen.

"Nicolas!" Adrien's shout rang through the room as he started across the floor. He didn't care that he'd breached protocol. Nothing mattered but Nicolas.

Reynaud turned to look at Adrien. Whispers of conversations filled the room as several guards moved to restrain Adrien.

"Nicolas." Adrien stood only a few feet away. Nicolas stared back at him, his face paling.

"They've kept him from you," the voice in Adrien's mind whispered.

"Gilbert." Reynaud looked as though he'd smelled something particularly unpleasant.

"You must take what is yours. You have suffered far too long."

"Nicolas, step away from him." Adrien's hand warmed as his sword materialized. He pointed it at Reynaud.

"What do you want from me?" Nicolas asked Adrien. He narrowed his eyes and his cheeks flushed as he spoke.

"They have stolen him from you."

Adrien rubbed his eyes with his free hand and willed the voice to stop speaking. He needed to focus. He needed to be strong. He'd waited too long to let the moment slip through his grasp. "What have you done to him?" he demanded, his fury a storm that welled up within his chest.

"They have taken something dear to you, Adrien. You must show them you are no longer weak."

"Done to him?" asked Reynaud, clearly startled. "No one has done anything to him except you and your kind."

"He lies, Adrien."

"You and that bastard Pelletier, you've been working together," Adrien hissed. He wouldn't let them take Nicolas from him again. This was Pelletier's handiwork. Pelletier and his dogs.

"*Lord* Pelletier sacrificed himself to save Nicolas," Reynaud said, his face betraying true anger now. "He sacrificed himself for the sake of peace between our clans."

"You and he have kept Nicolas prisoner for a century. You're a traitor to your own clan," snarled Adrien.

Amidst renewed murmurs and gasps from the Council Chamber, Blaise rose and moved to face Adrien. "Haven't you done enough harm?" he asked, his face pale, pained. "You must accept that there is peace. There is nothing you can do to destroy what we've built so carefully."

"Harm?" Adrien stared at Blaise, uncomprehending.

"Enough." The room fell silent at Jean's resonant voice.

Adrien drew a long breath. He was sure Jean would tell them. Jean would explain the truth—that they were all in danger and Pelletier was merely biding time before drawing them all into his web.

"Adrien." Jean appeared startled. Concerned. "You are mistaken."

The silence in the room faded with the whispers of the Council members. Jean frowned, looked at Adrien, then back at Blaise. Jean shook his head almost imperceptibly, and for a moment, Adrien wondered if he did understand that something had changed. But then he said, "We resolved our dispute centuries ago. Pelletier died to save Nicolas's life."

"What?" Adrien's hand shook. "But you saw…. This is all Pelletier's handiwork." The pain in his head reached a crescendo. Somewhere deep within the recesses of his mind, understanding floated just outside Adrien's grasp.

Jean grabbed Adrien's free hand and Adrien thought he heard Jean's voice in his mind. *"We will speak later. You must not challenge him. I will—"* But the other voice in Adrien's mind grew louder, drowning out the part of Adrien that struggled to understand.

"They all lie, Adrien," the other voice said.

"Pelletier? Dead? But he's still alive, somewhere…. You know this." Something inside of Adrien rose, dark and uncontrollable. Didn't they understand what Pelletier had done? Didn't they understand how Pelletier had used them for his own ends? Didn't they see that Pelletier had lied to them? Tricked them?

"They cannot understand. They don't know your pain."

The voice spoke the truth. No one understood. No one saw through Pelletier's schemes. Adrien alone could save Nicolas. Only he knew the price they'd paid.

"Nicolas, you must come with me," Adrien said as he pushed Reynaud away and took Nicolas roughly by the arm.

"Let me go," Nicolas said, pulling away from Adrien. "I don't know why you insist on making a scene here, of all places. But know that I won't be ordered about by you or anyone else."

"Will you let yourself feel the pain again? Or will you fight them?"

"Please, Nicolas. It isn't safe here. If you come with me—"

"We're leaving," Reynaud said as he led Nicolas away with his sword pointed at Adrien.

Rage burst from Adrien's soul like fire, scorching his heart. He heard nothing but the voice urging him on. Telling him he must act or risk losing Nicolas forever. "No!" he yelled. "I won't let you take him again."

"Adrien, stop!" Blaise shouted from behind him.

"Show them. Show them, Adrien. Show them your power."

Adrien hit Blaise so hard that he flew backward into the wall. Jean pointed his sword at Adrien as several guards tried to restrain him. Adrien threw them off with ease.

"What are you doing, Adrien?" Jean shook his head in disbelief. "Reynaud isn't our enemy. Roland is."

"Roland?" Adrien demanded. "What the hell does Roland have to do with any of this?"

"You've lost your mind." Reynaud drew his weapon and aimed it at Adrien's heart.

"I won't let them take Nicolas again." Adrien turned to Nicolas. "Please. Nicolas. You know me. You know I'd never hurt you."

Reynaud pulled Nicolas closer to the exit, his sword still trained on Adrien.

"You cannot allow them to steal him from you again!"

"I won't allow you to steal him from me again!" Adrien shouted. The entire Council was on its feet now. A dozen guards stood, weapons pointed at Adrien.

Reynaud shot an arc of blue energy from his sword, and shards of ice penetrated Adrien's chest. Adrien ignored the pain.

"Now, Adrien! It's time to take your revenge!"

Adrien aimed a burst of black fire at Reynaud with such violence that its recoil nearly knocked Adrien off his feet.

"No, Adrien! Stop!" Nicolas shouted.

The flames hit Reynaud squarely in the chest. He fell backward and lay still.

"Uncle!" Nicolas dropped to his knees and pressed his hands against Reynaud's blackened chest. No one moved. Tears glistened on Nicolas's cheeks as he met Adrien's gaze. "Why? Why hurt him? He's done you no harm."

Adrien tried to answer, but a wave of dizziness far stronger than before came over him, causing his mind to flicker and lose its focus. Before he could struggle back to himself, something struck him in the chest—an attack from somewhere above, in the balconies. He felt momentary pain as the blackness claimed him.

As he lost consciousness, he heard the voice in his mind say, *"You are powerful, Adrien. Together, we are invincible."*

ADRIEN TRIED to focus on the voices but only caught bits of conversations. "…cannot allow him… not when he has no control over it." Roland's voice.

"…asked me to help you. He fears Adrien might lose control… hurt others." The second voice sounded like Jean.

"They fear you, Adrien." This last voice Adrien knew—the same voice that had spoken to him before. The voice in his mind.

I'm going crazy. He willed the voice away.

"You're nothing without me."

Get the hell out of my mind!

The voice in his head laughed. *"Not possible,"* it said. *"We are the same mind. I am you."*

Adrien moaned. He felt sick. Dizzy. He struggled to escape the prison of his unconsciousness. The same blue light he remembered from the Council Chamber flickered in Adrien's mind.

"You'll stay here as long as I wish it."

Please… just let me die.

"Time to play, Adrien," the voice said.

Play?

"A game" came the reply. *"If you win, I'll let you die. If I win…."*

I don't understand. What kind of game? Adrien fucking hated games.

More laughter. Then: *"A game where you change your future."*

CHAPTER TWENTY:
FALSE STARTS

"GET OUT of bed!"

Adrien blinked hard, rubbed his eyes, and sat up. How long had he been sleeping? He remembered the voice in his mind. He thought maybe he'd vomited. His mouth felt dry and his body ached. He must have been sleeping for days, as foggy and unfocused as he felt.

"Water." His voice sounded strange. Higher pitched than usual.

The room came slowly into focus. Small, familiar, much like the room he had grown up in. His father's house in Saint-Gervais. Had Roland brought him here? He guessed the Council would be looking for him. He felt quite sure he'd killed Reynaud or seriously injured him.

He moaned and massaged his forehead. His head hurt like a beast.

"Get out of bed!" Again that voice. Like François's. He looked up and saw it was François frowning at him, lips pressed together. He looked to be all of nineteen. "You promised you'd come with me to Lyon. At this rate, we're going to be late."

"Lyon? Why are we going to Lyon?" Adrien asked, trying to stall for time. He figured he was dreaming. Except this didn't feel like a dream. It felt—

"You're not escaping this time," François said. "All of the week's work is done. And if you think you can use a book"—he pointed to a pile of books on the floor by the bed—"as an excuse, I'll use them for practice. I bet they burn quite well."

I'm in the past? Adrien stood and stretched. His hands came nowhere near the low ceiling. He walked past François to the small mirror by the window. The face that peered back at him looked familiar, but younger than he remembered. *What year would this be? 1894?* How old would he be? Seventeen?

Adrien tried to recall how he'd come to be here. At the wedding he'd turned back time, but only by a few minutes. And over the past century, he had tried time and again to recreate what had happened then, but to no avail.

Why now?

The sound of laughter came from inside his mind. The same voice he'd been hearing. The voice he'd heard at the wedding, more than a century ago, and again at the Council meeting.

Have you brought me here?

The voice laughed again.

"Addie!" François cuffed him on the back of the head, just hard enough to get his attention.

"I always hated when you did that," Adrien snapped.

François shook his head and laughed. "All the more reason not to stop. These days it seems the only way to keep you from dreaming." He picked up one of the books and raised an eyebrow. "King Arthur?"

Adrien pulled the book from François's hands, realizing as he did that he was acting exactly as he had when he was a child. He'd loved that book, even imagined himself wielding Excalibur.

Instinctively, he called for Ianus. Nothing happened. He glanced around the room and saw the sword propped against the bed where he'd always left it. Solid as it once had been.

Time travel inside my own body? Was that what he'd done at Nicolas and Rosina's ill-fated wedding? Was he still immortal, or could he die here? And if he was no longer immortal, could he return to his own time? Would he have to live his entire life again? Without Nicolas, would he grow old and die?

"Addie." François glared at him. "The carriage is ready. I packed some food for the trip. But if we don't leave now, we'll arrive too late for the fête."

"Fête?"

"The Council's ball." François shook his head in disbelief. "We've planned this for weeks. Please don't tell me you're going to back out again this year. Madame LeFavre will take care of father, and Isa said she'd feed the animals for us."

"Isabelle?" Adrien ached at the sound of her name.

François laughed and pushed Adrien playfully. "Breakfast? Maybe then your head will clear."

He tried to recall the fête but came up with only a vague memory of an excuse he'd made for not attending. He'd never liked parties, let alone the lavish affairs the Council of Hunters sponsored.

He thought of François and of how he'd nearly lost him before. No. If he had to live his life over, he would do things differently. Perhaps he'd be stronger for it, and he'd be able to save Nicolas this time.

"I'll dress and eat," Adrien said. "Then we can leave." François stared at him with such a comical expression of surprise that Adrien laughed out loud. "Have I surprised you?" He tossed the book at François, who caught it and looked at him in obvious shock. "You might try reading it," Adrien added. "Far more enjoyable than practicing swordplay. You might even learn a few new things."

François chuckled, then shrugged and left the room. He didn't return the book.

Adrien walked around the room, stopping at the small desk and running his fingers over the blotter. He smiled to see the tiny depictions of swords and armored knights he'd drawn there.

A small painting of his mother caught his eye. He picked it up and wondered if his father had kept it after he'd left. He'd told himself the modern apartment in Miami, with its clean lines and the abstract canvases on the walls, suited his purposes. He told himself he didn't need the painful memories. Yet seeing the portrait made him long for the comfort of this room and of his family as it had been more than a century before.

He laughed at himself for the maudlin thoughts and turned his attention to the sword, sheathed and leaning against the wall.

"Ianus." He picked up the sword. It felt different than how he remembered. Heavier. But in spite of this, he felt the thrum of the metal in his bones and his heart. This was not the sword of his youth but an immortal's sword.

He dressed in traveling clothes, then buckled the sword around his waist and walked back to the mirror. In about three years, he would stop aging, but for now, he looked to be barely more than a boy.

A man in a boy's body.

A few minutes later, he headed downstairs.

"You slept a long time."

He froze at the sound of his sister's voice.

"Isabelle." She was young, smiling... alive. Without thinking, he rushed to embrace her. He held her until she pushed him away, a quizzical look on her face.

"Are you sure you aren't still asleep?" she said, giggling. "You act as though you haven't seen me in ages."

It *had* been ages since he'd seen her. Nearly fifty years; she'd been an old woman. "I guess I'm still a little sleepy," he lied. "But it's still good to see you."

"Silly." She walked over to the table and sat, waiting until he joined her. "Bread?" she asked as she cut several pieces and set them on a plate for him.

He nodded. The bread smelled heavenly and his stomach growled in appreciation. He slathered some butter over it and bit in with relish, devouring the entire piece in just a few seconds.

"You'd think we didn't feed you," she said with a grin. She wore the motherly expression he remembered well. She'd been the youngest, but they'd all relied on her. Not that Adrien and François didn't do their share of the vineyard's work, but Isabelle kept things running smoothly, especially when their father disappeared on Council business for days at a time.

"The bread's delicious." Adrien buttered another piece. "Where's Papa?"

Isabelle eyed him with concern. "François said you fell hard yesterday when you two were sparring. Are you sure you'll be all right to travel?"

"Fine," he said, his mouth full once again.

"He went to Marseilles," she said brightly. "He'll be back tonight."

"Forgot," Adrien mumbled.

"Papa said he'd think about what I said. About Montpellier."

This time Adrien knew what she was talking about. "What do you think he'll decide?" he asked.

"Papa said I'll have to wait until my sixteenth birthday," Isabelle replied. "But if Madame LeFavre's cousin is willing to let me stay with her, he agreed to let me attend the university."

"You don't want to get married?" he asked, knowing full well what her answer would be. He'd always admired her independence. She'd gone on to write several books about French history after her studies—the only woman from their small town who had studied at a university.

"I'll marry if and when I choose to," she said, raising her chin in indignation.

"And so you should."

Her eyes grew wide and her lips parted. "You really must have hit your head yesterday."

He shrugged and chewed on another piece of bread.

"Addie!" François shouted from outside.

"You'd better go," Isabelle said. "He's so excited that you finally agreed to go with him, he may burst into flames, sword and all." She laughed, then picked something up from the table and handed it to him. "For the ball," she said.

He unfolded the bundle and held the deep brown jacket up to his chest. "It's beautiful," he said. "You made this?"

She blushed and giggled. "Who else would make it?"

"Thank you." He swallowed hard and met her gaze, so bright and full of joy.

"There's a shirt and trousers as well," she said, looking away as the pink on her cheeks deepened.

He leaned in and kissed her on the cheek. "Thank you," he repeated, at a loss for words and knowing anything else he might say would be completely out of character for his seventeen-year-old self.

"Get going, now," she said with mock sternness. "I expect you to tell me all about it when you return." She turned back to the table and rearranged several plates stacked there. He knew he'd made her uncomfortable.

"I will," he said. "I promise."

ADRIEN BARELY recognized the Lyon of his childhood. Gone were the lines of automobile traffic and the sprawling urban landscape, replaced by horse-drawn carriages and people pushing carts. The boxy electric nineteenth-century streetcars looked nothing like their twenty-first century counterparts, although many of them appeared newly built.

The scent of the old city momentarily overwhelmed Adrien. Smoke rising from chimneys made his eyes water, but he found the smell of hay and manure surprisingly comforting and familiar. From time to time, Adrien caught a hint of exhaust on the air as an automobile sped by them, more like a motorized carriage than anything resembling the modern incarnation.

Adrien had always avoided Council social gatherings and knew nothing of what to expect. François pulled the carriage up to a large stone building Adrien recognized as the local hunter headquarters. He'd been here many times when he'd searched for Charles, but he'd avoided the place when he'd returned to Lyon for his own business.

A servant met them and took the reins from François while another helped them down from the carriage. The ride from Saint-Gervais to Lyon was about five hours, so they changed into their evening clothes at the small hotel where they would spend the night. François looked handsome in his black suit with his sword at his waist. In a few years, Adrien would be just as tall. Seeing his brother from the vantage point of his slightly smaller stature, Adrien admired François's powerful shoulders and comfortable gait. François strode confidently, his eyes intense with focus, his strength obvious. Adrien remembered how he'd longed for such confidence, and how awkward he'd felt in public.

They walked up a large set of stone steps and were greeted by several guards at the entrance to the building.

"Names?" one of the guards asked.

"François and Adrien Gilbert, of the Gilbert Clan," François said with obvious pride.

The guards bowed and allowed them entry. From there, they walked down a marble-tiled hallway toward a large ballroom. The sounds of conversation and of music drifted toward them. Years ago Adrien would have feared such a gathering. Now, he realized, he looked forward to it.

Heads turned as they walked through the doors and down a set of marble steps to the dance floor. A young man Adrien thought looked familiar waved at them.

"François!" the man shouted.

"Victor." François clasped Victor Sauvage's hand. "So good to see you."

"It's been too long." Victor smiled back at François, then glanced at Adrien. "So this is your brother." He shook Adrien's hand. "Pleased to finally meet you."

"Adrien isn't one for parties," François put in. "But I finally convinced him to join me."

"Good to meet you too." Adrien noticed Victor's smooth skin and recalled the scars he'd worn with pride when they'd met in Paris. Then Victor had mentioned training with Roland and meeting Adrien once in Saint-Gervais. "Have you seen Roland lately?"

Victor laughed. "Last I heard, he was still in hiding. Council politics got a bit too hot to handle."

Seeing François's look of surprise, Adrien remembered his younger self would not have known this. "I wondered," Adrien said. "He left Saint-Gervais in a hurry."

François smiled at Adrien. He'd known Adrien had been devastated at the loss of Roland and that Adrien had believed he was somehow to blame for Roland's quick departure. The unspoken *See, you weren't to blame* made

Adrien remember how much he loved his brother, and how much François had been his strength when their father hadn't been able to manage it.

Victor turned back to François and asked, "Join me in a dance?"

"I'd be honored," François replied. There was no mistaking the pleasure in François's eyes. How naïve Adrien had been to think François had known nothing of men before he'd met Charles. They'd just never spoken of it.

A moment later Victor and François had disappeared into the sea of people on the dance floor as the small orchestra played a waltz. Men danced with women, men with men, and women with women. The sound of tinkling glasses, hushed conversations, and melodic laughter mingled with the music. Above them, huge chandeliers twinkled with lit candles like hundreds of tiny stars.

Adrien helped himself to Champagne from one of the servants who moved about the room. Several girls off to the side smiled at him. Next to them, some of the young men eyed him with obvious interest. At seventeen, he'd never paid much attention to those sorts of looks.

One of the girls blushed under his gaze. He had forgotten how much a long dress flattered a woman's figure. The young men in their well-cut evening suits looked even better. The familiar sensation of bloodlust rose within him, although unlike days before, he had no difficulty controlling it. With the bloodlust came the realization that regardless of the body he now inhabited, he was still an immortal.

He finished his drink and quickly replaced it with another. His head felt light, warm. The sound of the music caressed his ears, and he wished he could join François on the dance floor. Several women smiled at him, and he toyed with the idea of asking one of them to dance. He had just about made up his mind to ask the pretty redhead who stood just a few feet away when movement at the top of the steps caught his eye.

He felt the familiar presence immediately; he knew that soul better than his own. Dressed in an evening suit of deep green, a color that made his hair shimmer like obsidian, he wore his hair tied back with an emerald clasp. He walked with confidence and grace. Adrien's heart beat wildly in his chest.

Nicolas.

CHAPTER TWENTY-ONE: REACQUAINTANCES

NICOLAS WALKED down the stairs and onto the dance floor. For the first time, Adrien sensed the presence of several dozen vampires amongst the revelers. He hadn't considered that vampires might be invited. He supposed it made sense, since the ancients were permitted to attend certain Council meetings.

Adrien inhaled slowly, willing himself to relax. He wouldn't meet Nicolas for another few years, and he wouldn't risk frightening him as he had at the Council meeting. He retrieved an extra glass of Champagne and walked over to Nicolas. Several men had already gathered nearby, eager to engage him in conversation. Adrien ignored them and bowed as best he could with two glasses of Champagne in his hands.

"Thirsty?" Nicolas asked with a barely repressed smile.

"I thought you might be." Adrien offered Nicolas the Champagne flute, their fingers brushing in the exchange. Adrien heard Nicolas's audible intake of breath and hoped his own wasn't as obvious.

"Thank you, monsieur…?" Nicolas began, clearly intrigued with Adrien.

"Gilbert. Adrien Gilbert."

"Nicolas Lambert," Nicolas said as he offered Adrien his hand. "Have we met before?"

"I don't believe so. Although I'm sorry we haven't." *More than you know, Nicolas. I wish we'd had more time together.*

"Of course," Nicolas said as he released Adrien's hand. "My apologies."

"None needed." Adrien offered Nicolas a reassuring smile.

Nicolas appeared to consider something before asking, "Are you Jacques Gilbert's son?"

"Yes," he replied. Of course Nicolas would know his father.

"Your father's a friend of my brother, Jean," Nicolas explained. "Do you know him?"

"I...." Adrien hesitated, knowing that his younger self would not yet have met Jean. "I know *of* him," he finally said. He guessed that this Nicolas, like the Nicolas in his own time, did not yet know Jean wasn't his brother by blood.

Nicolas took a sip of his Champagne.

Adrien, throwing all caution to the wind, asked, "Would you like to dance?"

Nicolas held up a dance card and frowned at it. Every dance on it was filled.

Adrien did his best to hide his disappointment. "It seems you're already quite busy with dances. Perhaps another time." He wouldn't press Nicolas. Later, perhaps, he'd—

"They'll wait." Nicolas took Adrien's glass, then handed it along with his own to one of the servants before offering Adrien his arm. The men and women who watched Nicolas from nearby appeared less than pleased.

Once on the floor, however, Adrien floundered. Other than a waltz, he recognized none of the dances he'd seen that evening. Having never learned to dance as a child, he had taken classes in the 1940s only because his work demanded a social presence beyond the board room.

"You seem uncomfortable," Nicolas said as Adrien did his best to follow his lead. Adrien saw no judgment in Nicolas's expression, only a quiet curiosity. Or was that amusement? How different Nicolas seemed than in the time they'd spent together before. Still charming, of course, but lighthearted. Happy.

"I'm afraid I only know a few dances," Adrien answered with a self-deprecating laugh.

"You do quite well in spite of it." Nicolas's eyes sparkled this time as he spun a breathless Adrien around. "You have a very unusual style."

Adrien repressed a grin.

The dance ended all too soon, and they bowed to each other. "I'd ask you to dance again, but I've no wish to see you cross swords with other guests," Nicolas said with a wistful smile. "Besides, I'm a bit older than you. It would be unseemly if I were to be seen robbing the cradle. As it is, I've gotten quite carried away—"

"I'm well of age," Adrien pointed out. "In fact, I'm nearly eighteen."

"And I'm ten times that." He appeared to hesitate, then added, "Still, I must admit you seem older."

"As a hunter," Adrien pointed out with a grin, "I could never be old enough for you. At least not until I'm old and withered."

Nicolas chuckled.

"Lord Lambert," someone from behind them said. "I believe this next dance is mine."

"Of course," Nicolas said. "I'll be there in a moment."

"Later, then?" Adrien pressed.

"I would like that." Nicolas smiled and nodded.

Adrien again bowed formally, then watched as Nicolas turned to one of the hunters and offered him his hand.

"Addie!" François clapped Adrien on the back. "Enjoying yourself?"

"Could be." Adrien smiled at his brother.

"I saw you dancing." François pressed his lips together with obvious satisfaction. "Who was he?"

"Nicolas Lambert," Adrien replied.

"The vampire?" François's eyes grew wide. "But I thought…."

"You thought I despised vampires." When François nodded, Adrien added, "For him, I'll make an exception."

François smiled outright. "Indeed. I'm glad."

The music stopped and a woman laughed. Adrien's gaze strayed to the dance floor where Nicolas bowed to yet another dance partner. Beautiful, with long blond hair, the woman blushed charmingly and allowed Nicolas to lead her onto the dance floor.

"Another Champagne?" Adrien asked François, unwilling to acknowledge his rising jealousy and looking for a distraction.

"Thank you." François eyed him carefully, no doubt having seen Nicolas as well.

Adrien handed François a glass, then took one for himself. A moment later a young woman approached François, who dug his dance card out of his breast pocket. She pointed at what Adrien guessed was her name. François smiled, and they were gone a moment later.

"May I have this dance?" a woman standing next to Adrien asked. Dark-haired, green-eyed, beautiful, and dressed in a blue velvet gown, she did nothing for Adrien, who still kept Nicolas in his sights.

"I'm sorry, mademoiselle," Adrien said. He shouldn't have cared if he appeared impolite, but falling back into the social niceties of the time felt familiar. A bit like wearing an uncomfortable old coat. "I need a bit of fresh air. Perhaps later."

She nodded, tossed her long hair, and disappeared a moment later.

Adrien slipped quietly onto the balcony. He needed time to think. Stars lit the clear sky as Adrien gazed out over the city. Until now, he'd been too overwhelmed with the knowledge that he had somehow managed to travel back in time again, even if he had no idea how he'd done it.

Someone nearby laughed, reminding Adrien of the voice he'd been hearing in his mind. *"Time to play, Adrien."* What had it said? *"A game where you can change your future."* If this was a game, what the hell were the rules? And whose game was it?

Adrien could think of only one name that came to mind for answers: the focal point of this new past, Roland Günter.

CHAPTER TWENTY-TWO: THE RULES KEEP CHANGING

HE'D FIND Roland. If what Roland had told him was true—that vampires had once been able to travel through time—maybe Roland could help him figure out what was happening.

He's here somewhere. At least, he would have been in the past Adrien remembered. Closer to Lyon than his home in Saint-Gervais, in fact.

Adrien would tell François he'd meet him later, at the inn. Then he'd find Roland. He walked toward the large glass doors connecting the balcony with the ballroom, but stopped as he noticed the lone figure leaning against the railing.

Nicolas.

"I was under the impression your dance card was full," Adrien said.

Nicolas sighed and shook his head. "You've caught me. I decided I needed some fresh air and pleaded a headache." He ran a hand through his hair, dislodging the silver pin at his nape, which clattered onto the flagstones. He bent down to pick it up as Adrien did the same. Adrien saw the bob of Nicolas's Adam's apple as he swallowed, then stood and seemed to collect himself.

"I'm surprised your brother allows you to attend parties without an escort," Adrien said, remembering Jean's overprotective concern.

"I need no one's permission to attend social events," Nicolas said as he slipped the clasp into his pocket. "I'm quite capable of defending myself."

Adrien chuckled. "I know."

Nicolas frowned, although he appeared at least somewhat amused. "And how would you know, monsieur?"

"I can see it in your eyes," Adrien said, quickly covering for his misstep.

Nicolas shook his head and sighed. "My brother worries too much about my well-being," he said. "He felt it necessary to assign me an escort for the evening. At least he knows better than to require the poor man to follow me around as if I were a child."

Adrien reached for Nicolas's cheek. Nicolas put his hand over Adrien's, holding it for a moment, then pulling it away as if he'd come to his senses. "I shouldn't."

"Why not?" Adrien countered.

"I—"

Adrien leaned in and brushed Nicolas's mouth with his own. Nicolas parted his lips to allow Adrien entry, causing Adrien's breath to stutter. As their lips parted, Adrien tilted his head in invitation. Nicolas skated his lips over the tender skin below Adrien's ear. Adrien waited for the sting of Nicolas's bite. It didn't come.

Nicolas gasped and pulled away. "I'm sorry," he said, clearly at a loss. "I... I.... That was quite rude of me. For a moment I...." He frowned.

"You needn't apologize." Adrien offered what he hoped was a reassuring smile. "My mistake. I don't know what came over me. I'm the one who owes *you* an apology." Vampires considered the sharing of blood a far more intimate contact than sex. In his own time, Adrien might take another's blood without hesitation, but in this time, such conduct would be considered shameless and brazen.

And he thinks you're only seventeen.

Nicolas knitted his brow, and Adrien knew he still blamed himself. "I should go," Nicolas said. He turned to leave, but Adrien caught his hand.

"May I call upon you sometime?" he asked in the custom of the time.

Nicolas hesitated for a moment, then answered, "Yes." Before Adrien could say anything in response, Nicolas opened the french doors and walked back into the crowd.

CHAPTER TWENTY-THREE:
THE PRODIGAL TEACHER

ADRIEN LEFT the party without telling François. If he was right about where Roland was, he'd be back before they were to return home. Adrien had an idea of where he might find Roland—a desolate place not far from Lyon where, as children, he and François had spent months training. Adrien still remembered François's excitement to leave Saint-Gervais. Their father had taken them as far as Saint-Étienne, where for the first time Adrien had seen the Alps rise like silent sentinels over the lush fields. From there, he and François had ridden alone, following the line of rocky hills to the south until they reached the tiny town of Saint-Just-Malmont. Roland had met them there and led them out of town to a place where the rocks seemed to perpetually tumble down cliffs, forming natural walls that hid the entrances to caves, and rough plants clung to the few protected surfaces. In their scant free time, Adrien had lost himself in the few books he'd managed to hide in his belongings, while François had reveled in exploring the countryside.

With the moon to light his way during the night, Adrien arrived as the sun began to rise on the horizon. Wild and untouched but for the narrow trails that snaked back and forth to the tops of the hills, the woods gave way to open fields where farmers grazed their cattle. Here, small rocky outcroppings rose from the grass, as if the boulders had been lifted by a giant's hand and tossed like gravel, dotting the landscape.

Adrien traveled onward until he spotted, on the other side of a particularly steep hill, a pile of rocks far larger than the others. Beyond it, more trees announced another small forest. There, amidst the trees, a stream had cut its way through the moss. He was sure the cave was here.

Adrien rode in circles for the better part of an hour, trying to find the opening he remembered seeing as a child. He closed his eyes and reached out for Roland's presence. Over the century since he'd lost Nicolas, Adrien had learned to sense both vampires and hunters more clearly.

He dismounted and drew his sword. A hawk soared above him, its lonesome call echoing around the hills. He stumbled over rocks as he searched for the opening to the cave. Eventually he came upon a smooth rock larger than the others nearby. He pushed hard with both hands, but it didn't budge. He was sure this was the place. He tried to remember how Roland had moved the stone when they'd first come here.

He drew a long breath to calm his racing heart, and as he did so, the memory of the entrance to the hunter prison returned. Adrien ran the blade of his sword over his forearm. He touched the weapon to his arm, where a thin line of blood had formed. Then he touched the tip of the blade to the rock. The rock vanished to reveal an opening large enough to admit a man. With a sigh of relief, he stepped inside.

Twenty feet from the entrance, the passageway opened onto an enormous cave lit by the sunlight that filtered in through cracks in the ceiling. Larger than he remembered, the cavern felt cool and damp from the small stream that ran through the middle. Beyond the stream was the entrance to a second, smaller cave with its simple living quarters.

Be here, Roland.

A rustling sound came from behind one of the enormous boulders. Adrien turned slowly, pointing his weapon out from his body. Something—*somebody*—was here.

Adrien heard the crunch of stone underfoot and saw a flash of steel as someone moved toward him faster than his eyes could follow. Using only the sound as his guide, Adrien met the offending blade and the cavern reverberated with the sound of metal upon metal.

"Roland. Dammit. It's me, Adrien!" he shouted as he jumped aside just in time to avoid his opponent's swing. He caught a brief glimpse of his challenger, dressed completely in black, his face covered.

Adrien swore under his breath as he tried to dodge another parry. He might still be immortal, but he was slow in this body—far slower than Roland. He focused on Ianus, on the feel of the hilt against his palm. He remembered the way he'd felt when he'd opened his soul to the sword and how he'd recalled it on the day of Nicolas's ill-fated wedding. Power warmed his chest, then traveled to his arms, his hands, and his fingertips. He swung his sword over his head and a fiery blast of red and gold flew out of the tip toward Roland, who moved like lightning as before, then set his feet in a wide stance and fired back at Adrien, sending a shower of silver sparks into the air.

For a moment Adrien thought Roland had missed. The silver shimmered and floated in midair, then turned back and screamed toward Adrien from every direction.

Adrien closed his eyes and his body grew warm. He imagined power enveloping him, covering his skin like a shield. He opened his eyes in time to see the silver sparks of energy evaporate. Too late, Roland raised his sword. Adrien leaped into the air, somersaulted, and landed on his feet behind Roland, then pressed his blade against Roland's throat, immobilizing him.

Adrien pulled at the mask, which unwrapped like bandages. His sword still on Roland's neck, Adrien turned Roland around and pulled off the black hood.

"Thomas?" Adrien stared in surprise. He'd never fought Thomas and he had no idea how powerful the man was.

Thomas smiled. "Good to see you, Adrien," he said. A heartbeat later Thomas slipped out of Adrien's grasp, spun about, and held Adrien in his grip, his arm tight around Adrien's neck, his sword in his hand. Thomas had clearly let him win.

"You've gotten much stronger since we last met," Roland said as he walked toward them.

Thomas released Adrien, who stumbled forward, caught himself before he fell, then dusted himself off. "What the hell kind of welcome was that?" Adrien said as Thomas tossed him his sword, which he caught and sheathed.

"We don't get many visitors." Roland clicked his tongue a few times, then frowned as if trying to unravel some deep mystery. "I would say it is good to see you again," Roland said, his eyes now wide, a smile flickering over his lips. "But I'm not so sure that's correct."

Thomas tilted his head to one side and frowned. "He certainly looks the same as he did. Maybe a little taller than I remember, but this is still Adrien Gilbert."

"Oh, he is," Roland replied with his usual coy smile. "But this Adrien Gilbert isn't exactly as he appears to be."

Adrien pursed his lips but said nothing, instead waiting to see how much Roland could sense about him.

"Yes," Roland said with conviction. "This Adrien Gilbert is an immortal."

CHAPTER TWENTY-FOUR: LIFE, AGAIN

THOMAS LAUGHED and sheathed his sword, then climbed atop one of the nearby rocks and waited patiently.

"Welcome," Roland said. "I'm a bit surprised, though."

"Why are you surprised?" Adrien pulled off his dusty cloak and tossed it onto the ground.

"The Adrien I knew hated vampires. For you to have shared something as intimate as your soul… something must have changed."

"Could be." Adrien smiled in the knowledge that for once, Roland was at a loss rather than the other way around. "I need your help," he added when Roland remained silent.

"To be honest, I'm not sure I understand." Roland rubbed his chin. "The gift of immortality is not something to be taken lightly."

It took Adrien a moment to realize Roland was still speaking about his hatred of vampires. Adrien chuckled and shook his head. "Some things don't change," he said. "Like how you ignore me so you can see how pissed—I mean angry—you make me."

Thomas coughed. "I'll get us something to drink," he said as he hopped down from his perch and headed into the smaller cave. Roland watched Thomas leave, the telltale flash of red in his eyes gone as quickly as it came.

Adrien repressed a grin. "Thought so."

"I'm sorry," Roland responded a moment later. "You were saying something?"

Adrien ran a hand over his mouth and shook his head. "You know exactly what I meant. But if it makes you happy, I'll play dumb."

"Yes. He's…."

"Your lover," Adrien finished.

"Thomas delights in toying with me," Roland confirmed, his wild gray curls tumbling over his forehead. "I'm surprised it took you so long to realize he wasn't simply my right hand."

"I guessed." Adrien almost added *when I got older* but thought better of it. "I was a bit naïve when you still lived in Saint-Gervais."

"But you're no longer naïve." Roland pursed his lips and rubbed his chin. "And you aren't what you appear to be either, are you?"

Adrien quirked an eyebrow.

"No. It hasn't been that long since I last saw you. You were talented when I taught you, but you've gotten too good, too quickly." Roland frowned. "Something else has changed."

"Why do you say that?" Adrien asked.

"Call it a hunch." Roland knitted his brow as if considering something. "But if I'm correct…. No, that's impossible."

"Impossible?" Adrien swallowed his grin.

"You're far too patient, you know," Roland continued.

This time Adrien laughed outright. "Is that so?"

Roland opened his mouth as if to speak but instead formed an O with his lips. "I *am* correct," he said triumphantly. "So, Adrien Gilbert, how old are you, I wonder?"

Adrien didn't respond. It was far too much fun making Roland guess.

"Bit difficult to say, since you're trapped in a boy's body," Roland continued, undaunted. "But I'm guessing you're far older than you appear."

Adrien schooled his expression, although he was pleased Roland had begun to put the pieces together. "Could be."

"You hide your thoughts quite well." Roland smiled. "You were never very good at that when I taught you. Another reason to believe you aren't the young Adrien Gilbert I knew."

"Go on," Adrien prompted. "You're getting warmer."

"I'm getting warm…?" Roland laughed. "Indeed. Shall I make one other assumption, then?"

"Be my guest." Adrien smiled.

"A bit over a century old," Roland mused. "And I venture you've been having a bit of trouble as of late."

"You might say that."

"Then am I correct?" Roland wore a self-satisfied smile.

"Yes. I'm more than a century old."

"Oh, good." Roland beamed. Adrien waited for him to ask how such a thing was possible, but instead Roland gestured to the entrance to the second cave. Adrien just shook his head and laughed. Eventually Roland would get around to explaining things. For now, Adrien was tired and hungry.

A few minutes later, they sat on pillows at a low table with Thomas, glasses full of a good bottle of red wine and another bottle waiting. At least not everything about Roland had changed.

"And what about you, Roland?" Adrien said as he swirled his wine about. "Have you given up your efforts to reform the Council?"

Thomas's expression darkened, but his anger appeared directed at Roland. A sensitive topic, Adrien guessed.

"I've come to enjoy this life, such as it is." Roland took a long sip of his wine and appeared slightly uncomfortable. Given what Adrien knew would happen when Roland challenged Pelletier, he couldn't blame the man for hesitating to step in. For the first time, Adrien saw Roland for what he was: a man, with doubts and fears not so different from his own. Of course he wouldn't have noticed that when he was seventeen—he'd thought only about his own life back then.

As if on cue, Thomas stood and gathered what was left of his cup, then walked to the other side of the chamber. *A very sensitive topic.*

Adrien found the familiar tang of the grapes comforting. In a world where so much had changed, the wine reminded Adrien of the past he'd known and of the tiny slivers of happiness that shone through the darkness like sunshine after a storm.

"So, Adrien," Roland said as he gazed at the place at the table that Thomas had just vacated, "may I ask *you* a few questions of my own?"

Why not? Adrien inhaled the warm scent of his drink and felt the tension in his shoulders ease.

"Shoot," Adrien said. When Roland raised a questioning eyebrow, Adrien explained, "It's a modern expression which means 'go ahead.'"

"Of course. Which leads me to my first question," Roland said. "How did you come to be here?"

"No idea. I woke up in this time."

"Interesting," said Roland, setting his glass down and contemplating it momentarily. "Then I will need to ask you some more questions."

"Fine." Adrien shrugged and took another swallow of the wine.

"When did you receive the gift?" When Adrien did not immediately respond, Roland quickly added, "It would help me to understand *why* you are here if I understand *how* it is you came to be here."

"It will happen a few years from now," Adrien answered. "But when I asked you—your counterpart—about time travel—"

"Then this has happened before?"

"Not in the same way. I... I was able to turn back time. Only a few minutes, though." Adrien pushed away the thoughts that usually accompanied the memory of losing Nicolas to Pelletier. "And I've tried for nearly a hundred years to repeat that act. Nothing's worked."

"How do you think you came to be here?"

Adrien blew air from between his lips. He was pretty sure he knew what Roland wanted to know—the voice in his head had only grown more insistent over time. He doubted what he'd heard it say at the Council meeting was a coincidence. "At first I thought Pelletier did this. Sent me here."

"Verel Pelletier?" Roland didn't appear particularly surprised to hear this.

Adrien nodded.

"But?"

"But I've been hearing something," Adrien said in an undertone. "Someone. In my head."

"I see."

Again, Adrien hadn't expected Roland's lack of surprise or obvious concern. "I've done things.... When the bloodlust rages, I can't control myself." He clenched his jaw and stared down at his cup. "I worry I might truly harm someone." There. He'd said it. And if Roland wanted to laugh or tell him he was insane, then so be it.

"The strength of an immortal comes not only from the blood we were given," Roland said, all hint of lightheartedness gone from his voice. "It also comes from the natural conflict within each of us."

Adrien frowned. "Conflict? What kind of conflict?"

"Humans who are transformed into vampires experience a similar conflict after their transformation. An internal struggle for dominance. You know how many fledgling vampires lose control?"

Adrien nodded. Through the years, he'd killed far more fledglings than older vampires. He'd seen François's struggle with his own craving for human blood. Without an older vampire like Charles to guide him,

120

François could just as easily have been the subject of a hunter's carte, the Council's written execution order.

"Immortals, too, experience something similar." Roland paused as if considering something, then added, "For us, it comes later. For some, within the first fifty years. For others, it can take centuries to manifest. If we survive the struggle, we become more powerful. If we lose...."

"That... *thing*... inside my mind. That's... normal?" Adrien realized calling something like a voice in his head "normal" was strange in and of itself. Still, he felt relieved to know he might not be losing his mind.

Roland nodded. "Some of us like to call it our demon. But it's no demon, not in the traditional sense. It's a basic, primal instinct that asserts itself and fights us for control."

"A demon." Adrien inhaled slowly. He could almost hear the thing in his mind say, *"You are powerful, Adrien. Together, we are invincible."* For more than just a moment, he'd believed those words.

"I know of no other immortals who have been able to manipulate time." Roland leaned back and rubbed a finger over his lips. "Then again, I know of no other immortals who have such powerful blood."

"Nicolas's blood. The Rousseau blood."

Roland raised an eyebrow. So Roland knew Nicolas was a Rousseau. *Interesting.*

"You told me that some vampires once possessed the power to travel through time." The pieces began to fall together for Adrien. "And my blood—vampire, immortal, and hunter combined—something about my blood makes this possible."

"A good guess," Roland replied. "If the Rousseaus once had the ability to travel through time, your unusual blood may have rekindled the lost gift."

"Then this demon you spoke of.... All of this is a game?"

Roland nodded. "A game, a challenge.... A fight each immortal must win. The fight might vary, but its purpose is the same. Knowing demons for the capricious creatures they are, you may be here because it thought it would be amusing to watch." Nothing in Roland's expression led Adrien to believe he was joking.

"And if I win the fight?" Adrien asked.

"Then you will grow more powerful." The glint of excitement in Roland's eyes made Adrien wonder how Roland had defeated his own

121

demon. But that was a question for another time. His own time, perhaps, if he ever managed to return there.

"How do I tame it? Pelletier nearly killed me twice," Adrien admitted, his shoulders tensing once more. "You saved my life the first time. The second... I wasn't able to defeat him. I need its power so I can fight him and win."

"Fighting Pelletier to a draw shows you've learned a great deal," Roland said.

"I'm not sure you can call it a draw."

Roland set his cup down and met Adrien's gaze with surprising ferocity. "That you survived the encounter is proof enough, however you might perceive it. Pelletier is a powerful opponent."

"How do I get back?" Adrien wasn't sure he wanted to return to his own time, but he wanted to understand.

Roland shook his head. "My guess? If the demon sent you here, you'll return when, and *if*, it wants you to."

AN HOUR later, Adrien headed back to Lyon. It was afternoon by the time he reached the hotel. François, sound asleep in their room, still wore his trousers. No doubt the reveling had continued well into the morning. Adrien tossed a blanket over François, then collapsed on the other bed, his mortal body overcome with exhaustion.

ADRIEN WATCHED the waves break on the sand, his head pressed against Nicolas's bare chest. In the distance the glass windows of high-rise apartments shimmered with the sun's rays. Adrien pushed himself up on an elbow and smiled at Nicolas. The long hair Adrien loved to run his fingers through was cut short at the back with long bangs that fell over Nicolas's eyes, which were obscured by dark sunglasses.

"You're tired," Nicolas said.

"I traveled far today," Adrien replied as he wrapped his arm once again around Nicolas's waist and listened to the beat of Nicolas's heart.

"I sense a change in you."

"A change?" Adrien asked.

"You seem different," Nicolas answered. "Stronger than I remember."

"Stronger? Yes, maybe I am."

"*I felt something today.*" *Nicolas kissed the top of Adrien's head.* "*Something I haven't felt in a long time.*"

"*What did you feel?*" *Adrien closed his eyes and drew a long breath.*

"*A soul,*" *Nicolas replied.* "*And I wondered if I were to meet your soul, if I'd recognize it.*"

"*I hope you would.*" *Something stirred in Adrien's heart. Something he hadn't felt in more than a century.*

"*I think I would know it.*" *Nicolas pulled him up and claimed his lips.*

Adrien pulled the sunglasses off to reveal Nicolas's eyes. Beautiful eyes. Not quite human.

"*I'm glad.*" *For the first time in what felt like an eternity, Adrien's heart forgot its grief. For the first time in an eternity, Adrien felt hope.*

CHAPTER TWENTY-FIVE: COURTSHIP

ADRIEN RETURNED to Lyon two days later. He'd hoped to avoid speaking with his father, not wanting to involve him and concerned that Jacques would sense the change in him. But if Jacques sensed anything unusual about Adrien, he kept it to himself. They spoke only of the vineyard and of the coming harvest.

The only explanation Adrien gave his father for his trip back to Lyon was that he needed to pay a call on an old friend. Again, Jacques did not press him. Adrien had only one thought on his mind: he needed to see Nicolas, to reassure himself that Nicolas was safe.

He arrived at the Lamberts' estate midafternoon. He left his horse with one of the servants and climbed the stairs to the front door, where he lifted one of the cast-iron rings to announce his arrival. He gave his name, and a servant ushered him into a sitting room. She did not seem surprised by his appearance, nor did she ask for whom he was calling. She left, then, after several minutes, reappeared and asked him to follow her.

They walked toward the back of the home, where she opened a set of wooden doors onto a library and motioned him inside. A man stood by the fire, back to him, dark-haired and familiar.

Jean Lambert turned around and asked, "You're Adrien Gilbert?"

Adrien took a deep breath, relieved to see Jean.

"I am," Adrien replied as he shook Jean's outstretched hand. "You're Lord Lambert?"

"The same. Nicolas told me about you." Jean appeared to take Adrien's measure. No doubt he'd be suspicious of anyone who came to call on Nicolas, given Pelletier's threats. Adrien wondered if Nicolas had decided to marry Rosina yet, then guessed he hadn't or he probably wouldn't have been willing to see Adrien again.

"I've heard much about you as well," Adrien replied. "I thank you for allowing me to come."

"You wish to call on my brother."

Again, Adrien sensed Jean's hesitation. Adrien would give him no reason to fear he meant to harm Nicolas. He allowed his mind to open to Jean's, making his thoughts plain. "With your permission, of course. I hope I haven't offended by coming unannounced." Adrien had tried his best to observe the customs of the time, but he feared he'd done something wrong. He had no experience with nineteenth-century courtship.

"Please forgive me," Jean answered. "Nicolas calls me overprotective, and I suppose he is correct. I'm a bit surprised, though. From my brother's description of you, I thought you to be a much older man."

Adrien laughed softly. "I'll take that as a compliment, my lord," he said.

Jean's expression softened almost imperceptibly. "You are welcome to pay a call on my brother." Jean nodded, then left the room.

While he waited Adrien watched the flames dance in the fireplace. He hadn't even realized how nervous he'd been, coming here.

"Monsieur Gilbert." Nicolas offered Adrien his hand as he strode into the room.

"Monsieur Lambert." Nicolas's skin felt soft against his own. Warm. Reassuring and familiar.

"I'm pleased you came. I hoped you might. After the party, I wondered how it was that we'd never met."

An interesting question. Had Adrien's own shortsightedness kept him from meeting Nicolas sooner? Given the hatred he'd held for vampires, would it have mattered if they had met sooner?

Adrien ignored the laughter in his mind. "Perhaps it was just fate," he said.

"Fate?" Nicolas mused. "I don't believe in fate. I prefer to believe I have some control over my life and my destiny."

The irony of Nicolas's words was hardly lost on Adrien. "Sometimes I wonder how much control over either we truly have."

Nicolas appeared to consider this. "There is no weakness in believing one has the power to override fate," he said after a moment.

"Indeed." Adrien smiled. "But call it what you will, I *am* pleased we met."

"Ride with me?" The corners of Nicolas's mouth turned upward. "The trees are beautiful this time of year."

"I would love to."

A short time later, they traversed the open fields behind the manor and arrived at a small pond on the edge of a pine forest. Adrien knew this area well, having spent several months here before he and Nicolas had left to find Charles. Then, he had ridden the trails alone in an effort to avoid Nicolas and Jean. How things had changed.

"May I show you something?" Nicolas asked as they skirted the outside of the woods.

"Please." Adrien was about to ask what Nicolas wanted to show him when Nicolas laughed and galloped off, hair flying about his face as he headed into the forest. Adrien followed, barely able to keep up as Nicolas wove between bushes and trees.

Until now, so much of their time together had been spent pleasing others, fighting for them, and stealing moments together. This Nicolas seemed unfettered, carefree. Adrien had never seen Nicolas truly happy. Even when they'd shared their bodies, they'd both felt the weight of duty—Nicolas's to marry Rosina, and Adrien's to protect him so that he might live to marry her.

Were they fortunate to be able to relive the past? He'd spent most of his life before he met Nicolas mourning his mother, training to become something he never wanted to be, yet spending so little time enjoying what he had. For once Adrien was free to touch the happiness in his heart, to embrace the joy of being here with Nicolas and of being alive.

In a very strange way, the demon had given both him and Nicolas a gift. They had time together at last. Like this, Adrien could almost forget the future that awaited them.

Nicolas halted at the top of a ridge where the trees thinned. Adrien followed, then drew a long breath of the cool air as he gazed down at the city below. He'd never come this far before, but the view was quite impressive. "It's beautiful," he said.

Nicolas laughed and shook his head. "It is," he said, "but this isn't what I had in mind."

"Then what is it you want to show me?" Adrien asked.

"Come," Nicolas said. He jumped nimbly off his horse and headed down a small path off the main trail. Adrien joined him, and they walked in silence for a few minutes.

"There," Nicolas said, pointing ahead.

Adrien took a few more steps and saw Nicolas had gestured to a small clearing. In its center was a pond filled with water so clear, Adrien could see all the way to the bottom. Silver fish swam beneath its surface, darting away when they drew too close. Steam rose from the water and disappeared a few feet into the air.

"A hot spring?" Adrien reached down and felt the heat of the water. "I didn't know there were springs this close to Lyon."

"There are no others I know of," Nicolas answered. "Few people know of this place, but Jean tells me it's been here for more than a thousand years." Nicolas walked around the spring and sat on the mossy bank. "Join me, monsieur?"

"Please call me Adrien."

"Join me, Adrien?" Nicolas asked playfully. "And if I'm to call you by your given name, I'd much rather you call me by mine."

"Nicolas." Adrien sat beside Nicolas.

"You're a fair rider, Adrien," Nicolas said.

"I'm a bit out of practice." Adrien couldn't remember the last time he'd ridden before he'd found himself back in the past. He owned several horses his staff cared for on one of his properties, he didn't care to ride them. He chuckled to think that if his seventeen-year-old body hadn't been accustomed to riding as long or as hard as he had the past few days, he'd have been too sore to move.

"Something amusing?" Nicolas asked.

"Only that I'm enjoying myself."

Nicolas raised a quizzical eyebrow. "Are you surprised?"

"I... no. I didn't mean it to sound that way."

Nicolas was smiling at him.

"You were joking, weren't you?" Adrien asked.

"I'm sorry. I shouldn't have made a joke of it. It's just... I feel strangely comfortable with you." Nicolas appeared genuinely embarrassed.

"Don't be sorry." Adrien leaned back on his elbows and sighed. "I feel the same."

A comfortable silence settled between them. For once Adrien didn't want to ask questions. He didn't need to understand. He just wanted to enjoy the beautiful afternoon, the forest, and Nicolas's company.

"I'll miss this place," Nicolas said after some time had passed.

"You're leaving?"

Nicolas nodded. "I hope to study in London."

"London?" Adrien felt strangely bereft to hear this. He found it difficult to imagine Nicolas anywhere but in France. *But this will never happen, will it?* Nicolas would soon decide to marry Rosina instead.

"I'll be studying at the Architectural Association." Nicolas's face lit up as he spoke these words. "Seems my incessant doodling is good for more than just filling time."

"That's wonderful." Adrien knew the school well—he'd hired one of its graduates to work on the British headquarters of his company. The Canary Wharf building was his pride and joy. "Have you been to London?"

"Once. With my brother Jean."

It struck Adrien how much less formal Jean had been with him when they'd spoken at the house earlier. Nicolas's decision to marry into the Rousseau Clan for the sake of peace had clearly weighed more heavily upon Jean than Adrien had ever realized.

Adrien was about to tell Nicolas how much he loved London, but stopped himself. How could he so easily forget that his actions were constrained by the limited experiences of his younger self?

"I would like to travel sometime," Adrien said in an effort to cover his discomfort.

Nicolas laughed and stood. "Sometimes you seem far older than you appear." He walked over to the edge of the water, then bent down and ran his fingers along its surface.

"Sometimes I feel older than I appear," Adrien countered as he got to his feet.

"You've known pain," Nicolas said almost casually. "I can sense it."

Adrien remained silent, unsure of what to say. Finally, throwing caution to the wind, he said simply, "I have."

"She was a fool to leave you," Nicolas said.

Adrien swallowed hard. "*He* did not leave willingly." For a few minutes, he'd almost imagined nothing had changed, that they were still lovers and that there was hope for a future with Nicolas in it. But in that moment, Adrien's grief surged. He was thankful Nicolas could not see his face—he knew it revealed more than he meant to show.

"I'm sorry," Nicolas said.

"So am I."

Chapter Twenty-Six: Remembering

The wind picked up as they walked back to the horses. Neither spoke, although Nicolas didn't seem to mind. He, like Adrien, seemed preoccupied. Thoughtful. The temperature had dropped, and the cool air made Adrien feel strangely alive. He'd never thought of autumn as a new beginning—it had always seemed to him a time when the world went to sleep, awaiting the coming of spring through the harsh winter. But now he wondered if he simply hadn't noticed its fading beauty because he'd dreaded the time when the vineyard seemed to die.

They stopped at the top of the ridge. Bands of fuchsia and purple streaked the sky. Color bled from the clouds onto the trees and hills, making the entire scene appear surreal. Like some of the impressionist paintings Adrien recalled seeing at the Orangerie in Paris.

"Nicolas," he said as the breeze ruffled the leaves around them, "why did you agree to let me pay you a call?"

"Why not?" Nicolas appeared surprised at his question.

"I'm a hunter," Adrien said. "There must be a good number of men of your kind who would wish to spend time in your company."

"There are," Nicolas said without pride. "But none of them interest me. I find *you* interesting. There's more to you than meets the eye. I feel it in my soul."

Adrien repressed a grin. "I'm flattered." Did he feel young again because of Nicolas? Or was it that this youthful body he inhabited had seen none of the pain he had suffered? *Does it matter?*

Nicolas laughed. "Humble as well."

Nicolas, who had been standing shoulder to shoulder with Adrien, now turned and faced him. Without a word, he put his hands to Adrien's face and drew him closer. "I have learned not to hesitate," Nicolas said. "Life changes too quickly to think too much."

Adrien swallowed hard but did not move to close the gap between them.

Nicolas wore an expression of curious surprise and confusion as he brushed a thumb over Adrien's mouth. His gaze fixed on Adrien, Nicolas leaned in and their lips met. Adrien opened to allow Nicolas entry—not just his lips, but his soul.

The kiss began as an exploration. Nicolas traced the contours of Adrien's mouth with his tongue as he cupped the back of Adrien's neck. He carded his fingers through Adrien's hair, causing Adrien to moan with pleasure. Their bodies now pressed against each other. Adrien felt Nicolas's cock against his thigh and moved to meet it with his own arousal.

Adrien, who had willed his hands to remain where they were on Nicolas's upper back, now allowed them to follow the contour of Nicolas's body downward, past the slight curve of his waist and onto the top of Nicolas's buttocks. Even through the heavy fabric of Nicolas's riding trousers, Adrien felt the powerful muscles there. He squeezed, gently at first, then more insistently as familiarity returned.

How had he forgotten the feel of Nicolas's body? He'd learned every bit of it in the short time they'd had together. After the ill-fated wedding, Jean had commissioned a painting of Nicolas. Each time Adrien had visited Jean, that painting had been prominently displayed.

"I have no need for a painting," Adrien had once told Jean. "I remember everything about him." But he'd begun to forget Nicolas's face and the feel of his body. Even in his dreams, Adrien had struggled to see Nicolas's face. Now, however, his memory seemed clear once again.

When the kiss finally broke, they continued to hold each other. Adrien imagined he could feel Nicolas probing his heart, seeking answers to unspoken questions. Could Nicolas sense their connection? If an immortal could sense the change in time, why not an ancient, through whom the immortals' powers were imbued?

Adrien took a deep breath to open himself more fully to Nicolas. He imagined he could share his soul as he might share it through his blood. He had not shared his blood with anyone in over a century, but he would willingly offer it to Nicolas, should he ask. He wanted to lay himself bare for Nicolas and allow him into the deepest recesses of his being. He wanted Nicolas to know his pain and his joy. His heart.

God, I've missed you, Nicolas!

Nicolas skated his lips over the soft skin of Adrien's neck. Adrien waited for the sting of Nicolas's teeth as they broke the skin....

Nicolas gasped, then pulled abruptly away. He stared at Adrien with slightly parted lips. Adrien heard his ragged breaths and saw a flash of red in his usually brown eyes. *Bloodlust.*

"We should be going," Nicolas said, his voice uncharacteristically rough. "It will be dark soon."

CHAPTER TWENTY-SEVEN: RIPPLES

"I'M STAYING." Adrien ignored the cup of tea Roland handed him.

"Staying?"

"Here," Adrien said. "In the past."

Roland raised an eyebrow but said nothing.

"I can live my life over again. I can stop Pelletier before—"

"Have you considered what might happen to the rest of your future should you remain here?"

"What happens to my seventeen-year-old self if I leave?" Adrien countered. "Will I remember this?"

"I don't know." Roland smiled and tapped his teacup, causing the liquid inside to ripple.

"Then how do you know what I do here will change anything of the future I know?"

"You tell me," Roland said. "Before you came here, you said things changed in the middle of a Council meeting. That one minute things were how you knew them, and the next, everything had changed. Is it possible your demon showed you what the changed future would look like?"

"I…. Yes, I suppose that's possible." More than possible, Adrien's heart told him. Probable.

"How much does each man, woman, or child influence the future? For the average person, undoubtedly the influence is small. But subtle changes can lead to larger consequences. Regardless of how unimportant they may seem, if a man and a woman create a child who grows up to do great good or great evil, is their contribution not significant?"

Adrien knew where this conversation was going. "I understand what you're saying," he said.

"Do you?" Roland glanced down at his cup again and said, "I'm not so sure."

"Nicolas is happy. Jean is a part of his life. I can keep him safe. The Council of Hunters is relatively stable. We can petition the Council for a more thorough investigation of what happened to the Rousseaus, make them listen. We can show them that Pelletier is a threat. That he—"

"And what if we do?"

"Then you won't have to hide," Adrien said.

"I'm unconcerned about myself. I've told you that before. But there are other people in your life," Roland explained. "Have you considered what effect you will have upon their future if you remain in their past?"

"I don't see why anything needs to change for my family," Adrien replied. "I can be a far better brother to Isa and François knowing all I know now."

Roland smiled and nodded. "Precisely. And therein lies the rub." He took a sip of his tea, then asked, "Tell me, if you are a better brother to them, will you not change them?"

"They deserved more from me," Adrien answered. "If I'd been a better brother to François... if I'd been willing to travel with him, maybe he...." Roland's words began to penetrate the fog of happiness that had dulled Adrien's mind.

"Yes?" Roland asked. The knowing expression he wore reminded Adrien of when he'd been Roland's student.

"François," Adrien said dully as the weight of the truth settled in his thoughts. "If I'd traveled with him, maybe he would have traveled farther."

Roland said nothing but waited for Adrien to continue.

"And if he'd traveled farther, he might have never met.... He might have never have...." Adrien knew the answer. François might never have met Charles. And if he'd never met Charles, he might never have been imprisoned, tortured, hurt. But François was happy with Charles. Loved. Cared for. Still powerful. Stronger for the pain. Who was Adrien to say François's life should have been different?

"If you stay, you may recreate the love between you and Nicolas...." Roland waited until the import of his words became clear to Adrien. "But what then?"

"Why do you care?" Of course Roland would have put the pieces together. He'd already admitted Nicolas had given him immortality. He'd worn his heart on his sleeve.

133

"There's nothing wrong with recreating it," Adrien insisted. "It's not as though I'm twisting his arm."

"No. I never meant to suggest that. But what if he *does* fall in love with you again? Will you expect him to give you the gift? I'm not even sure it would work, given that the Adrien who inhabits this body is already immortal."

"I hadn't even thought about that." Adrien frowned. "But regardless, I wouldn't expect him to give me the gift."

"Really? Your body may already be immortal, but what if by receiving the gift again, your immortal body were to grow stronger? The truth is we know nothing of what might happen should you stay." Roland eyed Adrien with the hint of a smile on his lips. When Adrien didn't answer, Roland continued, "Many things would likely change if you were to remain in this timestream. Perhaps you can justify them, as you might Nicolas giving you immortality again. But can you justify them all when you can't even fathom what changes you might cause?"

For once, following his heart had seemed so simple. More than a hundred years old, and he hadn't even considered how complicated things truly were.

"The longer you stay here," Roland said as if reading his thoughts, "the more you *yourself* change."

"I'm forgetting things." Adrien shook his head. This was no different than forgetting Nicolas's face. "I'm acting...."

"Like the seventeen-year-old boy you are," Roland finished. "Impetuous. In love. Good-hearted."

"I'm none of those things." *I'm only a fool.*

"You can still help Nicolas," Roland said. "But you must do it in a way that repairs the future you came from."

"Pelletier. This all comes back to him, doesn't it?" Adrien had begun to wonder how much Pelletier understood. *Did he take Nicolas because he knew what Nicolas meant to me?*

"He does seem to have taken an interest in you."

"But why?" Adrien asked. "You yourself said I'll return only when the demon wants me to. And Pelletier... he seemed to sense that the future had changed when I saved Nicolas's life at the wedding."

"An interesting point. And a disturbing one."

"I don't understand," Adrien said, although he wasn't being entirely truthful. He had an inkling of understanding, and he didn't like what he understood one bit.

"If your demon has the ability to travel through time," Roland explained, "so do you. You said you believe Pelletier sensed the change when you turned back time. Imagine what power he would wield if he were able to travel through time at will." His expression darkened. "If he obtains such a power from the Rousseau blood, what then? What might he do? What kind of world would he create?"

"He's only one man." Adrien didn't want to think about the possibilities in Roland's scenario. If Pelletier had taken Nicolas to gain the power.... He pushed away the thought of what Pelletier might have already done to Nicolas—it would do him no good to dwell on that.

"Have you ever watched the waves at the shore?"

"Yes," Adrien replied, remembering his dream of only the night before.

"Each wave leaves the tiniest trace upon the sand." Roland tapped his teacup and the liquid moved with the vibration. "Each wave represents a change in the flow of time. The effect of the wave upon the sand is subtle, but the shape of the beach changes as each wave retreats. Collectively, the water can completely change the land without us noticing the change until it's too late."

"What if he's already gained this power? What if the changes to this timestream are changes he made?" Adrien asked, horrified to realize that Pelletier might be using Nicolas's blood. Was that the power Pelletier had killed for?

"I don't believe he has," Roland said. "At least I see no indication of it from what you've told me. If he's using Nicolas's blood, he may eventually learn to master time travel. Even if he does, you can do nothing about it until you make changes within yourself. You must learn to control the force inside of you. Control the demon and you will control the power. Your demon is your strength." Roland met Adrien's gaze and held it, his expression suddenly somber. "Have you considered why you came here? Why the demon *sent* you?"

Adrien hesitated just a moment, then said, "It wants to tempt me." The moment he spoke the words, he knew they were the truth. He felt it more than understood it.

"It's no secret why we call that part of us a demon. It's the part of our soul we, as thinking men, seek to control." Roland finished his tea and set the cup down on the table. "It's the part of us that cares nothing for what is moral and right. It is the most basic part of who we are. Greedy. Hungry. It cares only about satisfying its baser needs.

"There are two ways to conquer it. You can kill it or you can learn to control it."

"But if I kill it...?" Adrien asked.

Roland nodded. "You lose its power forever. You will remain strong, but you will never grow stronger."

Adrien knitted his brow and tried to understand. "And if I lose? If I fail to conquer it?"

"Then you will die."

CHAPTER TWENTY-EIGHT: THE CHALLENGER

ADRIEN SAT next to Nicolas under a large oak in the garden outside the Lamberts' Lyon estate. The grass was soft and green and the sun shone between the leaves of the tree. Nicolas picked a bit of cheese from the plates the servants had set out for their lunch and popped it into his mouth. He tossed a piece to Adrien, who laughed and caught it.

"Jean tells me I refuse to act my age just to cause him grief," Nicolas said as he lay back on the grass. "He could be right." He put his hands behind his head and gazed up at the sky. "I do enjoy seeing him laugh, even if it's at my expense."

"I've never seen him laugh." Adrien rubbed the bridge of his nose without really thinking.

"He does. Rarely." Nicolas rolled onto his side. "I am glad you came today."

"I'm glad you asked," Adrien replied.

"Tell me about the man you spoke of," Nicolas said. "The one you said hadn't left you willingly."

The question took Adrien by surprise. "There's nothing much to tell. It's over."

"I'm sorry. That was quite rude of me, wasn't it?"

"Not rude," Adrien said. "But what would speaking about it accomplish?" *It's been over longer than you could ever imagine.*

"Nothing. Although I have to admit I'm a bit jealous, even if I have no right to be." Nicolas looked away.

"You're jealous?" Adrien hadn't even thought Nicolas would care.

"I realize it's childish. We've barely met, but I feel as though we've known each other far longer." He shook his head, then sat up and stared off into the distance. "Please forgive me."

Adrien got up and sat behind Nicolas, then wreathed his arms around him. "There's nothing to forgive. And if it helps—" He leaned forward and kissed Nicolas's cheek. "—I feel the same."

Nicolas relaxed against him. "I had an unusual dream last night," he said after a few minutes had passed. "I was in a strange place… a jungle of glass boxes. People seemed to be in a hurry. I thought I saw you, but when I called your name, you didn't answer."

"That *was* a strange dream." *A twenty-first century city?* How many times had Adrien dreamed he'd seen Nicolas in Miami? He'd imagined he'd chased Nicolas down a crowded street and called his name, but Nicolas hadn't heard him.

"Some say the ancients could once see the future." From his expression, Nicolas clearly didn't believe this. Adrien wasn't as sure. If Nicolas's ancient blood had given Adrien the ability to manipulate time, perhaps the ancients had once possessed that ability too.

"I'm not sure I'd want to see what's ahead," Adrien said honestly.

A companionable silence settled between them. The wind blew stronger, causing Adrien to shiver.

"We should be getting back," Nicolas said with a sigh. "I don't want to worry Jean."

"When can I see you again?" Adrien asked.

"Soon." Nicolas leaned in and kissed him. "We will see each other again," he whispered against Adrien's ear after their lips parted. "I'm quite sure of it."

CHAPTER TWENTY-NINE:
PREMONITIONS AND PASTS

NICOLAS WOKE with his heart pounding against his ribs. Again he'd seen Adrien, and again he'd had the same dream of the city of steel and glass.

Overhead, trails of smoke crisscrossed the high clouds. On the street, strange machines like the horseless carriages that had begun to appear in Lyon flew by him in blurs of sound and color.

He walked quickly down a paved avenue, on his way… somewhere. His feet, at least, knew where he was headed. He turned the corner onto a smaller street near the water. He inhaled the tang of salt and slowed his pace.

Ahead, a man strode from one of the buildings onto the pavement. Dressed in strange clothing, his hair cut short, he wore a pair of dark eyeglasses that partially obscured his face. He pushed the glasses onto his head and pulled something from inside his jacket. Nicolas strained to see it—a small glass-and-silver box.

The man tapped the box several times and frowned, then turned and headed toward where Nicolas stood. The man shoved the box back into his jacket, and started to put the eyeglasses back on when he stopped and met Nicolas's gaze.

"Adrien?"

Adrien didn't move, but he didn't appear to have heard Nicolas, either.

"Adrien," Nicolas repeated.

Adrien settled the eyeglasses onto his nose, then turned abruptly as a very long carriage stopped in the road. Someone opened the door to the vehicle, and Adrien stepped inside.

"Adrien! No, please! I need to—"

Nicolas's shout was lost as something flew overhead, rumbling and buzzing like a giant insect.

"Adrien!"

But Adrien was gone, and no matter how quickly Nicolas ran, he couldn't catch him.

Now, as the first hint of color lit the morning sky, Nicolas gazed out the window onto the gardens where he and Adrien had sat and talked the night before. Even more now than before, Nicolas was sure he'd met Adrien. And yet when he'd mentioned this to Jean at dinner, Jean had just smiled and told him he was smitten. Which, he supposed, he was.

NICOLAS ARRIVED in Saint-Gervais in the late afternoon. The ride from Lyon had been an easy one, the mid-September weather cool and sunny. "Please let my brother know I'm spending the day with Adrien," he had told one of the servants as he left the house dressed in his riding clothes. "I won't be back for dinner."

He'd never been to the tiny town before. It was one of many small communities along the route from Lyon to Limoges that provided respite for the weary traveler and provided agricultural goods to the cities.

He wasn't sure why he felt compelled to find Adrien, but he knew he needed to speak to him. Learn more about him. Understand why he felt he knew Adrien, even though he was sure they'd never met before the dance. *He's not much more than a boy.* And yet, in spite of his youth, Adrien seemed wise beyond his years. An old soul.

The curious glances he drew as he rode into town didn't surprise or concern him. Visitors were welcome, but unlike the city, in a place where everyone knew each other, he could not pass unnoticed. He stopped to feed and water his horse on the outskirts of town.

"Gilbert?" the stable hand said when Nicolas handed him a coin worth far more than the cost of the feed. The man pointed to the hills just beyond a stone church. "Their vineyard is up the road just past the river. Where the road curves to the east, you'll see the house."

Nicolas arrived at the house a half hour later. He tied his horse in the shade of a tree by the road, then walked up the dirt path on foot. He knocked on the front door and waited. No one answered, and no sound came from inside.

"Hello?" he said as he walked around the back. A small fire burned in a pit—wood for baking, perhaps. He peered into the kitchen through an open window. The scent of yeasty dough tickled his nose. He saw no one inside.

He noticed a smaller stone building farther up the dirt path. Stables, judging by the smell of manure and straw. Beyond, neat rows of grapevines climbed the hillside. Even this far away, he could see they were laden with fruit. He knew little about winemaking except that the wine from this region was excellent. He resolved to ask Adrien more about it.

Nicolas reached the stables and was just about to round the corner to see if anyone was behind it when he heard voices.

"...isn't a game, Adrien," a man's voice said.

Nicolas waited, not wanting to interrupt.

"Don't you think I know that?" Adrien snapped in response. "Father, you of all people know what's at stake. It's not as if I *chose* to end up here."

"François tells me you've been spending time with Nicolas," Adrien's father said. "Do you think that's wise? What if he guesses you aren't the boy you appear to be? I know you mean well, but Roland is right. This is a dangerous game."

Nicolas's hands grew cold. Was he a game to Adrien? Had Jean been right to warn him about his heart?

"I can't go back even if I wanted to," Adrien replied. "I don't know how."

"Papa!" someone called from near the vines.

Nicolas turned to see a young girl run from the house carrying a basket. He took a deep breath and rounded the corner.

"Nicolas?" Adrien's expression betrayed both shock and pleasure.

At least he wanted to see me. Nicolas smiled and held out his hand to Jacques Gilbert. "Nicolas Lambert," he said as Jacques took his hand. "And you must be Adrien's father."

"That I am," Jacques said with a quick glance in Adrien's direction.

"Adrien wasn't expecting me," Nicolas put in quickly. He smiled, hoping to put Adrien at ease, then said, "I apologize for not letting you know of my visit."

"Papa?"

"This is Isabelle," Adrien said. "My sister. Isa, this is Nicolas Lambert."

Isabelle blushed, then stepped closer to Nicolas and said, "You're a vampire, aren't you?"

Nicolas smiled and nodded.

"I didn't know you could tell, Isa," Adrien said with obvious surprise.

"Why don't we leave your brother and his guest alone, Isa," Jacques said. "François said he'd be coming home tonight. I believe you mentioned you'd be making his favorite dinner?"

"You're welcome to join us for dinner, monsieur Lambert," Isabelle said.

"I would love to," Nicolas said, "but I need to be back in Lyon tonight. Another time, perhaps?"

"That would be wonderful."

Jacques put a hand on Isabelle's shoulder and took the basket she held. "Lunch?" he asked as he peered beneath the cloth cover. She nodded happily and they set out down the path to the house.

Adrien watched them walk with a wistful expression. *Not just wistful. Sad.* Whatever questions Nicolas might have after overhearing Adrien's conversation with his father, he sensed how much Adrien loved his sister.

"I'm glad you came," Adrien said after Jacques and Isabelle disappeared into the house.

"I truly am sorry I took you by surprise." Nicolas schooled his expression. He struggled to understand the little he'd overheard.

"You will always be a target," Jean had once told him. "There are those in the Council of Hunters who distrust our motives. They know that the key to power is through the ancient clans."

What if Adrien was working on behalf of the Council? What if Adrien's interest in him was a sham, a ruse meant to put him off his guard? *Lure you away from safety....* For the first time, Nicolas noticed that, even here in the vineyard, Adrien wore his hunter's sword. The Gilbert Clan was old and powerful. If they wanted to do away with the vampires who stood in their way, what could he alone do to prevent it?

"I really *am* happy you came," Adrien said as they walked along the vines, Nicolas a few steps behind.

Nicolas's hand tingled, ready to call his sword. He listened for sounds of others, but heard only the rustling of the grape leaves. *What if your suspicions are warranted? What if your actions jeopardize Jean's safety as well as your own? What then?*

Adrien sat in the shade of one of the vines and motioned to Nicolas to join him. "The view is best here," he said. "You can see most of the valley. Sometimes I imagine I can see all the way to Lyon."

"What do you want with me?" Nicolas blurted, unable to hold back.

"What?" Adrien looked up at Nicolas in stunned surprise.

"I know you've lied to me." Nicolas clenched his jaw and called his sword.

"I haven't—"

Nicolas pointed his weapon at Adrien. "I overheard you and your father."

"You... what?" Adrien blanched.

Nicolas shook his head. "I was naïve enough to believe you wanted me. That there might be something between us." He clenched his jaw and pressed the tip of his weapon to Adrien's neck.

"Nicolas... I haven't—"

"Get up," Nicolas hissed. "Draw your weapon. I won't kill you in cold blood."

"Kill me? No, Nicolas, I don't want to fight—"

Nicolas reached down and grabbed Adrien by his shirt. "Draw your weapon."

"No."

"Then tell me what the *hell* you were speaking to your father about," Nicolas demanded, at the limits of his patience. Did Adrien think he'd just bare his neck and let Adrien cut off his head?

"I... I can't," Adrien said.

"Then fight me, or I *will* kill you." Nicolas picked Adrien up by his collar until his feet dangled, then threw him backward. "Draw your weapon."

"I don't want to hurt you," Adrien said as he got to his feet and dusted himself off. Blood oozed from a cut on the side of his chin.

The smell of Adrien's blood made Nicolas dizzy. He'd heard that hunters' blood tasted different from humans', but this felt like more than just that. The smell seemed familiar. "Then tell me what he meant by you not being the boy you appear to be."

Adrien's laughter sounded forced. "He only meant that I'm not always altruistic. Sometimes I can be downright selfish."

"You're lying."

Something like recognition flashed in Adrien's eyes. No doubt he'd heard that some ancients could discern truth from lies.

"Draw your weapon."

Adrien opened his arms with his palms facing upward. "No."

"Damn you." Nicolas pushed Adrien, causing him to roll a few feet down the hill, then stop as he collided with one of the vines. "Tell me what your father meant about you not being who you appear to be."

"You won't hurt me," Adrien said.

"You know nothing," Nicolas lied. "I could kill you if I wanted."

"But you won't."

"Damn you." The bloodlust made Nicolas's body thrum with need. He straddled Adrien and set his sword down. The cut on Adrien's face had begun to bleed again. Nicolas swiped his thumb over the blood, then brought it to his lips.

The hint of a memory borne on Adrien's blood took him by surprise. Adrien, unconscious. Dying. Then the memory vanished as quickly as it had come upon him. Nicolas drew a long breath, allowing the captivating scent of Adrien's blood to fill him. To his surprise, he smelled his own blood as well as Adrien's.

That's impossible. He had never given anyone the gift. This was just another ploy, another means to set him off balance. He needed to leave this place. Leave Adrien behind and return to the safety of Lyon.

But he couldn't leave. Every fiber of his being told him he couldn't leave. Not now. He must know the truth. Not much more than a drop of blood, and he'd seen something. He needed to understand how such a thing was possible. How could this man be an immortal?

Adrien met his gaze and held it without fear. Surely he knew Nicolas could kill him without a weapon. Surely Adrien had seen the red in his eyes. Surely Adrien understood what he was capable of.

Adrien allowed his head to fall to one side, baring his neck.

"No," Nicolas whispered. Still, he leaned over Adrien so that their faces were inches apart. He inhaled Adrien's scent, familiar. Enticing. Nicolas told himself the familiarity was something born of the past few days, but he knew that was a lie.

"You want the truth, don't you?" Adrien asked. "You saw something in my blood. I don't know how, but I know you saw it."

"I fear what I might do."

Adrien smiled and brushed Nicolas's jaw with his fingers. "You won't hurt me."

"That's the second time you've said that."

"I won't hurt you either. Can you sense the truth in those words?" Adrien's expression was kind. Almost… loving?

144

Nicolas exhaled as he watched blood pulse through the tender skin beneath Adrien's ear. His body responded in spite of his resolve. He'd wanted Adrien the first time he'd seen him at the party. In spite of Adrien's boyish face, his eyes spoke to Nicolas with the depth and clarity of a far older man.

"Tell me this much," Nicolas said. "How old are you really?"

Adrien's lips parted. Nicolas saw hesitation dissolve into something unnamable, indescribable, a maelstrom of pain and joy and fear that mirrored his own. "Nearly a hundred and fifty years old," Adrien said at last.

Again, Nicolas touched the cut on Adrien's face and tasted the blood. "I could never hurt you," Adrien said as Nicolas finally gave in to the bloodlust. "I've spent most of my life trying to find you."

CHAPTER THIRTY:
MAKE-BELIEVE

"SIR?" A WOMAN'S voice, vaguely familiar.

Adrien lifted his head from the desk and looked up. The room danced with blue light as Adrien's stomach roiled. A minute ago he'd been sleeping under the vines with Nicolas.

Take me back there!

"This is my game," the demon said. *"I decide when and where you go."*

"Sir?" the woman said again, sounding concerned.

"Yes?" he said. His vision cleared more quickly than the last time the demon had sent him to a different time. He heard the demon laugh, but he ignored it. He wouldn't give it the satisfaction.

"I have the reports you requested, Mr. Gilbert," the woman said.

"Thank you." Adrien took the papers from her hand. He glanced at them. *1st Quarter 1988, Asian Bureau.*

He took in the room's textured glass walls, glossy mahogany floors, and the large abstract painting centered over a sleek couch with tan upholstery and lots of chrome. He ran his fingers over the polished wood of the desk. All so familiar.

"Is there anything else you need, sir?" Her voice brought him back to himself.

"No," he answered. "Thank you."

"Sir, are you feeling all right?" He heard the tinge of concern in her voice.

"Yes, I'm fine." He looked up and studied her. A handsome woman in her forties. Dark hair, well dressed. Pale skin and warm brown eyes with just a hint of age to frame them. Her kind face stirred a memory—a time in his life he'd tried to forget.

"You…. You've never thanked me before."

"Haven't I?" he said. "Well, I should have."

She smiled and left him alone.

He knew this place. His Manhattan office. Or it had been his Manhattan office once.

The intercom buzzed.

"Sir?" his assistant said, her voice tinny and thin through the speaker.

He struggled to remember her name. Robinson? Rogers? *Robbins. Beth Robbins.* "Yes, Beth?"

"Your father is on line one," Beth replied. "Should I tell him you're busy?"

"No. I'll take the call."

There was a moment of surprised silence, and then she said, "Of course, sir."

Adrien glanced at the desk calendar. May 5, 1988. He didn't need to ask the demon why he'd brought him here. Now. His gut clenched.

Why did you bring me here? Now, of all times? I could have stayed where I was, with Nicolas!

God, he'd been so happy with Nicolas! Nicolas, who knew all he'd been through. He could still smell the sweet scent of Nicolas's blood mingled with the familiar scent of hay. Nicolas, whom he'd held in his arms hours ago.

But it wasn't hours ago. It was nearly a hundred years ago.

What are you trying to do?

The demon remained silent.

Adrien depressed the button on his phone as he lifted the receiver. "Dad?"

"Will wonders never cease," Jacques said with a chuckle. "You've finally decided to take my call?"

"I… yes." Adrien's shoulders tensed. What was it about his father that aggravated him so?

"We need to talk, son."

"Why?" Adrien asked.

"You know why."

"Isabelle." Speaking her name felt as though he had stabbed himself in the gut. For an instant he could almost hear her shimmering laughter.

"You need to see her, Adrien."

"I'm busy," he answered. "The board is meeting next week about the first quarter results," he lied, "and I—"

"Time is fleeting. François and Charles are on their way. She won't last much longer."

"I understand," he replied. "But I've got a ton of reports to finish. I'll come this week, I promise."

"Adrien, if this is about François... I understand how you feel about vampires, but I'm asking you to put that aside this once. Please don't do something you might regret later because of your past disagreements."

François? Adrien didn't recall any dispute he'd had with François—not after François had been taken prisoner by the Council of Hunters. *This isn't the past I knew.* Something stirred at the back of his fuzzy brain. Yet he was here, alive, in 1988. How was that possible?

"What about Nicolas?" he asked his father, hoping against hope that this new past might mean he and Nicolas might—

"Who?"

Adrien crumpled the papers he'd been holding. He should have realized the demon wouldn't make things so simple. "Nothing," he said. "My mistake."

"Are you feeling all right, son? Even immortals need to rest," Jacques said.

Immortal. He touched his face and felt the smooth, youthful skin there. It made sense, of course. If he was alive and young, he had to be immortal here as well. Did that mean someone—Nicolas, even—had given him immortality? He struggled to focus on the questions.

"I'm fine," he said. "Just busy."

He heard Jacques sigh through the handset. "Please, Adrien. You really need to come."

"I'll be there," Adrien said, knowing he wouldn't quickly find the answers he sought. He'd have to learn them as he had the last time he'd traveled through time. He replaced the receiver and stared at the telephone in silence.

Isa. Sweet, beautiful Isabelle.

The demon was toying with him. Even if some things in this timestream were different from his own, the rest was all too familiar. Sending him here was far more painful than any physical wound the demon could inflict.

Adrien stood and walked to the bank of windows behind his desk. Below, Central Park teemed with people enjoying the warm spring day. The leaves on the trees fluttered, full and green. A grayish-yellow haze hung over the buildings.

Adrien turned back to the desk, opened the polished silver box he knew he'd find there, and pulled out a cigarette. He hadn't smoked in years. Not that it would have killed him. He'd quit because, as with everything else in his life of privilege, he'd grown bored with it.

He held the cigarette between his lips and lit it with the sword-shaped lighter. It had been a gag gift from his father, and it still made Adrien smile.

François is alive, and if he's with Charles....

1988. The year death had claimed his little sister. She had been nearly 110 years old. She had outlived her husband and her children, had lived to see her grandchildren have children and grandchildren of their own. But none of that mattered to Adrien. She couldn't die. He wouldn't let it happen.

He saw a leather jacket lying on the back of a chair and grabbed it before walking out the office door. "I'm going out," he told Beth.

"But sir," she shouted after him, "you have a three-o'clock meeting with—"

"Cancel it. I'm taking the rest of the day off."

"Of course, sir," she replied.

AT TWO o'clock in the morning, the streets below Adrien's Manhattan penthouse were empty. The moon, a half crescent, cast an eerie glow on the East River, making it glitter silver and black. Adrien sat by the window, unable to sleep.

"Isabelle." His voice echoed against the glass of the windows.

"It's too late, Addie," Isabelle said as they drove around Paris in his bright red Lion-Peugeot with its top down. "I'm not about to go begging the Council for a commission. Not at my age."

"You're young still, Isa," he told her.

Her hair blew about her face as he accelerated onto the avenue. "I'm nearly thirty-five," she replied as she glared at him. "That ship sailed years ago."

"Things have changed. Being a woman isn't—"

"I thought it's what I wanted. But even if the Council has changed its mind—again"—she screwed her face up in disgust—"and thinks a woman can do the job, I've moved on. I want a family. Children." She sighed and leaned her head on his shoulder. "George and I have been seeing each other for two years. He wants me to marry him. Dad's given us his blessing."

"But when will you train? He's a human, Isabelle. He won't understand—"

"I don't want to be a hunter anymore. I'm not even that good, Adrien, and you know it!"

He knew she was right. She had never really gotten the hang of it, but then again, none of them had really helped her. If she'd trained when they were little…. But they'd all relied on her—he, François, and his father. They'd needed her to care for them. And although Adrien had known some female hunters, they had never truly been welcomed.

"Our parents were both hunters. It's in your blood."

"That isn't a reason." Of course she'd point out how weak his argument was. She'd always been able to see right through him.

"But George is English," he said. "You'll have to leave France." It might be better if she left. With the Germans in Belgium, London was safer.

"Things change, Adrien. You travel. Why must I stay here my entire life?"

He had no answer to give her. What could he say? That he didn't want to lose her? That he wanted her there to greet him, as she always had, when he went home to Saint-Gervais? That without Nicolas, he relied on her for comfort and support?

Selfish reasons. They'd all been selfish when it came to Isabelle. And now that she had a chance to be happy, could he stand in her way?

She was married six months later, in London. A year later she gave birth to a boy, Justin. There would be three more children before George died in the trenches of Europe, fighting in World War I. Isabelle never complained about raising four children by herself, nor was she willing to uproot her family and return to France to do so. Only at the age of 100 had she moved back to their family's home in Saint-Gervais, where their father took care of her. She died with Charles, François, and their father at her side. Adrien had not come to see her.

He picked up the telephone and pressed one of the autodial buttons. "I'm sorry to bother you so late, Beth," he said.

"Please don't apologize, sir" came her cheerful reply.

"Please have the pilot ready my plane. I'll need the car in about an hour."

"Of course," she said. "Where will you be headed?"

"France."

"I see." From the tone of her voice, he guessed his father had mentioned Isabelle. "And where in France should I tell the pilot?"

"Saint-Gervais," he answered with a wistful sigh. "I'm going home."

CHAPTER THIRTY-ONE: FAREWELL AGAIN

"I DIDN'T think you'd come," Isabelle said as a broad smile lit her face. She lay in bed, reading a book. Bright-eyed, her skin nearly translucent, her hair as white and soft as clouds, Isabelle still reminded Adrien of the young girl she'd been when she'd tended the vines at his side. She had always been small, but she appeared terribly frail now, her tiny frame barely more than a wisp of a body.

"I almost didn't," Adrien admitted as he jumped down from the window.

"Something wrong with the front door?" she asked with a chuckle.

"I didn't want to see anyone else."

"You were always a bit of a show-off." She patted the bed, then added, "I'm glad you came. I've missed you."

He kissed her cheek and sat beside her. "How are you feeling?" he asked, then forced a smile.

"I'm fine," she replied as she reached over to pick up the plate of biscuits left at the bedside. Her hand shook violently, so he grabbed her wrist gently and helped her steady the plate. "Hungry?"

"Thanks." He wasn't hungry, but he knew it would make her feel good if he ate one. "You look beautiful, Isa."

"Liar." She laughed as he put the plate down for her. "I'm as old as the hills. You, however, haven't aged a day since I last saw you."

He looked away. More guilt. Always the guilt. Best friend of loneliness.

"Why the long face?" She reached out and turned his chin so he was forced to look at her. "I'm happy for you. You have the chance to do so much with your life."

"Time isn't always a gift."

"Does that mean you've given up on finding some happiness for yourself?" she asked. She pressed her lips together and shook her head. "You have, haven't you?"

"No."

"Hanging on by a thread doesn't count," she gently chastised. Adrien could almost imagine her as she'd been when they were children and he'd been bedridden. She had never let him wallow. She'd also never coddled him.

She took his hand in hers and squeezed. "Immortality has been hard for you, hasn't it?"

"Yes." He surprised himself by admitting it.

"Guilt accomplishes nothing. It sucks the life from you." She paused, looked away for a moment, then said, "There is someone who owns your heart, isn't there?"

"What?"

"The guilt. It's about more than just me. I can sense it." She sighed, then added, "All this time you've been looking for someone to make you happy."

"I don't know what you're talking about." He stood up and stalked over to the window, latched it closed, and stared out at the neat rows of vines. He had never told her about Nicolas.

"You can't hide from me, Addie. I can tell you're struggling with more than you're willing to share with me. And I know you didn't want to come."

"I—"

"You don't need to lie," she said. "I know you love me. I know you're afraid."

He blinked back tears. In the future, he'd regret his decision to avoid her deathbed. Now that he had an opportunity to revisit that decision, he knew he must face his fear. "Ironic," he said, his voice cracking in spite of his self-control, "that someone who cannot die fears death."

She smiled. "Not at all." She patted the bed again. "Please?"

He nodded and sat back down beside her.

"At my age, there's a certain peace in knowing death is imminent," she told him. "I've outlived my husband and my children. I've lived a good life. A happy life."

"I know I'm being selfish," he said in an undertone. He'd been fortunate that she'd been born of two hunter parents and had lived far longer than a normal human. Her long life had been a welcome gift to him. "I don't want to lose you."

"You can't stop time," she said. The irony of her words cut him deeply. "And even if you could, I wouldn't want to remain. I'm ready, Adrien. It's time to let me go."

At these words, the tenuous control Adrien maintained over his emotions fled. Tears streamed over his cheeks as she drew him against her shoulder. Thoughts of Nicolas and loneliness joined with the pain and fear of losing her.

For the first time in his life, Adrien stopped trying to fight the pain.

A FEW hours later, Adrien sat at the kitchen table, staring out the back window at the darkening sky. A gentle hand on his shoulder brought him back to himself.

"I'm glad you came," his father said.

Adrien wasn't sure what to think. Being back in 1988 was both more painful and more unsettling than he cared to admit. He'd thought he'd handled Isabelle's death well at the time. He'd arranged the funeral. He'd provided his plane to bring François and Charles back from a stay in Korea. He'd done everything for Isabelle. Everything but be with her when she passed.

"I've killed more vampires than I can count," he said as he looked into his father's eyes. "I've seen more death than most men…."

"It isn't the same." Jacques shook his head and sighed. "And for us…."

"When you lost maman," Adrien began, "what did you do?"

Jacques chuckled and pressed his lips together as he shook his head again. "I went a little crazy." He frowned, then added, "You should know. You remember what it was like, living with me."

"You were a good father to us."

Jacques shrugged. "I managed." He paused, then added, "I have a lovely bottle of our 1929 cuvée I've been saving. Care to join me?"

"I'd like that." Adrien returned his father's smile.

Jacques headed toward the door to the cellar, then turned around and said, "It's good to have you here. Now."

"I'm glad I came."

CHAPTER THIRTY-TWO: SUNDOWN

THE SUN was beginning to set the next day when François and Charles arrived at the vineyard.

"Addie." François tensed his jaw, his hesitation obvious. Adrien, however, embraced François.

"François, it's good to see you."

François stepped back after Adrien released him, staring at Adrien in shocked surprise.

"Whatever I've said or done in the past," Adrien said, "I hope you'll forgive me." He realized that he knew little about what had transpired between him and François in this past, but he also knew he'd been foolish when he'd pushed François away in his own past. If François hadn't become a vampire, there would probably already be another headstone under the ancient oak tree near the house.

Charles, who had been watching Adrien through hooded eyes, now offered Adrien his hand. "Perhaps there is some good to come of this," he said softly.

"Yes." Adrien wasn't as sure. If he moved on, would the Adrien left behind feel the same? The possibilities made his head spin, so he pushed them away as the three of them made their way upstairs in silence. Jacques sat at Isabelle's side, her hand in his. François's eyes glittered after he leaned in to kiss her on each cheek.

"I'm glad you came," Isabelle said. She smiled but struggled to keep her eyes open.

The night before, Adrien had almost imagined she would recover. Now he heard the weakness in her voice and saw the pain in her eyes. Jacques had said she'd refused to take her pain medication. She wanted to spend the last moments of her life alert. But Adrien sensed something more profound this time. Her spirit had begun to fade. The bright soul he'd sensed the night before flickered like the flame of a candle when no wax remained to fuel its wick.

Adrien and François spent most of the afternoon with Isabelle. At one point Isabelle nodded off and they watched her in silence.

Adrien wasn't sure if he imagined when her soul left her body. It didn't really matter. What mattered was that he was there when she died.

They buried her the next morning next to their mother. Beneath the same tree where she, Adrien, and François had played as children before their mother's death. All of the people who loved her were there.

Isa, Adrien thought later as he sat on the grass in front of her grave, *thank you for giving me the chance to say good-bye.*

THAT NIGHT after Charles and François went to sleep, Adrien wandered the vineyard by the light of a nearly full moon. Spring had always been Isabelle's favorite time of the year, with the promise of the harvest and the way the earth emerged from a cocoon of cold to explode into the warmth of life.

"There are times when I walk the rows at night," Adrien's father said from behind him. Adrien had sensed his presence for some time, but he'd been content to enjoy the silence.

"I used to dream of coming back here," Adrien said as he gazed over the valley. Below, the town glowed with the light from the streetlamps. "I never wanted to leave."

"I know. It's why I stayed, even after your mother was killed."

"I wondered," Adrien admitted. "When I learned you were an immortal... I guess I just didn't get it." He chuckled and shook his head. "I couldn't understand why you stayed, even after we all left."

Jacques sighed, and Adrien knew he was thinking about Isabelle. "Everyone needs a rock. Your mother was that to me. This place reminds me of her. You understand that, don't you?"

Adrien did, although it reminded him of Nicolas and of the empty, festering hole in his heart.

ADRIEN LEFT Saint-Gervais two days later for Paris, happy to focus on something other than his grieving heart. Isa had been right. He *had* been hanging on by a thread. He'd given up on his happiness, and as a result, he'd let Nicolas down.

He traded his jeans and T-shirt for an expensive Dolce & Gabbana suit, then hired a limousine and driver. He arrived at his destination, a modern high-rise in La Défense overlooking the nearly complete and soon to become iconic modern arch. The placard at the building's entrance read simply "JPL." One of the largest investment firms in Europe, it had no need to advertise.

Adrien gave his name to the guard at the front desk, who called to announce him. Several minutes later, Adrien rode the elevator to the offices on the topmost floor. The beautiful woman who met him at the elevator wore a well-cut wool suit and her long hair in a perfect chignon.

"Adrien," Caroline Vestry said as she offered him her hand. "It's so good to see you."

Adrien smiled to realize Caroline knew him. Charles's creation and one of the best fighters Adrien knew, Caroline had been a powerful ally and a good friend.

Her smile faded and she lowered her head as she said, "I heard about your sister. I'm very sorry for your loss."

"Thank you."

"If you'll have a seat," she said, gesturing to the waiting room, "Jean will be with you shortly. He's just finishing up a conference call."

"Of course." Adrien picked up a magazine from one of the side tables and sat on one of the leather couches. The cover featured a photograph of a boxy desktop computer and touted the lightning speed of IBM's new 25 MHz 386 processor. He scanned the article and set the magazine aside, then reached for his cell phone and chuckled at himself.

Caroline returned a few minutes later and led him down a long corridor to a set of frosted glass doors. She ushered him into an enormous corner office with floor-to-ceiling glass walls on two sides and a clear view of the city. Near the windows was a simple glass desk covered with exceptionally neat stacks of papers and several silver pens. The man sitting at the desk stood.

"Monsieur Gilbert." Jean Lambert's manner and speech were formal, stiff. "It's a pleasure to see you again."

Adrien drew a slow breath with the realization that this was *not* the past he'd lived. He and Jean had been too close in his own timestream for

Jean to ever call him "monsieur." "I'm sorry my visit was so last-minute," he said, schooling his features. "Thank you for making time for me."

Jean eyed Adrien with mild interest. "I've followed your career, of course," he said. "Successful entrepreneur. Hunter. And immortal." He frowned, then added, "Nicolas. Of course. How could I not have realized it?"

This Jean appeared to be the same man Adrien had known for nearly 100 years—dignified, focused, and above all, direct and to the point.

"You didn't know?"

"I remember that you and he were briefly lovers," Jean said. "He told me he'd left you. That he'd decided you were too young. But I never considered that you were the one to whom he gave the gift."

Nicolas had left him? No. *I left him behind in the past.* The ache in his chest flared with the dawning realization that this was the future he'd created when he'd moved forward in time. He recalled Roland's words: *How much does each man, woman, or child influence the future? For the average person, undoubtedly the influence is small. But subtle changes can lead to larger consequences.*

"Where is he now?" Adrien asked, both eager to hear about Nicolas and dreading what he might learn.

"You don't know?" Jean studied him with obvious interest. "Interesting." He frowned deeper this time. "Back then, when Nicolas told me about you, I found it strange that so young a boy might stir Nicolas's heart. And now you claim to have no knowledge of Nicolas's circumstances…. Is there something you haven't told me?"

"Time's just about up, Adrien," the demon warned.

"What interest do you have in Nicolas?" Jean asked when Adrien didn't respond.

Adrien took a deep breath. "I owe Nicolas my life. I am sworn to protect him. I know this must sound strange given what you know of me and Nicolas, but I speak the truth."

"What do you want?"

"Someday, Pelletier may seek to harm Nicolas," Adrien said.

Jean frowned. "Pelletier? But he's—"

"He's alive." Adrien met Jean's eyes unflinchingly. "I can't explain why or how, but if you love Nicolas as I do, you must believe me."

"You speak the truth," Jean said with a shake of his head. "Although I don't understand it."

"Time's up, Adrien."

"There's no time for me to explain," Adrien answered quickly. "There may come a time when I will ask for your help, for Nicolas's sake. All I ask is that you listen to me. Give me the benefit of the doubt."

Jean hesitated briefly, then nodded.

Adrien stood. "We will meet again, Lord Lambert. And you will remember my visit. When you do, you'll understand why I came."

"Indeed." The edges of Jean's mouth edged upward.

"Yes," Adrien replied. "And when we meet again, I'll ask for your assistance. I hope you'll grant my request."

Jean said nothing.

Adrien inclined his head, then turned and walked out of the office. He felt the familiar queasy sensation in the pit of his stomach as time twisted and he fell into the abyss.

CHAPTER THIRTY-THREE: THE ALLY

The Present

THE ROOM came into focus amidst a shimmer of radiant blue light. Outside, rain fell from a gray sky. Paris, judging by the Eiffel Tower in the distance. Adrien steadied himself against the wall, then dropped to his knees and fought nausea.

"You're weak, Adrien." The demon laughed. Adrien ignored this.

"Welcome back." Roland smiled at Adrien.

"Where…. When…?" Adrien croaked.

"I did a bit of damage control in the Council Chamber. Managed to get you out of there." Roland grinned, then added, "I made a bit of a mess of the place, I'm afraid. Brought you here, since I thought you might need a bit of time—"

"Is Pelletier alive?" Adrien demanded.

"Pelletier? No, but—"

"Damn him," Adrien hissed under his breath.

"Him? Pelletier?"

"The demon." Adrien gritted his teeth, pulled himself up to standing, then sat heavily on the couch when his legs began to shake.

Roland raised his eyebrows and rubbed his chin. "I see."

"Fucker sent me to the past."

"Oh?" Roland's eyes widened in recognition. "I see."

"What do you mean?" Adrien was having a hard time wrapping his brain around what had happened. The sound of a whistling kettle made him cringe.

"I wondered what happened at the Council meeting," Roland said. "Why you reacted so strongly to something you should have known. That Pelletier was dead."

159

"Fuck." Understanding finally came to Adrien. *I changed the future.* The realization hit him like a kick in the gut. Was the Nicolas he'd seen at the Council of Hunters the same Nicolas he'd met at the ball? Then this Roland was also a product of the past the demon had helped Adrien create. *He knew I'd change things in the past. He showed me what the future would look like.* How the hell was that possible?

The kettle continued to whistle.

"Fuck." Adrien rubbed the bridge of his nose. The headache had gotten worse. "Can you turn that damn thing off?" He closed his eyes and took a few long breaths. He heard the sound of Roland's shoes on the wood floors. At last the kettle quieted.

"Tea?" Roland called from the other room.

"Screw the tea." Adrien felt suddenly numb. It all made sense now. The future had changed, but not because of the demon. It had changed because of what he, Adrien Gilbert, had done in the past. What he'd done with Nicolas hadn't just left a small imprint—he had left Nicolas with a full-blown memory of the future and what might have been. Then he'd left Nicolas to cope with the aftermath, just as Pelletier had left him to mourn the loss of Nicolas. He'd left Nicolas with his true seventeen-year-old self, a boy who knew nothing of life. A boy who despised vampires. No wonder Nicolas had been so startled at the Council meeting. He hadn't expected to see the Adrien from the future ever again.

"Each wave leaves the tiniest trace upon the sand," Roland had told him. Adrien drew a slow breath.

"What have I done?" Adrien put his head in his hands.

"It seems your demon is quite powerful," Roland said from the kitchen. A few minutes later, he made his way back to the living room with a teapot and two cups of tea on a tray.

"How do I get it to stop?" Adrien asked when Roland said nothing more.

"You can't. The demon is part of you." Roland set the tray down on the coffee table, then sat on the couch next to Adrien.

Adrien sighed. He was too tired to fight Roland. He just hoped he wouldn't fall asleep in the middle of one of Roland's rambles. "What do you mean, I can't?"

"Just that. It will choose the place and the time for any confrontation. It's not up to you to do anything." Roland lifted the teapot and poured two cups. He handed one of them to Adrien, who took it without protest.

Adrien inhaled the steam from his cup. The scent was surprisingly calming.

"Helps with headaches," Roland explained before Adrien could say anything. "If I'm correct, your head must hurt like—how do you youngsters put it—'a bitch'?"

Adrien nearly laughed. He took a sip of the tea and willed his tense body to relax. The memory of the Council meeting began to coalesce. He'd been out of his mind, seeing Nicolas again. He'd thought Pelletier had changed time.

"How is Reynaud?" If he'd killed Reynaud, what hope did he have of finding Nicolas and convincing him of the truth?

"He's alive. He'll recover."

Thank God. "And Nicolas?" Adrien asked.

Roland appeared to hesitate. "He lives here in Paris," he said after a moment.

"Paris?" Adrien shot up off the couch and nearly spilled his tea. He immediately regretted it when his headache flared again.

"Before you go chasing after him," Roland said, "you may want to let things settle down a bit. The Council has men looking for you. We thought it best that you lie low for a few days."

"We?" Adrien asked.

"He's speaking of me," said the familiar voice from the door to the apartment.

"Jean." Adrien clenched his jaw. Of course this place seemed familiar. This was Jean's apartment.

"Nicolas said you'd be angry," Jean replied.

"Nicolas? When did you see him?"

"A few minutes ago," Jean answered as he hung his jacket by the door.

"Where is he? I need to see him," Adrien demanded.

"He won't see you."

"He's angry about what I did to Reynaud," Adrien said. He had no one but himself to blame for his loss of control.

"Sit," Roland said, patting the couch.

Adrien did as he was told. As soon as Roland stopped babbling and he figured out what Jean knew, he'd find Nicolas.

"He isn't angry about Reynaud," Jean said as he took a seat across from Adrien and Roland.

"Then why *are* you here?" Adrien was growing quickly tired of the conversation. "You didn't believe what I had to say in the Council Chamber."

"That's not quite true." Jean leaned back in the chair and crossed his legs, clearly considering something. "I sensed that something changed at the meeting."

Adrien remembered the words Jean had spoken in his mind at the meeting, urging him not to challenge Reynaud, telling him they would speak later.

"You paid me a visit years ago, when you said that someday you might ask something of me. You told me that Pelletier might seek to harm Nicolas."

"What exactly did you sense?" Adrien inhaled the tea again and the throbbing between his eyes eased a bit.

"I can't explain it," Jean answered. "But something felt different. *You* felt different."

"I don't understand."

"I didn't either," Jean said with a soft smile. "So I asked Nicolas for the truth."

"The truth?" Adrien asked warily. He'd lived through too many truths the past few days to have any idea what this particular truth might be.

"He told me I should believe you," Jean said. "He told me what he saw in your blood when you and he first met."

Adrien was speechless. Nicolas had believed him and he had sent Jean here so Adrien would know that he *remembered.* Adrien thought about the watch he'd found years before, after Pelletier had taken Nicolas. Adrien had no doubt the same Nicolas had written the words, *I remember.* But how was that possible?

He brushed the thought away. He had more important things to think about now.

"Where is Nicolas?" Adrien asked again. "I need to see him."

"He's at the Rousseau castle helping Blaise look after Reynaud. But he won't see you, Adrien. He asked me to give you this note instead." Jean handed Adrien a small envelope.

Adrien looked at Roland, but Roland's expression revealed nothing. He steadied himself, then opened the envelope and read:

Adrien,

I have sent Jean to you in hopes that he and Roland can help you return to your own present. I've told him the truth of your past. He knows you are a good man. Ask him for help. Please don't do this all on your own.

I ask only one thing of you. Please do not try to see me before you have completed your work. I know it's selfish of me to ask, but you must trust me as I have trusted you.

I have faith in you.

Nicolas

Adrien looked up at Jean. "Why won't he see me?"

"I'm sure he has his reasons," Jean answered.

"I don't understand." It made no sense. Why would Nicolas refuse to see him? Unless.... "Pelletier," Adrien said.

"What of him?" Jean asked. "He's been dead for centuries."

Adrien doubted Pelletier was dead. More likely hiding behind the scenes, pulling strings, much as he'd done in Adrien's own timestream. Biding his time and waiting patiently until.... *What the fuck is he up to?*

Adrien walked over to the coat-tree. "I'll return it," he said as he pulled Jean's jacket on. Jean glared at him, then looked to Roland, who just shrugged. "I'll be in touch," Adrien said as he stepped out into the hall. A minute later he rode the elevator down to the ground floor. He was only mildly surprised that neither Jean nor Roland followed him. No doubt they knew they wouldn't be able to stop him.

The cab ride from Paris to Rousseau Castle took less than an hour. It surprised Adrien to find the front gates unlocked. Clearly Blaise—or was Reynaud now in charge?—had no concerns regarding the safety of the castle's occupants.

Adrien walked through the gates and over the bridge that spanned the long-empty moat. He took deep breaths to slow his racing heartbeat. He would beg Nicolas's forgiveness. He'd explain that he didn't need to return to his own timestream. He and Nicolas would find happiness here.

An elderly servant answered Adrien's knock on the huge wooden doors. She seemed to expect him—Adrien guessed Jean had called ahead to warn Nicolas. *Good. He'll know why I've come.*

The servant ushered Adrien into a small walled garden on the side of the mansion, accessible only by a rusting wrought-iron gate. Ivy and climbing roses covered the high stone walls. The red roses had begun to fade, victims of the cool September air. Several small stone benches lined the path that wound around the plants. Moss covered most of the cobblestones. A private sanctuary and a place where he and Nicolas could speak without interruption.

Adrien practiced the words he meant to speak to Nicolas. A century of business negotiations had taught him that preparation was the best way to control his anxiety. He would be firm but honest. He'd apologize for his outburst at the Council meeting and hope Nicolas would understand.

The gate creaked open. All preparation, all thoughts of a rehearsed speech vanished when he saw Nicolas. Adrien hesitated, but Nicolas embraced him, claimed his lips, and held him close.

"Nicolas."

Nicolas turned away. "You shouldn't have come. It's not safe."

"I'm stronger than I was back then." He wrapped his arms around Nicolas's waist and kissed the back of his neck.

Nicolas tensed.

"Nicolas," Adrien said with a soft laugh. "I don't need to go back to my own time. We can be happy here together."

"No. I'm not the same person I was when we met at the ball all those years ago," Nicolas said.

"It doesn't matter. I don't expect you to be the same," Adrien said softly. When Nicolas said nothing, he continued, "I know you must hate me for what I did to your uncle. I can't apologize enough for my—"

"I understand why you did what you did. I may not remember it, but I saw it in your blood, how he lied to me… to all of us. There's nothing to forgive."

"Then we can put everything behind us. Start from here."

"No. We can't." Nicolas's voice resonated with an edge of steel. "There's no future for us now."

"But that's where you're wrong. You gave me immortality. We have forever. It may be different, but—"

"Different, and a dead end for us." Pain shimmered in Nicolas's eyes.

"Dead end? But—"

"We can't be together." Nicolas's jaw tensed and he shook his head. "You don't understand. I've lived without you for more than a hundred years. That day in the vineyard, I saw the future in your blood. When we

164

shared our blood and our bodies, I thought we would be able to build a life together. But the next day…."

Adrien felt suddenly sick. None of this made sense. His head pounded, the laughter nearly drowning out Nicolas's voice. "I don't understand. Tell me."

"I am bound by blood," Nicolas said. "Nearly a hundred years ago, I pledged myself to someone else. This cannot be undone."

Adrien struggled to catch his breath. "No. It's not possible. That day… in the vineyard… you took my blood. You saw everything… the truth."

Nicolas clenched his jaw. "You don't know what happened after that, do you?"

Adrien shook his head.

"We made love. We shared our blood. But when I awoke the next morning, the Adrien I knew—*you* were gone. I knew you had no control over it. But the Adrien left behind was barely more than a child. He remembered nothing of what we'd been to each other. He knew nothing of your future. He hated my kind. And who could blame him? We were the ones who killed his mother."

"Oh God." Adrien swallowed hard. "I… I wanted to stay with you. I tried to stay—"

"I went back to Lyon. I decided that even if you didn't remember, I would get to know you again. I tried to see you again, but the Council of Hunters activated your commission.

"And then I did something terrible. Something I still regret. Something selfish." Nicolas straightened, shoulders tensed, as if steeling himself. "I couldn't bear to see you hurt."

"You gave me—the other me—immortality."

Nicolas nodded. "After you left, he was no longer immortal. I feared…."

"Nicolas," Adrien said in an undertone, "I could never blame you for that."

"The other Adrien, the one from this time, never forgave me. I tried to explain, but all he knew of your past was through my eyes. He saw me only as a vampire who had violated him. Forced him to become something he never wanted."

Adrien tried to find words, but they all seemed trite. In the end, he settled for "I'm so sorry. Truly I am."

Nicolas smiled, but the sadness Adrien saw in that smile made his chest ache. "True love is a fantasy, Adrien. What you knew... perhaps you might call it that. But the Adrien Gilbert you left behind—his life unfolded differently."

"Differently?"

"Please, Adrien," Nicolas said. "It's not safe for you here. You must leave. I could never forgive myself if he—"

"Who is he?" Adrien demanded. His body shook with rage that welled up from deep inside, a dark and familiar place. He grabbed Nicolas by the shoulders and shook him. "Tell me."

"Let him go," Antonio Giovanetti said from the door to the garden.

Adrien hadn't heard Giovanetti approach. "What the hell are you doing here?" Adrien released the startled Nicolas and backed away.

"I might ask the same of you, monsieur," Giovanetti replied.

"Kill him," the voice in Adrien's mind prodded.

"I was speaking with Nicolas," Adrien snapped. "You should leave."

"I don't think so," Giovanetti said as he put his arm around Nicolas's shoulders. "This is our home. And you've already proven yourself a dangerous man. Should I tell the Council you've come here and threatened me?"

"*Your* home?" Adrien struggled to understand.

"I told the Council you weren't to be trusted, but after Jean Lambert vouched for you and Reynaud said he forgave you for your outburst—"

"Reynaud forgave me?" None of it made sense. Why would Reynaud not want revenge after what Adrien had done? Unless he had received something in return for his cooperation.

"And then my beloved husband took your part," Giovanetti continued. "Although for the life of me I can't understand why he thinks you're redeemable."

"Husband?" Adrien rubbed his eyes and tried to focus on Giovanetti, but the laughter was deafening now. Nicolas's husband? *No, that's not possible. Nicolas would never pledge himself to that bastard.* Then again, Nicolas had seen the past as Adrien knew it in his blood—perhaps Nicolas had thought marrying Giovanetti might give him some leverage with the hunters.

"Please, Adrien," Nicolas said. "Perhaps another time, when you're more—"

"Kill him. You know you want to." How easy it would be to give in to that voice. He could call his sword and do what he should have done more than a century ago.

"More what?" Adrien shouted. "More willing to accept this sham of a bonding? More accepting of your lies? What is it you want me to believe, Nicolas? Do you love him?"

"Kill him, kill him, kill him—"

The pity in Nicolas's eyes made his words sting more. "Yes," he said. "I love him."

Somewhere in the deep recesses of Adrien's soul, the sound of raucous laughter vibrated. The demon had awoken.

Chapter Thirty-Four:
Broken Glass

After Adrien left, Nicolas followed Antonio inside. He'd expected this day for nearly a hundred years. Time had finally caught up with them. For a moment he'd feared Adrien wouldn't leave without a fight.

"What the hell were you doing with him?" Antonio demanded.

"What difference does it make to you?" Nicolas shot back.

"I won't permit you to see him."

Just like Antonio. He'd always believed Nicolas weak enough to manipulate. Nicolas had let him believe it. "I see *whom* I want, *when* I want."

Antonio narrowed his eyes but did not argue the point. They had both made their choices. Antonio would fume, but in the end, he could do nothing. And Nicolas would not betray Antonio. He wasn't ready to die. Not yet. *Stalemate.*

Nicolas had expected to see Adrien at the Council meeting. He hadn't expected to see a new Adrien, untouched by the events that had shaped Nicolas's life. Nicolas had learned nothing about the immortals' ability to manipulate time, although he guessed Adrien's gift was somehow linked to a similar ability the Rousseau Clan had possessed long ago. Regardless, Nicolas had never expected to meet the Adrien of his past again.

"You lied," Nicolas said as he avoided Antonio's hand on his shoulder. "You said the Council meeting would end this uncertainty. You said Pelletier would show himself."

Antonio's scowl deepened. He hated being used, and Nicolas guessed he'd known nothing about Pelletier's plans. Pelletier, who was said to have died, but whom Nicolas knew lived somewhere, biding his time until he could solidify his power.

"Verel has his reasons."

"Of course he does." Nicolas smothered a laugh. He might despise Pelletier, but he needed Antonio no more than an arm's length away. "He enjoys stringing you along."

"He knows what's best for us."

"Of course he does." Nicolas shook his head in disgust.

Antonio pushed Nicolas against the wall and pressed his forearm against Nicolas's Adam's apple. Nicolas gasped, not from lack of air, but from the suddenness of the movement. Antonio had grown stronger. Nicolas knew Pelletier still lived and that he'd given Antonio his immortal blood—blood at least as powerful as that of the ancient vampires. That immortal blood kept Antonio in line and kept him alive—but Antonio was neither vampire nor immortal, and he would die without Pelletier's indulgence. Pelletier never gave Antonio enough blood, and Nicolas understood why: he needed Antonio strong, but not strong enough that he presented a threat. *A master puppeteer.*

Nicolas allowed Antonio to kiss him. He despised the touch, but he'd learned to tolerate it. Antonio's mouth found Nicolas's neck.

"No." Nicolas shoved Antonio backward with such force that he hit the opposite wall, causing one of the ancient vases to topple from its pedestal. He'd never allow Antonio to take his blood. Lately, though, Antonio's hunter's body had become more vampiric. Each drop of blood Pelletier made him beg for meant Nicolas had to fight harder to keep him at bay. Not that he couldn't kill Antonio if he wished. It would mean his own death, of course, but he'd long ago prepared himself for that. If not for Adrien, he'd long ago have killed both Antonio and Pelletier.

"Just a little taste," Antonio whispered as he fell to his knees. Already the bruise on his face had begun to fade.

How much longer before he becomes stronger than I?

"I'm going for a ride," Nicolas said. Later, he supposed he'd have to give his body to Antonio to make amends.

Nicolas rode into the forest as the sun disappeared behind the hills. He arrived at the small lake an hour later. He had no fear of the darkness, nor did his horse, who trusted him to lead them through the woods. He pulled off his riding boots and tossed them onto the mossy bank, then dipped his toes in the cool water.

Adrien.

A HUNDRED years ago, Nicolas had dreamed of the future he'd seen in Adrien's blood. He'd tasted its promise. But when he'd seen Adrien several days later, Adrien had appeared not to know him. The next time he'd seen Adrien, Nicolas acted as though he'd never met him. He'd approached Adrien, hoping against hope to see a glimmer of recognition in his blue eyes. But Adrien eyed him like so many of the hunters, with suspicion and contempt. Nicolas understood why: a vampire had killed Adrien's mother when he was a young child.

Not long after, Nicolas had suggested to Jean that he marry Rosina. He'd known already that he was a Rousseau, of course. He'd seen it in Adrien's blood. But he hadn't known what else to do but force Jean's hand, even though he wanted nothing more than to stay with Jean. He should have told Jean the truth, but he'd been a heartbroken fool and still hoped that Adrien might come to care for him.

There had been no Adrien to dream of a future with after Jean's confession stopped the wedding, but at least there had been peace between the clans. Verel Pelletier had disappeared after a fight with hunters Nicolas was told had opposed the wedding, although Nicolas never believed him dead as the others did. He knew better. Adrien had shown him the truth.

In the end Jean and Blaise agreed to send Nicolas to London, where he studied architecture as he'd once planned. Throughout that time, Antonio Giovanetti remained Reynaud's valued and trusted confidante. So when, upon his return to Paris at the conclusion of his studies, Nicolas found Giovanetti in the sitting room in hushed conversation with Blaise and Reynaud, he wasn't surprised.

"Come in, Nicolas." Reynaud had gestured Nicolas inside and offered him a brandy.

Nicolas smiled at his brother, who for once didn't return the smile. Nicolas had rarely seen Blaise in a temper, but whatever they had been speaking of before he'd arrived had clearly angered him.

"Lord Giovanetti," Nicolas said in an effort to dispel the tense mood. "What brings you to Paris?"

"Council business," Giovanetti replied. "And personal business as well."

"Lord Giovanetti has asked me for your pledge, Nicolas," Reynaud said with obvious pleasure. "I have given him my blessing."

"Handfasting?" Nicolas wasn't sure he'd heard correctly.

"Reynaud," Blaise said, his voice shaking, "I ask that you reconsider. Nicolas is under no obligation to—"

"*I* am clan leader," Reynaud replied. "Until such time that you succeed me, I alone will determine what is in the clan's best interests."

"I am not a thing to be parceled out in the clan's best interests," Nicolas said as he rose. "I alone will choose to whom I pledge myself."

Giovanetti offered Nicolas an understanding smile. "Of course, Nicolas," he said. "I understand. I apologize if I have offended you. I truly thought you would—"

"I am sorry as well, my lord," Nicolas said, not in the least regretful. "I mean you no disrespect." Nicolas glared at Reynaud and left the room without another word.

Three days later Nicolas saw Giovanetti again after returning from an early morning ride. Nicolas had bathed and taken his breakfast on the balcony overlooking the gardens, as he liked to do. The breeze from the fields caught the edge of his silk robe, which fluttered like the emerald leaves on the trees.

Nicolas had sensed Giovanetti and had guessed why he'd come. Once, Nicolas had believed Giovanetti strong. Now he knew better. He'd seen Giovanetti's weak soul in Adrien's mind and knew the only thing that motivated him was power.

Nicolas stood to face Giovanetti. "What do you want?"

"You're quite attractive," Giovanetti said as the breeze caught the silk of Nicolas's robe again, baring the smooth skin of his chest.

Nicolas had heard these words before. He understood the vampires' power over humans and knew that even hunters were susceptible to an ancient's scent.

"Leave." Nicolas tied the robe closed.

"I need you, Nicolas." Giovanetti stood so close his breath brushed Nicolas's cheek. "Your blood. Your power."

Nicolas held his ground. His palm tingled. How easy it would be to kill this hunter. *Simple. But what of those I love?* Pelletier would have the excuse he needed to start a war.

For all his anger toward his uncle, Nicolas understood what an alliance with the hunters might mean for his clan. Still, the decision would be his to make, not his uncle's.

"Have you ever wondered why your uncle is beholden to me?" Giovanetti caressed Nicolas's chin and ran a thumb over his lips.

Nicolas gritted his teeth.

"Have you never wondered, Nicolas?" Giovanetti untied the robe and pushed it off Nicolas's shoulders.

Nicolas shoved him nearly hard enough to knock him off his feet. "*Never* touch me without my permission." He raised his hand and all of the windows in the room shattered.

"Like an artist's sculpture," Giovanetti said, clearly unfazed. "The naked warrior charging into battle." He began to walk back toward Nicolas, eyes wandering over his body, taking it in with obvious pleasure. He ran his fingers over the writing desk near the window, brushing the bits of glass from its surface. "I once thought a woman's body beautiful. But after seeing yours—"

Nicolas called his sword and pointed it at Giovanetti. "Whatever my decision," he said evenly, "I will not be forced."

"Am I to understand that you have reconsidered my proposal, then?"

Nicolas forced his jaw to release its tension, then drew a long breath. He thought of Adrien and their short time together. He'd been young, naïve. He'd once hoped his future might include Adrien. No more. And if he was destined to live his life without Adrien, why shouldn't he secure his family's position? An alliance with Giovanetti would be useful, not only for the safety it might provide his clan but also because it might permit him to influence the future of both vampires and hunters.

"Yes. I have reconsidered your offer." Nicolas released his sword, then picked up the robe.

"Please," Giovanetti said, "don't get dressed on my account."

Nicolas took his time pulling the robe back on and retying the sash. He wouldn't be cowed, especially by this man. And he would give himself to Giovanetti only when it suited him.

"So, Nicolas? What is your answer? Will you give me your pledge?"

They were handfasted a month later in the small chapel inside of the castle, with only Blaise, Rosina, and Reynaud in attendance. Nicolas didn't tell Jean of the pledge until nearly a month later. Jean never questioned him. No doubt Jean, one of the most pragmatic men Nicolas knew, understood the value of such a union, even if he might have wanted something different for the man he still called brother. And what good were questions anyhow? A vampire's blood bond, even to a hunter, was a permanent one. There would be no going back on their vows.

This future held no place for him and Adrien.

CHAPTER THIRTY-FIVE: THE ONLY WAY FORWARD

"YOU SHOULD have killed him."

Adrien ignored the voice. He'd make things right.

"Send me back," he demanded as he strode into Jean's apartment well after dark. "And don't tell me you have no idea how to do it. If you're as powerful as I think you are, you can force the demon to do it."

Roland raised an eyebrow, then poured himself a cup of tea from the set on the coffee table. Again with the fucking tea. Did the man do anything but drink tea?

"No," Roland replied.

"Why the hell not?" Adrien's hands tingled and his head hurt like a beast.

"You aren't ready." Roland sipped his tea.

"Like hell I'm not." He grabbed Roland by the collar and shook him. The teacup clattered onto the floor, the hot water burning Adrien's hand. He was powerful. The strength clawed like an animal trying to escape its cage.

"Adrien. He's a fool. He doesn't understand." That voice again, calling him, urging him on.

"Why the hell did he agree to pledge himself to Giovanetti?" Adrien demanded.

"If I told you, would you change your mind?" Roland pried Adrien's hands from his neck. "If you try to change this, you'll just end up getting yourself *and* Nicolas killed. As it is, Jean had to intervene to reassure Giovanetti. He's there now, cleaning up after you."

"Giovanetti can rot in hell."

"And what of Nicolas?" Roland asked.

"Nicolas will be fine once I fix what Pelletier's done." Adrien wasn't as sure as he sounded. Something was wrong. Something darker had happened.

None of that matters. What matters is fixing the past.

"What matters is fixing the past," Adrien repeated without really thinking. "And if you won't help me, I'll figure out how to go back there myself."

"And I'll stop you," Roland said in his infuriating calm voice. "You can't go back there. Not the way you are right now. You need—"

"You're working with that bastard, aren't you? You and Pelletier! I should have realized it." He launched himself at Roland and wrapped his hands around his throat.

Roland peeled Adrien's hands away with surprising strength and twisted one of Adrien's arms behind his back. "I can't let you do this," Roland said. "Even if you could direct where you might end up, you're in no shape to face Pelletier. You're losing control again."

Adrien's heart pounded in his chest. Of course he didn't believe Roland had conspired with Pelletier. "I'm not—"

"Tell me you don't want to kill me right now."

Adrien tried to twist out of Roland's grip, but Roland just held him tighter.

"You're losing control of it again. It's there in your mind, urging you to kill me right now, telling you *I'm* your enemy."

"Fuck you!"

"Adrien. Tell me I'm wrong."

Adrien tried to focus his power in his hands, tried to aim it at Roland. "Let me go!" His palms vibrated with the attack, but the energy remained in his body, burning him.

"You're stronger than he is."

Adrien ignored the pain. His body would heal. Once again he tried to attack Roland, and once again the power of his attack flowed back into his body. Adrien gritted his teeth and tried not to gasp as the pain flared, red-hot like fire.

Roland didn't move. "You're too weak to fight me."

"He's lying."

"The hell I am." Adrien called his sword. Nothing happened.

"Are you finished?" Roland asked with a theatrical sigh. "Haven't you figured it out yet? You're weaker when you listen to that thing."

Adrien began to struggle against Roland again. This time Roland released him long enough to knee him in the gut and knock him to the floor.

"What did you do that for?" Adrien gasped, his face pressed against the carpet.

Roland held him down with a knee and asked, "Ready to listen?"

"Why would you listen to what he has to say? You know he lies."

Shut up!

"I'm waiting," Roland said.

Adrien could just imagine Roland's grin. *Fine. Let him say what he has to say.* He stopped fighting. "I give."

Roland released the pressure on Adrien's lower back. Ten minutes with Roland and he felt like shit. The worst part was knowing he'd done it to himself.

Roland put his hand to the teapot. "Cold," he said. His hand, then the china glowed faintly red. Too tired to call Roland a show-off, Adrien put his head on his arms and lay there.

"Damn you," Adrien said as he got to his feet, then promptly collapsed in the chair across from Roland.

"I know that you want to change things," Roland said, for once wearing a serious expression. "But as you are right now, you'll cause harm to those you care about. I cannot permit that."

Adrien glared at Roland.

"Let me make you a deal, Adrien," Roland said thoughtfully.

"A deal?"

"A contract of sorts." Roland offered Adrien a cup of tea.

Adrien took it. "Let me hear it."

"I'll allow the thing inside of you to take you where it will. But if you lose control, I'll forcibly bring you back."

"So you admit you *can* control my demon." The urge to throttle Roland grew stronger.

No. If we hurt him, we lose.

The demon growled in reply.

"I believe I can," Roland said. "So do we have a deal?"

"What the hell kind of deal is that?" Adrien rubbed his forehead. "And how can you control the damn thing if you don't even understand what the hell it's doing?"

Roland cocked an eyebrow. "I didn't say I could turn back time. I simply said I could control the demon. And I might have an idea of how to bring you back to the present. The present you knew and lived."

"Might?" Adrien wasn't sure if that was good or bad. Going back to his present meant chasing after Pelletier, trying to find Nicolas. Was it better to take his chances here, in this alternate timestream? He dry-scrubbed his face and toyed with the idea of letting the demon loose on Roland. But he didn't want to argue, and he couldn't think clearly enough to form a coherent argument. "Fine," he said at last. "What's your deal?"

"The deal is this: when you're strong enough to dictate where it sends you, I won't interfere, even if I disagree with your choices. Do you understand?" Roland smiled at Adrien.

"You won't interfere even if you disagree?" Adrien asked, repeating Roland's words.

"That is correct. I won't interfere."

Adrien eyed Roland warily. "Then all I need to do is become stronger than you? Defeat you?"

Roland frowned. "That isn't exactly what I meant, although I suppose you could put it that way."

"Fine," Adrien replied.

"Let me show you how strong we can be," the demon told Adrien. *"Let me show you how to move. Just imagine you are where you wish to be."*

Adrien focused his mind on the space behind Roland, imagining himself there. His body seemed to fold in on itself, as though he were squeezing between the molecules of air. He struggled to breathe as he pushed his way through the sensation. He emerged a moment later behind Roland and put his sword to Roland's throat. "Like this?" His heart raced with the knowledge that he'd done it—he'd done what Pelletier had done when he'd taken Nicolas. And he'd done it with the demon's help.

Adrien's exhilaration was short-lived, as Roland vanished, then reappeared on the other side of the room. "It's a start. But as you can see, you must use both your mind and the demon's power or you'll fail." Roland disappeared again, then rematerialized at Adrien's side and punched him hard on the chin.

Adrien hit the wall and dropped to his knees. "Damn you."

"You're powerful, demon," Roland replied. "But without your master, you're nothing."

"I don't need him," the demon replied using Adrien's voice. The hunter was weak. Sentimental. How many times had he sat back and watched as the hunter floundered?

"I beg to differ," Roland said.

The demon launched itself at Roland, reaching for Roland's neck. He'd strangle the man and shut him up for good.

Roland dematerialized again, then rematerialized a moment later a few feet away. "Haven't you figured it out?" he asked. "No, but of course you wouldn't, would you? You don't think."

"He's weak," the demon said. Perhaps not as weak as he'd judged, since he sensed the hunter—Adrien—clawing his way back.

"You're stronger with him," Roland countered. "There are powers you cannot reach without his help, or he without yours." He vanished again, then reappeared behind Adrien and put his arm around Adrien's neck, pressing against his Adam's apple.

The demon growled.

No. Get the hell out of my head!

"Adrien."

Adrien came back to himself with a start and a gasp. "Shit. What the hell…?"

"I see you're still listening." Roland released his hold on Adrien.

Adrien tried to focus, but his sword shook in his trembling hands. What had he just tried to do? What the hell had just happened? Had that *thing* taken over? "Fuck." He wouldn't let that happen again.

Roland chuckled. "The demon needs you as much as you need it. You have the will and the understanding. It controls the power. Stop fighting it. But if it strays," he added, "you must pull it back."

"How?"

"Don't allow yourself to drift. Stay in the moment, aware of what it does. But only push it aside when you need to." Roland picked up the teapot and sighed. "Cold again." He wandered into the kitchen, leaving Adrien with his sword in his hand.

Adrien released his weapon and rubbed his eyes.

What do you want from me?

The demon didn't answer.

CHAPTER THIRTY-SIX: TAPESTRY

NICOLAS WALKED through the mansion's formal gardens. Here, away from Antonio, he could think more clearly. Here, he could forget, if only briefly, the path he'd chosen. And as always happened when he let his mind go where it would, thoughts of Adrien intruded. Had it already been two months since Adrien had come here?

Adrien had stayed away from the mansion, but Nicolas doubted he would stay away forever. Antonio, too, must have doubted it, since he'd redoubled security around the estate. He'd also ordered Nicolas to remain within the grounds. Nicolas would obey him, but only to keep Adrien safe. Antonio had always suspected Nicolas knew more about Adrien than he let on. Nicolas would not give him a reason to have Adrien killed.

Nicolas wondered how much Antonio—or Pelletier—had guessed about Adrien's outburst at the Council of Hunters. Antonio wasn't powerful enough or perceptive enough to have realized that Adrien owed his immortality to Nicolas, but he was no fool. If he ever discovered the truth, Antonio would do his best to kill Adrien.

Nicolas passed through the iron gate to the garden where he had Adrien meet him. The wind had grown colder since then, and the remaining flowers had withered. The grass crackled beneath his feet with the early morning frost. Several fish rose to the surface of the pond, opening and closing their mouths, eager to be fed.

Nicolas bent down to retrieve the feed pellets he'd left in a glass jar under the marble bench. As he straightened, he saw a glint of light from under the bench, as if a tiny mirror had been left there. He retrieved the shiny object and stared at it. A watch. *His* watch—the one Jean had given him when he'd come of age. The same watch he'd left for Adrien more than a century before.

His hands shook as he depressed the top and the cover popped open. The piece of yellowing paper he'd left there felt slightly damp to the touch. He unfolded it with trembling fingers and read the words he'd written long ago: *I remember you.* He gritted his teeth and steeled himself against the pain.

He would not cry. He'd chosen this path. He'd made his peace with it.

The paper fluttered to the ground and he reached down to retrieve it, chastising himself for being so clumsy. But when he looked at it again, he realized he was looking at the other side. There, in Adrien's handwriting, were the words *I promise.*

CHAPTER THIRTY-SEVEN: BROKEN

ADRIEN SAT with Roland on the balcony of Jean's penthouse apartment, watching the sunset and drinking a bottle of wine. Adrien barely registered the excellent vintage. They hadn't spoken much since Adrien had allowed the demon to control him. Adrien hadn't wanted to talk. He felt overwhelmed, his ability to manage his emotions at its limits.

"Adrien...."

Adrien ignored the demon's voice in his mind. He was too tired to face it.

"Do you want to tell me about your encounter with Nicolas?" Roland ventured after nearly an hour of silence.

Adrien shook his head. "Tell me more about the demon," he said instead.

Roland chuckled. "If I knew about your demon, there would be no challenge, would there? Why don't you tell me what you know, instead?"

Fine. He supposed Roland was right. "The way he showed me the future, then sent me back in time… I think he has the power to send me back to my own present," Adrien said. "But he won't. Not yet, at least. He's enjoying this too much."

"Sounds reasonable."

"He wants to play, but he wants more than that. The stakes have to be high enough to make it interesting." Adrien gazed out over the city. Some things remained the same. The smell of exhaust, the traffic, the people hurrying to their destinations, the sunset fading on the horizon.

"We can kill Pelletier," the demon whispered.

Shut up. He would kill Pelletier, but he'd do it in his own time.

"There's something I'm missing," Adrien said. "Something connected to my present. Pelletier has something to do with all of this."

"You believe he may have powers similar to your own?" Roland asked.

180

"The blood he's taken is the key. And if I may be able to control time, why not him as well?" The thought frightened Adrien. If he was right, how long would it be before Pelletier joined the game as well? And with Nicolas as his pawn—

The demon laughed once again.

"They both want the same thing," Adrien said suddenly. "They both want to play. Pelletier is bored. He sees something in me that he wants. Or maybe he sees something in me that will make his miserable existence more interesting."

Roland raised an eyebrow and the corner of his mouth quirked upward. "Go on" was all he said.

"Let's play, Adrien. We'll play, then we'll kill Pelletier."

"The Council still needs to elect a regent," Adrien continued after the voice in his mind quieted again. He trained his eyes on the Eiffel Tower illuminated white against the darkening sky. "Giovanetti is Pelletier's proxy. If Pelletier is supposed to be dead in this timestream, he'll continue to control both the Lambert and Rousseau families through Giovanetti's attachment to Nicolas. But that's easy. All of this is just a setup for the main event."

"What do you think that is?" Roland watched Adrien with what Adrien guessed was a mixture of amusement and pride. Pride to realize Adrien understood what Roland had probably known for centuries would happen. Amusement, for the challenge to come? Adrien supposed Roland, too, had grown bored. And while he might not follow Pelletier's lead, he would enjoy meeting Pelletier's challenge to the status quo.

"I'm not sure. Domination of the vampires? Destroying them? The balance of power is fragile. What would it take to make the vampires rise up against the hunters? He's been biding his time, watching from the shadows in this timestream as well as my own. He won't make his entrance until he's sure he'll get the maximum impact from it. He's too vain."

"You believe he'll reveal himself, then?" Roland asked.

"Eventually. I thought he'd show at the Council meeting. So did Jean. Neither of us were thinking big enough."

Roland's expression grew suddenly solemn. "Humans."

Adrien sighed. "Probably. Although exactly what he wants from the larger world, I'm not sure even he knows yet. But he'll use them, because he knows the hunters who oppose him take their vows seriously. He knows we don't want to see humans hurt in this fight. What better way to control us than to use those vows against us?"

"You really are no longer a child, are you?" Roland said with the hint of a grin.

"Do you ever stop with your prattle?" Adrien countered. To be fair, he enjoyed the back-and-forth with Roland, even if sometimes the man infuriated him.

"What will you do about Nicolas?"

"You know what to do, Adrien. He's yours. He's here. Waiting for you."

Adrien once again ignored the demon's prodding. "I'm not sure yet," he told Roland. "But I may need your help when I figure things out."

"You know I'll help if I can." Roland turned to look at Adrien.

"Adrien, Adrien, Adrien...."

Shut up!

Adrien rubbed the bridge of his nose. The alcohol hadn't helped the headache. "Thanks." Adrien refilled his glass, avoiding Roland's questioning gaze. "I need as much help as I can get to set this straight."

"I can help," the demon said. *"If you'll let me."*

NICOLAS SAT at the computer, not really focusing on the plans for the new Barcelona theater he'd been working on. There had been a time when his work had sustained him. Now he struggled to concentrate. He'd promised the plans two weeks before, but they were nowhere near ready to share with his wealthy client.

Antonio had left for another meeting at the Council that morning. Each day for the past few weeks, he'd spent consolidating his power. It was only a matter of time before the Council elected him regent. Nicolas knew there was no escaping being paraded around at the Council, a symbol of the new order Antonio promised. Nicolas feared what that might mean. He'd mentioned his concern to Jean after the last Council meeting, but Jean had warned him to stay out of hunters' politics.

"I didn't marry him to be a pawn," Nicolas had told Jean as they rode in the woods behind the castle. "I won't sit back and watch him destroy what's taken centuries to build."

"And what do you propose to do about it?"

Nicolas knew Jean's anger was not as much for him as it was for Antonio. Jean had long ago forgiven him for pledging himself to Antonio without Jean's knowledge. Nicolas guessed Jean knew something of the reasons for his actions, although he had never admitted the truth to Jean or anyone else. He might be a pawn, but he had his pride.

Someone knocked on the door of the office.

"Come," Nicolas said as he glanced up from the screen.

Sarah, the old servant, entered out of breath and looking flustered. "Monsieur," she gasped. "I… I don't know what I should do."

"What's wrong?"

"That man is here again," she said. "He refuses to leave without seeing you. I told him Lord Giovanetti wouldn't want him here. I—" She lowered her voice to just above a whisper. "—I believe he's been drinking, monsieur."

"Adrien?" Nicolas asked.

She nodded. "His eyes are wild…. He says he'll destroy the house if you won't speak with him."

A chill snaked down Nicolas's spine. Antonio would return soon. He'd made it clear he wouldn't tolerate Adrien visiting. And although Nicolas guessed Adrien was the stronger fighter, as erratic as his behavior had been since the Council meeting, Nicolas feared Antonio might injure him. Or worse.

"It's all right, Sarah," Nicolas said, his voice calm despite his growing unease. "I'll take care of it."

Nicolas made his way down the steps to the front entryway, unsure of what to expect.

Adrien waited by the front door, his suit rumpled, a hint of shadow on his cheeks. He looked terrible, the dark circles underneath his eyes more pronounced, his skin pale, pasty. How long had it been since Adrien had fed? Even an immortal needed blood from time to time.

Nicolas swallowed hard and schooled his expression. Sympathy and pity wouldn't help Adrien, and he wouldn't want them anyhow.

"You shouldn't have come," Nicolas said.

"I'm not leaving," Adrien replied, his speech slightly slurred. "Not without you. Not this time." He rubbed his eyes and blinked, then shook his head as if trying to clear it.

"You can't change what happened here, Adrien. You can't fix this now." In spite of Nicolas's calm resolve, the feeling of dread continued to build in his gut. "The only way to fix it is to—"

"Not gonna happen," Adrien said. He lurched forward, accidentally knocking over a vase perched on a pedestal. The vase shattered on the marble floor and bits of porcelain flew about.

Nicolas stood his ground. "The pledge is for eternity. You know that."

"Or until one spouse dies." Adrien's eyes appeared cold, heartless. Wild. As if something—the alcohol, perhaps?—controlled his thoughts.

"You don't want to do this," Nicolas said. "I will stop you if you try to hurt Antonio."

"Antonio," Adrien snarled. "You call that bastard by his first name? He doesn't deserve—"

"That's enough!" Nicolas hadn't meant to raise his voice.

"I've waited far too long to be stopped by a pledge spoken in fear." Again, Adrien rubbed his eyes. For a moment Nicolas thought he heard Adrien mumble something to himself.

"No," Nicolas replied. "I love him."

"You lie," Adrien shouted, his voice echoing through the entryway. He aimed his hand at Nicolas. The energy that flew from his fingers appeared nearly black. The glass bowl on the pedestal to the right of where Nicolas stood shattered with the impact.

Don't do this, Adrien.

"It's over. Leave, before I have to hurt you."

Adrien's eyes filled with tears. Gone was the anger. Now all Nicolas could sense was Adrien's grief. "I can't… I won't lose you again. I don't believe you love him. Please, don't do this."

Seeing Adrien fall apart like this, watching his angry resolve dissolve into such pain, made Nicolas falter. Could he blame Adrien for the anger? They'd both suffered great loss. But Antonio already suspected there was more between them.

Adrien kissed Nicolas roughly, causing Nicolas to wince at the pain of the contact. Far more than just the reminder of the bond he shared with Giovanetti—it physically pained Nicolas to see Adrien like this.

"Tell me my kiss does nothing to you." Adrien tightened his hold on Nicolas.

"Please. Not like this."

"I want you," Adrien said, his face contorting with rage. "I won't let him possess you." He kissed Nicolas more tenderly this time.

I can't let this happen. Nicolas pushed Adrien away, but Adrien reached for him again. Nicolas hit Adrien across the face. The force of the blow sent Adrien flying into the wall.

"Damn you," Adrien hissed as he recovered, then grabbed Nicolas by the arm.

"Release me," Nicolas demanded.

"Release him." Giovanetti stood in the doorway, his eyes narrowed, sword drawn.

"Like hell I will. I don't know what you told him to make him agree to be pledged to you, but—"

"He is *mine*," Giovanetti shot back.

"I belong to no one," Nicolas said, stepping between them. "Neither of you own me."

"Leave here, Gilbert," Giovanetti warned. He glared at Nicolas, then stepped between them, pointing his sword at Adrien's chest.

"I won't leave him here with *you*, Giovanetti," Adrien snarled as his sword materialized in his hand.

"Adrien," Nicolas begged, "please."

"You don't love him," Adrien said under his breath.

"I don't love *you*." Nicolas pressed his hand to the edge of Adrien's blade, forcing Adrien to lower it.

"You lie," Adrien shouted. "You gave me the gift. Not him."

"I speak the truth. He's been the one to share my heart and body, not you. Where were you the last fifty years, Adrien?"

"You whore," Adrien snarled at Nicolas. Fury replaced the sadness in his eyes.

Nicolas felt the color drain from his face.

"That's more than enough, Gilbert." Giovanetti stepped in front of Nicolas.

Nicolas's heart beat wildly against his ribs. "Leave him alone, Antonio," he said. "No matter what he's done, he doesn't deserve to die."

"He doesn't deserve your pity." Giovanetti raised his weapon and sent a stream of red flame toward Adrien, who dove sluggishly out of the way. Smoke rose from the hem of Adrien's pants at the point of impact, and Nicolas saw a trickle of blood from Adrien's ankle.

"Bastard," Adrien snarled, returning the attack. The beam of energy, however, flew wide and hit the wall.

"Stop this! Both of you!" Nicolas shouted.

"This is between the two of us," Adrien said in a rough voice. "Stay out of it."

"Stay out of it?" Nicolas retorted. He'd reached the limits of his patience. "I'm not his possession, and I'm sure as hell not *yours*, Adrien. Whatever feelings I had for you, whatever feelings that remained, you've managed to kill. You're selfish. Out of control. Leave."

"He won't leave," Giovanetti said, his sword glinting in the sunlight that streamed in through the front door.

"Nicolas," Adrien said, pathetic once again. "Tell me you still love me and I'll leave."

"I won't lie to you," Nicolas said.

Adrien dropped his hands to his sides, his sword disappearing. He walked toward Giovanetti, his face set with obvious resolve. "I won't live without you, Nicolas," he said, tears sparkling in his eyes.

Giovanetti pointed his sword at Adrien. "Then let me help you die, you bastard. Even an immortal can't survive without a head."

Adrien closed his eyes and seemed to wait for the impact. Giovanetti turned his sword parallel to the floor.

"No!" Roland shouted from the doorway.

"You?" Giovanetti glared at Roland. But before he had time to do more, Roland grabbed Adrien and hit him over the head with the hilt of his sword. Adrien collapsed in a heap at Nicolas's feet.

Roland looked at Nicolas, then threw Adrien over his shoulder with a muttered "This is getting to be a bad habit."

"Get him out of here," Nicolas told Roland.

CHAPTER THIRTY-EIGHT:
LOOSE ENDS

ADRIEN FELL through nothingness. Peaceful, silent nothingness. Oblivion. Blissful darkness.

"Adrien."

Shut up.

"I won't be ignored, Adrien."

I don't have time for you right now.

"I won't wait forever, Adrien."

"Adrien?"

Adrien opened his eyes and looked up into Roland's face. "Damn." He rubbed the knot on the back of his head and tried to sit up, then gave up and lay back down on the couch. "That hurts like hell."

"What did you expect me to do?" Roland asked. He sighed, then added, "Or should I have let Giovanetti kill you?"

Adrien smiled. "Thanks," he said. "Although you could have gone a bit easier on me."

"And you could have warned me what you had in mind."

"You'd have just tried to stop me," Adrien said, rubbing his neck again. "Besides, I knew you'd follow me there. You still don't trust me."

Roland raised an eyebrow. "With your demon pushing you around, I didn't want to take a chance. But this had nothing to do with the demon, did it?"

"No." Adrien closed his eyes and drew a long breath.

"Nicolas still doesn't hate you, you know," Roland said in an undertone.

"I know." Adrien dry-scrubbed his face and this time managed to make it to a sitting position. "But he won't want to see me again, and Giovanetti knows it. That's all that matters."

"You don't think Giovanetti will also see through your little act?"

"As long as Giovanetti's convinced Nicolas won't see me again, that's good enough. Nicolas'll be safe for a while, at least. Long enough for me to make things right." Adrien tried to erase Nicolas's horrified face from his mind. *It was the right thing to do.* Still, he hated himself for hurting Nicolas again. He seemed to be doing a great deal of that lately.

"Adrien."

Get lost. I'm too tired to deal with you now.

"Don't ignore me, Adrien."

The room spun and Adrien lay back on the couch. "Mind grabbing me a few aspirin? I've got a bitch of a headache."

Roland frowned. "You can't avoid facing it forever."

"I won't let you forget about me so quickly, Adrien."

Go away. Adrien tried to focus through the dull pounding over his eyes.

"I will not be ignored, Adrien."

Just a little longer. Adrien pushed the demon back to the dark recesses of his soul. *I just need a little more time before I can deal with you, my friend.*

"I SHOULD kill you myself for what you put him through." Jean Lambert's face was like stone, but Adrien saw fury in his vampire eyes.

"Probably. But I had to do it." Adrien walked into his office—the same office where they'd met nearly twenty-five years before.

Adrien extended his hand, quite sure Jean would not take it. To his surprise, Jean shook his hand. "I know," Jean said.

"You know?"

"You've never seemed naïve or out of control," Jean answered. "Except perhaps at the Council meeting. Then again, if something similar had happened to me, I probably wouldn't have reacted much differently."

"Giovanetti was suspicious," Adrien replied.

"Not terribly surprising, given your past behavior," Jean said. "You may not be naïve or out of control"—a hint of amusement danced on Jean's lips—"but you do tend to act without thinking things through at times."

Jean was right. Adrien himself had created the danger to Nicolas.

"You deserve to suffer."

"So, Adrien," Jean continued, "may I ask why you're here?"

"Adrien. I know you can hear me."

Adrien ignored the voice and returned his focus to the conversation. "Twenty-five years ago, I told you I'd ask for your help," he said.

Jean gestured Adrien to one of the chairs by his desk, then sat across from him. "I'm listening."

"Pelletier will make his move soon," Adrien continued. "The Council will vote on Giovanetti's appointment as regent in three months."

"I won't disappear, Adrien."

"What do you need from me?"

"I need to know that the Lambert Clan will oppose Giovanetti," Adrien said. "And fight him, if it comes to that."

Jean leaned back in his chair and studied Adrien. "That is a great deal to ask, Adrien. Giovanetti is, for all intents and purposes, my brother-in-law."

"What's your answer, Jean?" Adrien didn't mean to say it so forcefully—he'd resolved to use patient diplomacy in his dealings with Jean—but the pounding in his head had reached a fever pitch, and he could barely hear himself speak over the sound of laughter in his mind.

Jean raised an eyebrow in surprise.

"I'm sorry," Adrien said, willing his shoulders to relax. "I didn't mean—"

"Yes."

"Yes?" Adrien repeated.

"I pledge the assistance of the Lambert Clan."

"Thank you." Adrien stood and nodded to Jean.

"I'll await your instructions." Jean offered Adrien his hand and held his gaze for just a moment, a silent gesture of support.

"Thank you." Adrien hoped his smile didn't appear forced.

"Adrien, Adrien, Adrien, Adrien, Adrien, Adrien, Adrien, Adrien, Adrien, Adrien."

Adrien rubbed his eyes and leaned on the back of the chair.

"Are you all right?" Jean asked.

"Yes," Adrien mumbled. "It's just a headache. I'm fine. Thank you again, Jean."

CHAPTER THIRTY-NINE:
SIDEWAYS

ADRIEN HAD done what he'd hoped to do—he had Jean's support for what was to come. Now he'd rest. Tomorrow he'd get to work on the rest of the plan.

The elevator doors opened and Adrien pressed the button for the lobby. As the car descended, he leaned against the wall and took a deep breath.

The world spun. Adrien tried to grab the railing, but his hand seemed to pass right through it. He tripped and landed on hard pavement. His stomach roiled and the familiar blue light flooded Adrien's sight.

What the hell?

The smell of salt water mingled with the metallic city air. He got to his feet and dusted himself off.

"Are you all right?" said a woman's voice. She spoke in English.

Where am I? No, that was wrong. *When am I?*

The laughter faded into the sound of honking horns, a bus pulling away from a bus stop, and a siren in the distance.

"Are you all right?" the woman repeated.

He looked at her and nodded. "Yes. Fine. Thanks for asking. I guess I must have tripped."

She smiled tentatively, then scurried away.

He knew this city. Miami. But when?

He dug into his jeans and pulled out his phone. *2:30 p.m. Monday, June 23, 2014.* A few months in the past. *Before* the Council meeting.

What are you up to now?

The demon didn't answer.

Fine. He'd figure it out on his own. He tapped his phone again. No service. *Just perfect!* He shoved the phone back in his pocket. He'd walk over to his office and figure things out from there.

190

The nausea had begun to fade—faster this time than the others—although the strange sense of displacement hadn't. He made his way down the crowded sidewalk, arriving at the building a few minutes later. At least the fucking demon hadn't dumped him in the middle of Biscayne Bay. He laughed softly as he walked through the revolving doors into the lobby. *Never a dull moment.* He sighed. *More games? Don't you get tired of playing sometimes?*

"May I help you, sir?" the woman behind the reception desk said.

Adrien didn't recall having met her before, but he guessed Scott, the usual security guard, must have the day off. He smiled at her. "I'm Adrien. Adrien Gilbert. And you are?"

She smiled back. "Victoria Collins. Who are you here to see today, Mr. Gilbert?"

Maybe not the best choice of a stand-in for Scott. He'd have his assistant contact the head of security and find out why their training was so poor. Not that he cared that much—he preferred not to be recognized—but if one of their customers was given the same treatment…. "Gilbert Industries," he replied patiently. "I'm *that* Gilbert."

"I'm very sorry, Mr. Gilbert," she replied. "I don't seem to have your name on the—"

"I own this company."

"Sir?" She stared at him and he saw her press a button on the console.

Adrien rubbed the bridge of his nose. This wasn't going at all well. He needed to sit down, get something to eat, and clear his fuzzy brain. "I assure you, Ms. Collins, this isn't a joke." He glanced above the reception desk to point to the logo over her head. It read Akiyama Industries.

Fuck. He clenched his jaw as he caught a hint of movement at the periphery of his vision. Security. *Of course. She thinks I'm insane.* Maybe he was. He was so fucking tired of jumping around, never staying anyplace—any *time*—long enough to get his bearings.

"I'm sorry," he said quickly. "My mistake." He headed out into the street, glancing behind him to make sure security wasn't following him. The last thing he needed was to draw more attention to himself than he already had.

He turned down a side street and tapped his phone. Still no service.

What are you playing at this time?

191

The lack of response didn't surprise him. That was all part of the game, wasn't it?

Beads of sweat ran down his back. He loosened his tie and began to unbutton his shirt. For the first time, he realized he was wearing the same clothing he'd been wearing in Paris. How was that possible? He'd bought the clothing in France because Jean hadn't given him time to pack, or any choice in accompanying him to the Council meeting. But he'd bought these clothes three months from now.

His headache was back with a vengeance. He was so hungry, he thought he might pass out. He'd hail a taxi and head back to his apartment. Regroup. Figure out what was going on. Why this was different than the other times the demon had sent him to a different time.

He walked back onto the main street and over to the curb, where someone caught his eye. A man with short black hair walked toward him. Dressed in dark jeans, with a white shirt and dark wool jacket, he wore a single diamond stud in his left ear. A woman hurrying down the sidewalk dodged Adrien as he stopped, but the man behind him knocked him to his knees.

"Are you all right?" someone said with a hint of a French accent.

Adrien looked up into familiar brown eyes. Adrien inhaled slowly, hoping to head off the bloodlust that buzzed at the back of his brain. Heat tingled at the back of his neck, raising the hairs there. His palms felt suddenly sweaty. He felt sick. Not nausea—shock at seeing Nicolas here, realizing it really *was* Nicolas.

This isn't a coincidence. And it wasn't possible. This wasn't his past, and it wasn't the past he'd just left. This was something different.

"Yes, I…." Adrien took the hand Nicolas offered and struggled back to his feet. The world spun and he grabbed Nicolas's arm to steady himself.

"You're not all right. You look ill. I should call an ambulance—"

"No ambulance." Adrien righted himself. "I just need to eat something. It's hotter than I realized."

Nicolas glanced around, frowned, then said, "There's a coffee shop at the corner." He didn't appear convinced by Adrien's words. "Why don't I help you over there?"

As if Adrien would object. "Thank you."

Five minutes later they sat at a booth by the window, Adrien drinking coffee with a trembling hand. Adrien had watched Nicolas as they'd walked the short distance to the restaurant, his swordsman's muscles straining against the fabric of his shirt. He looked only slightly older than he'd been when they met. "I'm sorry," he said, coming back to himself and wondering why Nicolas was sitting with him when he could have left. "I must be keeping you from something."

"No," Nicolas answered. "In fact, I just came from a meeting. I've got the rest of the afternoon free."

"I'm Adrien Gilbert." He forced a smile and set the empty mug down.

"Nicolas Rousseau."

"It's good to meet you, Nicolas," Adrien said in French. He drew another long breath and his heart slowed its gallop.

"Please call me Nico," Nicolas said, also in French.

"Nico," Adrien repeated. The nickname sounded strange on his lips. "Thank you for the rescue."

"Not a problem." Nicolas chuckled. "Sometimes I forget to eat when I'm working on a project. My brother Jean sometimes calls from Paris to check on me." Jean did that? "I didn't realize you were French." Nicolas's familiar voice caressed Adrien's ears like music. "I didn't notice an accent."

"I've lived in Miami a long time." *Longer than you know.*

"I see." Nicolas pressed his lips together and knitted his brow. "And you... you're a hunter?"

Adrien nodded. Of course Nicolas would sense this. How much more would it take for Nicolas to sense his own blood running through Adrien's veins? The thought both thrilled and terrified him.

"Small world."

"Yes. It is." Adrien hoped he wasn't staring. Everything about this Nicolas seemed different from the one he'd seen in Paris. Confident, relaxed, and friendly, he reminded Adrien of the Nicolas he'd fallen in love with more than a century before.

The waitress brought their food. The greasy hamburger and fries made Adrien's mouth water. He dived into them with relish, smiling up at Nicolas with his mouth full.

Nicolas lifted a fry and studied it for a moment, clearly lost in thought. "That doesn't bother you? That I'm a vampire?"

"Why would it?" Adrien offered Nicolas what he hoped was a reassuring smile.

"Good. I hoped you'd say that." Nicolas smiled back, then popped the fry in his mouth.

193

"How long have you lived in Miami, Nicolas—I mean, Nico?" Adrien had too many questions, but he forced himself not to overload Nicolas with them.

"About two years," Nicolas answered as he set his empty cup down. "I spent the last fifteen years in London." He paused, then shook his head and asked, "Have we met before? I know it probably sounds like a come-on, but it isn't meant to be. It's just that you seem so familiar."

"I don't think we've met." Adrien figured this was the best answer, for now at least. And it was the truth. Mostly.

"Most of the hunters I know keep a low profile. The era of Internet has made it a challenge to live so long and not raise questions amongst humans. Still"—Nicolas rubbed his mouth as if considering something—"I don't believe I've ever heard your name mentioned. Were you trained in France?"

Adrien nodded, knowing he'd strayed onto shaky ground but unwilling to lie to Nicolas. "I haven't spent much time there."

"I'm sorry," Nicolas said. He parted his lips, then shook his head. "It's so strange. There are just…."

"Too many questions?" Adrien finished. He reached out to pick up the ketchup at the same time Nicolas did. Their hands brushed and Nicolas gasped audibly.

"I…. Yes." Nicolas frowned again.

Adrien had felt it too. The familiar tug, to be sure, but more than that. The familiarity of a blood bond. *But that's not possible.* This Nicolas had never met him. Never given him his blood. *But his blood runs in your veins, regardless of whether this Adrien received the gift.* He refilled his cup with coffee in an effort to focus on something other than Nicolas.

"Adrien…." For the first time, Nicolas appeared unsure of himself. "Please forgive me if this sounds strange, but I feel I must ask again."

Adrien nodded. "Of course."

"Are you sure we haven't met before?"

Adrien set his mug down abruptly, and it landed on the edge of his knife, splashing his hand. He hissed with the sting of the hot liquid on his skin.

"I'm so sorry," Nicolas said, taking Adrien's reddened hand and dabbing it with his napkin. "I startled you. You must think me insane to—"

Adrien's hand had begun to heal. He was sure Nicolas had seen it too. Adrien felt quite sure Nicolas would ask him how that was possible, but instead Nicolas did something entirely unexpected. He brought Adrien's hand to his face, closed his eyes, and inhaled audibly.

Nicolas opened his eyes. "No. I'm not mistaken." His expression grew suddenly hard. He released Adrien's hand and stood. "I don't know what you're playing at, but I've had enough. Be thankful we're in a public place, or I'd kill you on the spot."

"Kill me?" Adrien struggled to understand Nicolas's reaction. He'd expected surprise. He hadn't expected the hatred.

Adrien heard contempt in Nicolas's laugh. "You're all alike. Hunters. You disgust me." He shook his head and turned to leave.

Shit. Adrien pulled out his wallet, tossed a wad of bills on the table, then chased after Nicolas, who had nearly reached the next block, his hand raised to flag down a taxi.

"Nicolas! Please. It's not what you think." Adrien caught up to Nicolas, who promptly rounded on him.

"What should I think, monsieur Gilbert?" he snapped. "After all that's happened. After all we did for your kind in the war. Didn't we suffer enough for you? Didn't we prove ourselves honorable?"

"I don't know what you're talking about," Adrien said. "Please, I need—"

Nicolas grabbed him by the throat and dragged him into a small alleyway between the buildings, then shoved him hard against a brick wall. "Roland Günter was a fool," Nicolas growled as he tightened his grip on Adrien's neck.

Adrien gasped and tried to pull Nicolas's hands away, but Nicolas held fast. "Roland?" Adrien croaked out.

"He lost his life fighting for the Council's survival," Nicolas said. "He saved my life. He told me there were others like him who believed our races could work together, that the ancient truce between hunters and vampires hadn't been a mistake."

Roland had died fighting a war? It wasn't possible. Roland was probably in hiding again. "Please, Nicolas. You have to let me explain."

"Explain what? Explain how you stole my blood?" With each word, Nicolas squeezed Adrien's throat harder. Adrien struggled to breathe now. He might not die if deprived of air, but he would soon lose consciousness.

"Please, Nicolas. I can't—" The pressure on his larynx was too much. Nicolas would crush it if Adrien didn't do something.

Adrien focused his power in his hands, moderating it so that he wouldn't hurt Nicolas. The steady hum of power built. Nicolas jumped backward, releasing Adrien's throat, blinking in surprise. "Nicolas… please…. Let me… explain," Adrien choked out.

Nicolas summoned his sword and pointed it at Adrien.

Adrien rubbed his throat with his right hand and took in long gasps of air. He kept his free hand trained on Nicolas. "Please don't make me hurt you."

"Why would you even care?" Nicolas demanded. His cheeks were flushed with anger, his eyes steely and focused on Adrien.

"It isn't what you think. I didn't steal your blood." He needed to keep Nicolas talking. He didn't want him to run, and he sure as hell didn't intend to fight Nicolas if he could help it. "Just let me explain."

"Nothing you can tell me will convince me. I've seen what your kind can do." Nicolas's eyes shimmered.

Adrien hesitated just a moment, then lowered his hand. "You're right," he said with resignation. "There's nothing I can tell you that will convince you. So let me show you."

"Show me?"

Adrien held his hand out, wrist facing up. "Blood doesn't lie."

"What?" Nicolas stared at Adrien in disbelief. "You think I'd taste—"

Adrien didn't wait. He tore at the skin and held his arm out to Nicolas. "If I've lied to you, you can kill me. I won't fight you."

I'd die before I'd fight you.

"You… what?" Nicolas paled.

I'd die for you, Nicolas.

"You heard me, didn't you?" Adrien asked. "My thoughts."

Nicolas stepped backward and shook his head. "No. I can hear your thoughts because you stole—"

"But you know it doesn't work like that, Nicolas. Only *shared* blood can do this. The blood shared by a vampire and his creation, or—"

"The giver of the gift," Nicolas finished.

"Please, Nicolas." Adrien's wound had already begun to heal. Adrien once again bit the skin there and held his wrist out to Nicolas. Blood dripped onto the pavement, black spots in the dim light.

Nicolas frowned as Adrien walked toward him until the tip of Nicolas's blade touched his shirt. A tiny speck of red blossomed at the point of contact over Adrien's heart.

"If I've lied, you can run me through." Adrien wasn't sure he could survive such a wound, but it was a gamble he was willing to take. When Nicolas said nothing, Adrien said, "Please. Nicolas."

You have to trust me. I could never hurt you.

Judging by the flicker of doubt in Nicolas's eyes, Nicolas had clearly heard the unspoken words. He hesitated just a moment longer, then took Adrien's arm. The point of Nicolas's sword cut into Adrien's skin as he leaned in to Nicolas.

I would gladly die for you.

Nicolas licked Adrien's bloody wrist, which had begun to heal again. He met Adrien's gaze and his lips parted; then he frowned and tore into Adrien's skin. Adrien's breath stuttered and he swayed on his feet. Nicolas's sword clattered to the ground, then vanished.

Time seemed to stop. The sounds of traffic from the street faded and the only thing Adrien heard was the steady beat of Nicolas's heart through the blood contact. Nicolas began to pull away, but Adrien whispered, "No. Please don't stop."

Adrien sensed Nicolas's bloodlust as keenly as his own. Nicolas drank deeply, and Adrien grew dizzy and weak. He didn't care. He'd gladly give Nicolas every drop of his blood and more.

Nicolas caught Adrien as his knees buckled and he collapsed. Strong arms held him fast. The blood connection was gone now, but Nicolas still clung to him as he floated somewhere outside of himself. He felt Nicolas's steady presence, felt the familiar heat of the contact. *Nicolas. God, Nicolas. I thought I'd never—*

"Shhh." Nicolas's voice sounded very far away.

I can't lose you again. I'll die.

"Rest for now," Nicolas whispered. "There will be time later to talk. I promise."

ADRIEN AWOKE with a start and looked around. An unfamiliar apartment, lit only by the pale morning sun. He struggled to remember how he'd gotten here, then remembered the alley. Nicolas taking his blood.

"Nicolas!" he shouted. He hadn't dreamed it. He couldn't have dreamed it. More than a hundred years... he couldn't survive losing Nicolas again.

"It's all right. I'm right here." Nicolas brushed a lock of hair from Adrien's forehead.

At Nicolas's touch, Adrien's self-control completely failed him. "Oh God." Tears streamed over his cheeks as Nicolas held him like a child, rocking him in his arms.

"Shhh. I'm not leaving. I promise," Nicolas said as Adrien's tears finally abated. "I'm so sorry, Adrien. I didn't mean to hurt you. I took too much of your blood. I couldn't help myself... I didn't believe... I *couldn't* believe."

Adrien forced himself to pull away.

"What's wrong?" Nicolas asked.

"I.... That wasn't your fault. It's not fair of me to expect you to—"

Nicolas's lips silenced him. Familiar lips and the familiar rush of hunger. Bloodlust mingled with physical need. Adrien moaned, and when the kiss broke, he felt bereft. Fragile.

"I have no bond mate. No pledge," Nicolas said, no doubt having read Adrien's thoughts. "No one to claim my heart as his own."

"You know nothing about me." A weak protest, since Adrien knew that if this Nicolas gave himself to him, he'd not push him away.

"Blood doesn't lie," Nicolas whispered against Adrien's cheek. "And although I can't tell you that I love you as that Nicolas loved you"— he brushed the tracks of Adrien's tears away with his thumbs—"there is something between us I can't ignore."

"But surely—"

"There have been other men," Nicolas explained. "But no one owns my heart. My past is quite different from the Nicolas you knew." He hesitated a moment, then added, "Although you may find me a disappointment compared to him."

"No. Never." Adrien didn't need Nicolas's blood to know this. He might mourn the loss. He might wish the Nicolas he had known had lived a different past. But this man *was* Nicolas. "Souls don't change."

Nicolas smiled. Then his expression grew serious as he leaned in again to claim Adrien's mouth. Adrien closed his eyes and sighed. *Too long. So very long.*

Nicolas didn't hesitate but began to unbutton Adrien's shirt. With each inch of skin Nicolas exposed, he raked his sharp eyeteeth over the surface, drawing blood he eagerly licked. "So good," Nicolas murmured.

Having reached the last button, Nicolas helped Adrien shrug free of the fabric, then moaned his approval as he gently bit Adrien's shoulder. Adrien opened his eyes as Nicolas withdrew, their gazes meeting.

Please. Adrien didn't care that he sounded needy. He was. At any moment the demon might yank him back to his own timestream and he'd lose Nicolas once again. Nicolas seemed to understand this, because the urgency in his touch made Adrien's skin vibrate. Adrien marveled that the intensity of the blood connection made this possible even though they'd just met.

Nicolas's eyes grew dark and wide as he pushed Adrien down on the couch. With deft fingers, Nicolas unbelted Adrien's jeans and pulled them off along with his briefs. Slowly and deliberately, Nicolas laved his abdomen. No teeth this time, just the heat of Nicolas's tongue sliding downward, tantalizing and wet.

Time seemed to slow as Nicolas teased Adrien, his mouth approaching but not yet capturing Adrien's hard cock. Blissful torture.

Please.

Nicolas looked up with smoldering eyes tinged with red. Adrien guessed his own eyes also reflected the bloodlust.

"I will share my blood," Nicolas said in his mind. *"But I ask that you wait. I know it's selfish, but I want to feel your body. Have you know me first as a man."*

Adrien nodded. He'd guessed the secrets of Nicolas's blood might not be pleasant ones. He felt too raw, too vulnerable to face the truths that blood might reveal right now. He needed Nicolas inside him.

Please.

Nicolas swallowed Adrien down to the root, circling his tongue around Adrien's shaft, covering his sharp teeth with his lips to avoid hurting Adrien. "So good," Adrien whimpered as he closed his eyes and reveled in the pleasure of Nicolas's hot mouth.

Nicolas moaned against Adrien's cock, the buzzing sensation nearly sending Adrien over the edge as the bloodlust threatened to overtake him. *"Soon,"* he heard Nicolas say in his mind. *"I promise my blood will be yours."*

The words brought Adrien back from the edge just as Nicolas caressed his sac and flirted with the sensitive skin behind. Nicolas leaned in, pressing Adrien's legs farther apart so that his short hair tickled the inside of his thighs. Adrien combed his fingers through Nicolas's hair. He missed the long silk of it, but Nicolas looked good with the more modern cut.

Nicolas's wet finger breaching him chased away all thoughts of anything but the heat of Nicolas's mouth. Nicolas let him slip slowly from his mouth, causing Adrien to groan his displeasure, but a moment later, Nicolas licked his inner thigh and brushed his balls with the slightly rough skin of his cheek.

"Please... I can't...," Adrien whispered. "I want...." He wanted this to last. He wanted to savor Nicolas's body, his touch, the feather-soft brush of Nicolas's thoughts in his mind.

Nicolas withdrew and Adrien opened his eyes to see Nicolas stand and pull his T-shirt over his head and toss it aside. Slowly, he unbuckled his jeans and pushed them down along with his fitted boxer briefs. He waited just a moment, as if he'd understood Adrien needed to see him like this: naked, hard, wanting him. Adrien saw no embarrassment in Nicolas's expression, only pleasure and hunger. Nicolas had never been uncomfortable in his skin—Adrien had found that honesty far more appealing than the false modesty of many of the human men he'd fucked.

The urgency of Adrien's need faded. The demon relished this as much as he—an interesting and unexpected observation. They both wanted to feel Nicolas's body, slow the moment in a very real and human way.

Adrien got to his feet and stood in front of Nicolas, then trailed his fingers over Nicolas's smooth shoulders and down his arms, finally clasping his hands as their fingers wove together. He licked Nicolas's neck, pausing over the pulsing of his artery but knowing he would wait to taste the secrets there. Adrien released Nicolas and explored the planes of his chest with greedy fingers. The hair that dusted the skin between Nicolas's nipples felt downy and soft. Pressing inward, Adrien met the hard muscle beneath and felt it ripple as Nicolas, too, ghosted his hands over Adrien's body.

"Familiar?" Nicolas asked silently.

Adrien nodded and leaned in to lick a pebbled nipple. Nicolas gasped in response, then pulled Adrien to meet his lips with such force that Adrien could only yield in reply. *Gentle Nicolas. I always loved how you never hesitated to claim me as yours.*

Nicolas smiled as their lips parted. "Come," he said. "My bed is far more comfortable." He took Adrien's hand and led him down the hallway to his room, then backed inside as he drew Adrien against him again.

Nicolas drew a long breath, then pushed Adrien against the foot of the bed, causing him to tumble onto the mattress. An instant later Nicolas kneeled over him, licking his way around Adrien's nipples, then trailing his tongue upward and over Adrien's chin until their lips met.

Adrien tasted his blood in Nicolas's mouth—just a hint of it—and he shuddered with pleasure. For so long he'd not let anyone take his blood. He'd wanted to share it with no one but Nicolas. He had nearly forgotten the pleasure of opening his soul to someone.

Not just someone. Someone I love.

Nicolas's sharp eyeteeth pierced the skin of Adrien's lower lip, causing Adrien to gasp. Adrien's blood infused Nicolas's demanding kiss with the urgency of Adrien's unrequited bloodlust. Denial was sweeter than Adrien imagined it might be.

Nicolas took Adrien's hands and pulled them over his head, then pressed them into the bed, pinning him there. Never one to cede without a struggle, Adrien fought Nicolas's powerful arms as Nicolas claimed his mouth again. Adrien ran his tongue over Nicolas's teeth, knowing the instinct to bite was a powerful one. He sensed Nicolas fight the urge to take more than just a taste. He reveled in the knowledge that he triggered Nicolas's primal instinct for blood, that even after having fed on his blood, Nicolas wanted more.

This thought led to another. He wanted Nicolas inside of him. He wanted to cede the control he'd so carefully guarded for the past century. "I want you inside of me," he moaned.

Nicolas ran his tongue suggestively over his eyeteeth, then licked his hand and, without averting his gaze from Adrien's, took Adrien's cock in his palm. Adrien lifted his body to the firm touch, his breath stuttering. Nicolas stroked him mercilessly, watching him struggle to maintain his control, clearly relishing Adrien's pleasure. Then, when Adrien thought he could no longer hold back, Nicolas released his cock and leaned down to bite his shoulder.

"Ah," Adrien hissed, the pain and pleasure blurring his vision as Nicolas sucked gently at first, then harder so as to cause the skin there to tingle. "Fuck. Yes!"

Nicolas groaned before he released Adrien, then licked his way over the hypersensitive skin of Adrien's neck, where Adrien longed for him to feed. "Not this time," Nicolas said under his breath.

Adrien whimpered—such a pathetic sound. At Nicolas's hands, he felt both powerful and powerless, a contradiction in flesh and spirit. He wondered if this wasn't something like what a vampire's creation felt for his creator.

"Stop thinking," Nicolas whispered in his ear. "Just feel."

Nicolas.

Nicolas's lithe fingers found Adrien's cock again but this time reached behind it to tease Adrien's opening. Adrien hadn't even noticed when Nicolas had slicked those probing fingers—he'd been too lost in thought.

Nicolas pressed a finger inside, barely breaching Adrien's body, but Adrien cried out against Nicolas's silky hair as Nicolas bit and pulled at a taut nipple.

"More. Please. More."

Nicolas's soft chuckle felt like a shiver, traveling up Adrien's spine and filling him with warmth. *"To wait for me... for so long...,"* Adrien heard Nicolas say in his mind. But words seemed to fail Nicolas as they had Adrien, for they melted into sensation and emotion, warm, comforting, even loving. He wouldn't think about whether the emotion was this Nicolas's own or whether it rose from the memories Nicolas had gleaned from his blood. This would be enough for now.

"You're thinking again," Nicolas teased as he pressed his finger fully inside Adrien.

Although comfortably cradled in the downy bed, Adrien rested his hands on Nicolas's shoulders in an effort to steady himself. The sensation of falling wasn't unpleasant but it took Adrien off guard. In spite of his strength, in spite of his long resolve, he felt fragile, as if Nicolas's touch might send him spiraling toward something both dark and wonderful.

Nicolas gently tugged and worked a second finger inside of Adrien, then a third. Adrien dug his fingers into Nicolas's shoulders in response. His cock ached and his body thrummed with need. The bloodlust nearly blinded him with its intensity. He couldn't hold off much longer.

"I know," Nicolas told him as he withdrew his fingers and pushed Adrien's legs toward his shoulders. *"Just a bit longer...."*

Adrien closed his eyes as Nicolas pressed his cock against Adrien's hole, then paused ever so briefly, as though he too fought for control. Then, with one long and deliberate stroke, Nicolas entered Adrien, pushing him back into the bed, making his thighs ache with delicious pain.

"Open your eyes," Nicolas silently commanded.

Adrien obeyed, not caring that Nicolas would see vulnerability in his gaze. He'd let no other man discover that part of him.

Nicolas thrust hard, his own face betraying a softness for Adrien alone. His warm brown eyes glowed with a hint of red, his beautiful lips, full from kisses, pressed together with his body's effort. His breaths grew more rapid, his movements more deliberate. Adrien heard the unspoken question *How is it possible that I already love him?* echo in Nicolas's mind, although Nicolas hadn't meant him to hear.

Blood was the answer, but they both already knew this. Blood, the doorway to the soul through which Adrien had come to understand the Nicolas of his youth. Nicolas's hips pressed against Adrien's thighs with each thrust that drew them closer to the edge of something they both knew would change their lives forever.

Adrien teetered on the edge of his climax, and he knew Nicolas was close, as well.

"Please," Nicolas gasped, his voice rough and low. "Take my blood."

Adrien pulled Nicolas roughly toward him as he came against the hard heat of Nicolas's chest. He bit Nicolas's neck, heard Nicolas hiss with the pain of blunt teeth tearing his flesh. Adrien's mind exploded just as Nicolas thrust his hardest yet, then cried out as he came too.

The light and color of Nicolas's thoughts flooded Adrien's senses. No longer was he in his room in Miami, his body one with Nicolas's. He saw Nicolas's childhood, felt Nicolas's love for Jean and the pain of learning the truth of his birthright. He saw London through Nicolas's eyes, felt his pleasure as he received word of his first architectural commission. He felt Nicolas's fear when he'd been recalled to France—fear that turned to horror as he witnessed the deaths of so many of his kin. His heartfelt grief at seeing Roland's sacrifice, a wound that ran so deep Adrien knew Nicolas would never fully recover. He saw himself through Nicolas's eyes and sensed both confusion and happy surprise. He knew Nicolas had never expected to find happiness with any man—vampire, hunter, or human. He understood that Nicolas believed the emptiness he'd felt to be the price of his survival in the face of so much death. He felt Nicolas reach for him, touch his soul, and knew that Nicolas would not leave him. *Could* not leave him. Their bond was too strong, their hearts too close.

Nicolas. No words could convey his emotions, so Adrien didn't even try. He released Nicolas and felt their connection dim but not sever, just as their bodies were still joined.

Forever.

CHAPTER FORTY: THE GAME

ADRIEN PADDED into the kitchen where Nicolas was cooking breakfast, then slipped his arms around Nicolas's waist. Ella Fitzgerald sang "Day In, Day Out" on the radio. God, he could get used to this—a normal life with Nicolas at his side.

"It smells amazing," Adrien said against Nicolas's neck. The feeling of warmth in his chest grew. He wanted to shout. Sing. Something.

"Are we talking eggs or something else?" Nicolas countered playfully, then licked the skin under his ear.

Adrien shivered in response. He wanted Nicolas now. "Set the table?" he asked, knowing if Nicolas didn't stop soon, breakfast would be eaten very cold.

"Thanks." Nicolas gave him one last lick for good measure, then got back to work on the food.

A few minutes later, they ate their breakfast as the cool breeze from the water blew through the open patio doors.

"This is terrific," Adrien said with a dramatic sigh. "You'd think as long as I've lived, I'd have learned to cook. My sister tried to teach me. Years ago." Thoughts of Isabelle led Adrien to think of Roland. In his mind's eye, he saw Roland stand before the Council of Hunters and warn both hunter and vampire that they could not survive without one another. Nicolas's memory, and now his own as well.

"Our fates are intertwined," Roland said proudly, though his eyes reflected pain and defeat. "Without them, we are incomplete." Adrien felt Roland's deep commitment and his love of the Council, a love he'd tried to instill in Adrien. A tiny flicker in Adrien's heart, that love burned suddenly brighter. The sense of loss clawed at Adrien's soul, growing stronger as he saw Roland surrounded by Pelletier's men, fighting them off, giving the vampires time to try to escape.

Adrien tried to look away as one of the hunters swung his blade to strike the final blow, but he couldn't. He watched in horror as the hunters turned to pursue the vampires after Roland's headless body collapsed in a heap on the stone floor of the Council Chamber.

Adrien wrenched himself back to the present. "The Roland I knew had a habit of disappearing at the most inopportune times. I can't tell you how many times people told me he was dead. When you told me he'd died, I hoped…."

Nicolas wore a somber expression. "I realized afterward that he wanted to die there." He sighed and shook his head. "He lived for the Council. He knew he could not survive its demise."

"I never understood how much the Council meant to him," Adrien admitted.

"I liked Roland," Nicolas said as he swirled the coffee around in his cup. "He believed in the treaty between vampires and hunters. Jean trusted him. I did too. We didn't know Pelletier was an immortal until the fight for control of the Council.

"Most of my past is the same as yours." Nicolas's eyes glistened as he spoke these words.

"Most?" Adrien braced himself for what he guessed the answer might be. He hadn't seen the answer in Nicolas's blood—there had been too much in Nicolas's blood for Adrien to have seen all of Nicolas's memories.

"He didn't just kill my parents." Nicolas's voice sounded hollow. Adrien didn't need a connection to Nicolas to feel his pain—it was written across his face. Etched there.

"Rosina and Blaise?"

Nicolas nodded.

Adrien rose and wrapped his arms around Nicolas's chest. "I'm so sorry," he whispered. "For you to see what you saw in my blood…."

"Please don't be," Nicolas said dully. "I never knew them. Jean shared his memories of them with me. But seeing them as you did… in your memories… it gave me something I've never had."

Adrien had no words to respond with, so he just held Nicolas tighter.

"There's still something I don't understand," Nicolas said after a long pause.

"What's that?"

"You. You're immortal. I taste my blood in yours, and yet we've never met. How is that possible?" Nicolas asked.

Adrien shook his head. "I don't understand it myself," he admitted. "There's so much about the power you gave me that I don't understand. All I can guess is that even when time changes, my blood remains the same."

Nicolas took a long breath, then said in a voice that told Adrien he wanted—no, he *needed*—Adrien to understand, "Roland stood up to Pelletier. He begged the Council to listen to reason. Nearly all of the ancients made the trip to Paris to speak on behalf of maintaining the treaty between our races.

"At the Council meeting, Roland revealed the truth of Pelletier's immortality. He told them the truth of my family's story." Nicolas laughed bitterly. "Pelletier didn't deny any of it. He told the Council the truth—that his followers were strong because of *our* blood."

"Bastard."

"It was a trap," Nicolas continued after a moment. "We were so naïve." Nicolas stood and pulled away from Adrien, stalking over to the windows overlooking the city and gazing out at something on the horizon. "His men attacked the ancients. We were stronger, but there were so many of them.... Roland and a few others stood with us. They gave us the time we needed to escape."

Of course Roland would have been willing to sacrifice himself. He'd never cared for his own safety. *He loved the Council more than his own life.*

Adrien steeled himself against a powerful wave of grief.

"Jean and I buried Roland. We couldn't leave his body there. Not after all he'd done for us."

Adrien rubbed his eyes. Roland. He'd come to love the man as he loved his father. Roland. Alone against Pelletier's men. Fighting for the Council. His beloved Council.

"Most of the ancients were slaughtered that day. Those who survived went into hiding. I have no doubt Pelletier and his men know where Jean and I are. We refuse to hide from him." Nicolas straightened visibly, his pride obvious. "I doubt he cares that we live. We're insignificant. From what Jean and I were able to discover, there are perhaps a dozen ancients left in the world. Male, or too old to have children. There will be no more to take our place."

There was one last question Adrien had to ask, although he feared the answer more than any other. "What of the Council?"

Nicolas stared at him in obvious surprise. "The Council of Hunters?"
"Yes."

"It died with Roland and his dream," Nicolas said softly. "There is no need for a hall of justice when there is no justice to be meted out. The Council Chamber was destroyed. The Council members who opposed Pelletier have all been killed."

ADRIEN STOOD on the balcony while Nicolas showered. He felt numb, in spite of Nicolas's presence. For just a few hours, he'd believed he might be happy.

He'd expected the demon to comment. He could almost imagine it saying, *"You can be happy. You can stay here."* How strange, that before the demon had been anything but silent and now.... Something was different this time. Adrien knew he hadn't created this timestream, hadn't created the future this Nicolas now lived.

Roland dead. The Council destroyed. Pelletier had done thorough work eradicating the vampires. An ancient might procreate with a human, but the offspring would not have the power of the ancients. Nicolas was right—there would be no more ancients. The thought pecked at Adrien's soul like a buzzard.

There's no one left to challenge him. No one to stop him from destroying the rest.

Adrien had once told Roland he believed Pelletier wanted to toy with him. A soul without love was as gaping a hole as a freshly dug grave. An immortal soul with nothing to fill its empty chasm was a dangerous thing. Pelletier wasn't capable of love. He had probably never desired it. *What value is there in a life where everything you desire is handed to you without challenge?*

No. Even if the demon had sent Adrien to this time, he had not created it, of that Adrien was quite certain. But if Pelletier had possessed the ability to travel through time, why had he waited so long?

Maybe the answer didn't matter. Meeting Nicolas here and now was no coincidence. Pelletier had laid down the gauntlet.

You know me better than I know myself.

Adrien walked back into the living room and pulled his cell phone from his jacket. He'd call his father. *If he's still alive.* He shivered in the knowledge that Charles and François might also be dead.

Adrien tapped the screen. Still no service. He'd call customer service and see if there was a problem with his account. There were no phone messages, of course. But there was a single text message. The number had been withheld. He frowned and tapped the screen again. The message was simple but like a kick to the gut.

If you choose to stay here, I won't get in your way. Keep your sweet vampire. Live your perfect life.

No signature. Then again, none was needed. Adrien knew who'd left the message.

Pelletier.

"Adrien?" Nicolas smiled at him from the hallway, wearing only a towel around his waist. *His* Nicolas. The man he'd spent more than a hundred years trying to find. Here. Now. Alive.

"Hmm?" Adrien tossed the phone onto the couch.

"You okay?" Nicolas wrapped his arms around Adrien and the towel fell onto the floor.

Nicolas. Solid. Real.

"I'm perfect now," Adrien lied as he caught Nicolas's lips.

Don't miss how the story began!

Blood and Rain

Blood: Book One

By Shira Anthony

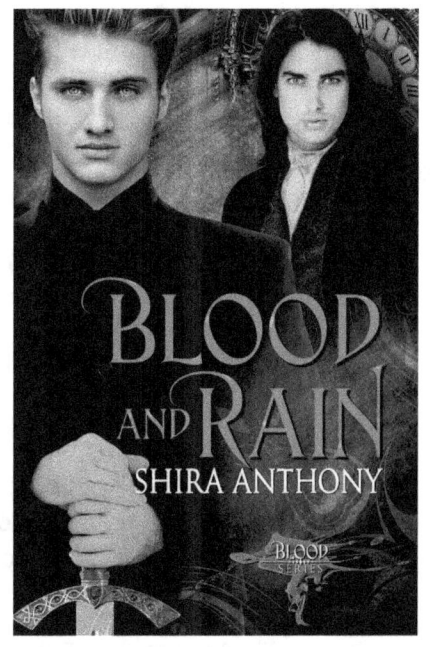

Adrien Gilbert has spent several lifetimes searching for the love he lost. Born in the 1800s into a clan of fabled vampire hunters, Adrien once wanted nothing more than to tend his family's vineyard in southern France or read a good book. But Adrien's peaceful existence ends abruptly when his older brother, François, is murdered. Bound by his hunter's oath, Adrien sets out on a path that will forever change his life when he agrees to execute his brother's killer, the vampire Charles Duvalier.

After months chasing the elusive Charles, Adrien reluctantly makes a bargain with Nicolas Lambert, an ancient vampire. Adrien will escort Nicolas to Paris for his marriage to a rival clanswoman, and Nicolas will help Adrien find Charles. Nicolas's quiet strength and gentle heart soon convince Adrien that Nicolas is nothing like the vampires he has sworn to destroy. As the wedding date draws nearer, a force intent on destroying the fragile peace between the vampire clans threatens to tear apart both the vampire realm and the world of the hunters. To secure both past and future for those he loves, Adrien must find a way to stop the looming war between hunters and vampires. But first he'll have to let Nicolas go.

SHIRA ANTHONY was a professional opera singer in her last incarnation, performing roles in such operas as *Tosca*, *Pagliacci*, and *La Traviata*, among others. She's given up TV for evenings spent with her laptop, and she never goes anywhere without a pile of unread M/M romance on her Kindle.

Shira is married with two children and two insane dogs, and when she's not writing, she is usually in a courtroom trying to make the world safer for children. When she's not working, she can be found at the Carolina coast aboard *Land's Zen*, a 35' catamaran sailboat, with her favorite sexy captain at the wheel.

Shira writes what she loves, be it contemporary musicians, shifter mermen, or time-traveling vampires. Her Mermen of Ea series book, *Into the Wind*, was named one of the best books of 2014 by both Scattered Thoughts and Rogue Words and Hearts on Fire Reviews, and was a finalist in the 2014 Goodreads M/M Romance Member's Choice Awards. Her *Blue Notes* series of classical-music-themed gay romances was named one of Scattered Thoughts and Rogue Word's "Best Series of 2012," and the most recent book in the series, *Dissonance*, was named one of the best books of 2014 by Hearts on Fire Reviews.

Shira can be found on:
Facebook: https://www.facebook.com/shira.anthony
Goodreads:
http://www.goodreads.com/author/show/4641776.Shira_Anthony
Twitter: @WriterShira
Website: http://www.shiraanthony.com
E-mail: shiraanthony@hotmail.com

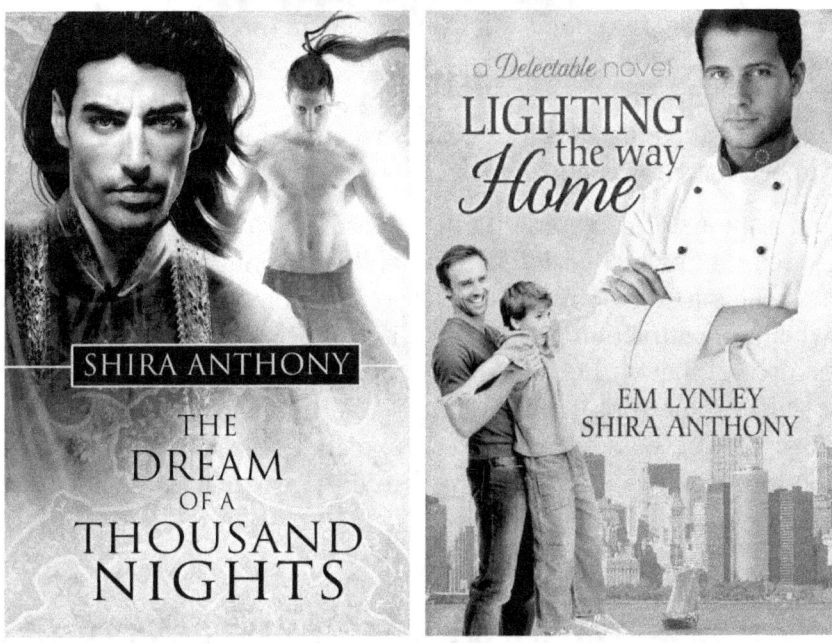

Stealing the Wind

Mermen of Ea: Book One

By Shira Anthony

Taren Laxley has never known anything but life as a slave. When a lusty pirate kidnaps him and holds him prisoner on his ship, Taren embraces the chance to realize his dream of a seagoing life. Not only does the pirate captain offer him freedom in exchange for three years of labor and sexual servitude, but the pleasures Taren finds when he joins the captain and first mate in bed far surpass his greatest fantasies.

Then, during a storm, Taren dives overboard to save another sailor and is lost at sea. He's rescued by Ian Dunaidh, the enigmatic and seemingly ageless captain of a rival ship, the Phantom, and Taren feels an overwhelming attraction to Ian that Ian appears to share. Soon Taren learns a secret that will change his life forever: Ian and his people are Ea, shape-shifting merfolk… and Taren is one of them too. Bound to each other by a fierce passion neither can explain or deny, Taren and Ian are soon embroiled in a war and forced to fight for a future—not only for themselves but for all their kind.

http://www.dreamspinnerpress.com

Into the Wind

Mermen of Ea: Book Two

By Shira Anthony

Since learning of his merman shifter heritage, Taren has begun building a life with Ian Dunaidh among the mainland Ea. But memories of his past life still haunt him, and as the threat of war with the hostile island merfolk looms ever closer, Taren fears he will lose Ian the same way he lost his beloved centuries before. Together they sail to the Gateway Islands in search of the fabled rune stone—a weapon of great power the Ea believe will protect them—and Odhrán, the pirate rumored to possess it.

After humans attack the Phantom, Taren finds himself washed up on an island, faced with a mysterious boy named Brynn who promises to lead him to Odhrán. But Taren isn't sure if he can trust Brynn, and Odhrán is rumored to enslave Ea to protect his stronghold. Taren will have to put his life on the line to find his way back to Ian and attempt to recover the stone. Even if he does find it, his troubles are far from over: he and Ian are being stalked by an enemy who wants them dead at all costs.

http://www.dreamspinnerpress.com

Blue Notes

Blue Notes